SING WITCH, SING DEATH

Roberta Gellis

Thorndike Press • Thorndike, Maine

Copyright © 1975 by Roberta Gellis

All rights reserved.

Published in 1999 by arrangement with
Spectrum Literary Agency.

Thorndike Large Print ® Romance Series.

The tree indicium is a trademark of Thorndike Press.

The text of this Large Print edition is unabridged.
Other aspects of the book may vary from the original edition.

Set in 16 pt. Plantin by Rick Gundberg.

Printed in the United States on permanent paper.

Library of Congress Cataloging in Publication Data

Gellis, Roberta.
   Sing witch, sing death / Roberta Gellis.
     p.   cm.
   ISBN 0-7862-1922-X (lg. print : hc : alk. paper)
   1. Large type books. I. Title.
   [PS3557.E42S56 1999]
   813'.54—dc21   99-14359

SING WITCH,
SING DEATH

CHAPTER 1

"Witch . . ."

Lady Pamela Hervey turned her head and strained her eyes. Had she really heard that word, or was it a whisper of wind, a distorted bird cry? She stood listening while the light grew dimmer, not sure whether or not she was frightened but quite certain she was wildly excited, vividly alive. Silent, still listening, she lifted her face to the wailing wind, lifted her eyes to the wheeling sea birds.

Witch. The word had not been repeated, but Pamela considered it. She did not believe in witchcraft, not in this enlightened year of 1816, but here and now anything was possible. For days she had been ravished by the wild, unbelievable beauty of Cornwall. First she had been fascinated by the improbable scenery, then entranced, and finally enslaved.

It was not pretty. The hills were barren and untamable. Fangs of rock gleamed through the broken earth and sparse vegetation. There was no timber. Gnarled and distorted by the wind that never seemed to stop, the dwarfed trees stretched longing arms in toward the warm and fertile heart of England. Again and again they had passed areas in which the earth was ripped open to expose naked ribs of rock where tin and copper were torn from its bowels. Yet even that was not ugly. It was hard and grim, as were the visages of the few people they saw, but somehow both suited the country — and therefore both were beautiful.

The landscape might well inspire a belief in witches. Even the rich valleys that threaded the barren hills and were both well-timbered and well-cultivated had a mysterious rather than a peaceful air. Pagan spells, said in the dark of the moon, could easily account for the abundance of those glades nestled under the bitter crags. Here, where the wind keened and where black shadows were cast by the broken hills even when the sun shone, one could believe in witches and warlocks.

Pamela laughed softly, the sound hardly audible above the sibilant whisper of the steady wind. Perhaps the bittersweet pleasure of a short escape from a situation that was growing steadily more unpleasant was causing her imagination to smolder. Nonetheless, she had an impulse to investigate the sound; surely she had heard something. She had not yet moved, however, when the beat of hooves forestalled her intention. She drew to the side of the road, her generous mouth curving in a smile of amusement at her childish desire for "something to happen."

Of course, a day spent in the coach traveling with her employer was enough to disorder anyone's imagination. Not that it was Hetty's fault. No one could help being travel sick. Pamela considered her employer objectively. To give her credit, she did not deliberately torment her hired companion; to give her even more credit, she did not vent her resentment on Pamela either. And, from Hetty's viewpoint, she had much to resent. She had been the only daughter of one of the wealthiest families of the West Indies. Then an honorable, the youngest son of the Earl of St. Just, had been "bought" to be her husband.

Pamela frowned slightly. That was an ugly way to put it, although it was perfectly true. The trouble was that Hetty had explained it that way. Not in public, only privately to Pamela; still, it should not have been said at all. Am I being a hypocrite, Pamela wondered, and then decided the criticism was just. Marriages of convenience were extremely common, but they worked out better if both parties allowed the original basis of their union to become obscured by time and by a growing respect and regard. In any case, the fact that Hetty did voice such things, and not always in private, and that she had a tendency to display her wealth in vulgar and ostentatious dress, accounted for the fact that Pamela, a lady by birth, was in the position of companion, and for their presence in Cornwall. Hetty, countess though she was, was not a lady. Pamela had been hired to give her the outward semblance of one.

The situation was very uncomfortable for everyone involved. Hetty, Countess St. Just, bitterly felt that she had been betrayed. When her husband's father and two elder brothers had died in a tragic accident, making Vyvyan the earl, she thought she would come to England and take her place in the forefront of society automatically. Instead she found herself being hustled off to Cornwall. On the other hand, Pamela understood Lord St. Just's position. Partly he did not wish to be embarrassed by his wife, but largely he was concerned for her sake. His friends and sporting companions would accept him no matter what Hetty did. If she tried to force her way into the ton, however, she would be ostracized. In fact, although Pamela needed employment because her father's folly had left her penniless, she would not have taken a position so fraught with explosive qualities had she not felt sorry for both Hetty and Lord St. Just.

He was an interesting man, a giant with eyes of a strange clear green, startling against a sun-browned complexion. A hard mouth, distorted by bitter lines, aged his face, and his whole being gave forth an aura of enormous energy forcibly leashed. Pamela understood that; her own life, of late, had been one long effort to curb her nature. It was, indeed, an echo of St. Just's frustrated energy that had sent Pamela out to fight the wind on the lonely road. Tall, deep-bosomed, and broad-shouldered, Lady Pamela's figure told the same tale of leashed energy — only she did not have the outlets of a man.

Under her pelisse she was dressed most fashionably, but without the bows and knots of floss with which most women adorned their clothing. Her hair, which was very long and thick, was looped in two heavy coils, con-cealing her ears and framing her handsome, large-featured face to perfection. Pamela knew she was good-looking, knew she dressed well, knew she moved with a leonine grace that drew eyes — just as well as she knew that she was too big to interest men who, in these days, were oriented to desire delicacy in a woman. Fortunately, in spite of her size, Hetty had taken to Pamela and had shown

11

herself far more docile to her companion's tutoring than to anyone else's.

Hetty's travel sickness was the greatest misfortune, Pamela thought. Not only had it condemned them to poor accommodations and sent Lord St. Just scouting ahead to find a better inn, but it had exposed problems between the earl and countess of which Pamela would have preferred to remain in ignorance. She had had plenty to think about from the very first day on. Hetty had been sick and had forced Pamela to stop the carriage so often that St. Just, who was riding ahead, had resumed to remonstrate with his wife. Pamela got down to make room for him and heard him say, "I am sorry you are unwell, Hetty, but it will take months to make this journey if you do not control yourself."

"I don't want to make any journey," Hetty snapped. "I want to go back to London."

"You know we cannot do that," the earl replied sharply. "It is not sensible. We would merely have tripled the travel, because we would have to set out again tomorrow."

"Then let me go back alone."

"No, Hetty."

Pamela had seen the countess's pale eyes light with fury, and started off down the road to stretch her long legs after her confinement in the carriage. Her relations with Hetty and her husband would be much simpler if she could pretend to be unaware of their disagreements. She was not quite far enough away, however, to avoid hearing Hetty scream, "Murderer! I hate you! You'll kill me for my money as you killed —" The door of the carriage slammed shut, and the words became unintelligible. Pamela started back toward the coach. Everyone would be out of temper after this scene, and she did not wish to cause any more trouble by delay. Hetty seemed to say the most inexcusable things in a rage. She would have to be impressed with the need to govern her temper better.

When St. Just leaped down from the coach a few moments later, however, Pamela could almost credit that there was some truth in Hetty's accusation. The narrowed, glittering eyes and thinned mouth made him look very dangerous.

"How much of that did you hear?" he asked in a vicious undertone.

Pamela at first considered telling him that she had taken a walk and heard nothing, but she could not. "Too much," she replied, "but do not trouble about it. I know hysterics when I hear them."

The overlying expression of fury had disappeared from St. Just's face, and Pamela was surprised to see how much pain it covered.

The earl had given her no reason to believe that he loved his wife. In fact, he had once remarked that he was "obliged" to Hetty. This confirmed what Hetty had already told Pamela of the marriage, as being one of convenience. One is never "obliged" to a person one loves. The consideration Lord St. Just had always shown for Hetty had not shaken the belief that he did not care for her; it had merely improved Pamela's opinion of him and confirmed her conviction that he was a gentleman.

"I wish there was less truth in it," he muttered.

Pamela felt a sudden chill of fear, but rejected it along with Hetty's remark as ridiculous. She forced a laugh. "Do you mean to tell me that you *are* a murderer?"

"In fact, if not in deed, I suppose I am." The green eyes were strangely misted and withdrawn. St. Just shuddered and rubbed his hands together as if they were cold; then he focused his eyes on her. "That's the devil of a thing to say," he added with a twisted smile, "but I have never deliberately planned a man's death for my own profit — in spite of what you may hear."

The hoofbeats Pamela had heard became loud enough to break into her memory. They slowed as they approached her, and she could make out the shape of horse and rider even in the deepening twilight. As she expected, it was Lord St. Just.

"Lady Pamela," he exclaimed harshly, "what are you doing alone here? It is dangerous to be abroad in the dark of the moon in Cornwall. Put your foot on my boot. Give me your hand." When she had done so, he pulled, and Pamela rose smoothly to sit on the saddle in front of him. "Hetty will be miserable if you have left her alone for long."

It had seemed like a long walk, but on horseback the inn soon came in sight. Pamela went to Hetty at once. The countess was sitting huddled in a chair, so subdued that she did not even ask where Pamela had been.

"Vyvyan, I do not like this inn," she burst out as soon as St. Just came through the door.

Her husband sighed. "I knew you would not, Hetty," he said in a voice that, surprisingly, held no exasperation. "I rode ahead to see if there was a brighter or larger place we could stay, but there was nothing."

"Vyvyan, I'm frightened."

"Cornwall is a frightening place in the dark of the moon, but no one could wish to hurt you, Hetty. You are a stranger here. You have neither made, nor marred, nor meddled. Whatever is in the air is not directed at you."

"Voodoo, Vyvyan? Here?"

Pamela was startled at how close Hetty's thoughts had paralleled those she had when she believed she heard "Witch" float by on the wind. Hetty had given the West Indian name for witchcraft, of course, but Pamela noticed how St. Just's lips tightened. It was as if he had forgotten that Hetty was familiar with the aura surrounding witchcraft.

"Not really," he replied to his wife's question, "although it is something along the same line. Cornwall is a very backward place. Old things die hard here."

"Vyvyan," Hetty teased, the fear dying out of her face. "Are you telling me you *are* a believer?"

"I certainly believe that the covens have power among the locals. There can be no good in offending these people." St. Just replied rather coldly.

"But what is done about this, Lord St. Just?" Pamela asked, thinking that it was time a less personal and more general note was needed in the conversation.

"Very little can be done. The gentry are very seldom troubled by the covens in the first place. In the second, they would not care to make laughingstocks of themselves by bringing such charges in this day and age. The witches' power is over the ordinary

16

people — farmers and fishermen, because the witches sing fertility to the crops and quiet to wind and wave — and the simple folk will not say a word against them."

"I can understand why the local people wish to keep on good terms," Pamela said. "The wind and the sea are certainly of importance to them, and I must say that the valleys are unusually fertile."

"Oh, Pam, now he has you believing it," Hetty giggled.

"Not, perhaps, in the efficacy of the spells," Pamela replied seriously, "but if the local people believed that someone had offended a coven and the witches then refused to cast their spells, or threatened to cast the wrong ones, the people might become dangerous."

They were called to dinner before Hetty could reply, and spoke of trivialities while they were served. When they were at last able to rid themselves of the obsequious innkeeper, Hetty looked disdainfully at the dishes before her.

"You will have to get a cook from London, Vyvyan. You know I cannot eat such crude fare."

"It is impossible to get London servants to come to Tremaire. You know that, Hetty. Why, your maid gave up her post even when you offered double her wage when she learned she would need to stay in Cornwall for near a year."

"You mean after you had threatened her if she dared to come!" Hetty spat. "I do not believe that London servants will not come to Cornwall. You do not want them, Vyvyan. You want me to be isolated, surrounded by your creatures. All this talk of witches and Cornwall being dangerous! I am sure you mean it to be dangerous to me. You want me dead like my brother so that you —"

"Hetty!" the earl bellowed, leaping to his feet and raising his hand.

Hetty cowered, and Pamela interposed her own strong body between the countess and her husband. "Do not dare strike her," she hissed. "She is sick and tired and over-wrought." His green eyes glowed with rage, but Pamela's bright hazel ones met them unflinchingly, and his hand dropped. "Come, Hetty," she said softly. "I will take you to your room and give you your drops. Tomorrow you will feel much better."

CHAPTER 2

Traveling became steadily worse. They left the main road — not that it had much to identify it as such — at Penzance, and the track they now followed was so pitted with holes and ruts that Pamela expected the carriage to be overturned from one minute to the next. She kept her fears to herself, however, since Hetty was growing more and more unmanageable. The carriage lurched again, and Hetty was thrown against the frame of the window.

"Stop!" she screamed.

Pamela pulled down the window and relayed the order to the coachman.

"His lordship said I wasn't to stop again, my lady, not for nothing, not until we come to the house," the coachman called over his shoulder.

The next hour was the most horrible that Pamela had lived through since her father's death. Hetty screamed until she was sick, fainted, and recovered only to begin screaming again. Pamela never saw the village of St.

Just. She saw and heard nothing but her charge until at last the carriage stopped. When St. Just wrenched the door open, Hetty lunged forward. He caught at her and went staggering back under the unexpected impact. Instinctively he pushed Hetty backward toward the carriage as he strove to regain his balance. Simultaneously, fearing that Hetty would fall and be hurt, Pamela grabbed for her. To Hetty it seemed as if her husband and her companion had joined forces to keep her in the carriage.

"No, no," she screamed, "I will not go back in there."

She struggled violently in her husband's arms. St. Just had all he could do to keep her from flinging herself on the ground. Pamela scrambled down to assure Hetty that they had arrived, but as she reached out, Hetty screamed and fainted again.

"Hallo, what's all this?"

A willowy young man with an astonished expression on a normally gentle face had appeared on the steps.

"My wife is ill," St. Just snapped. "She is a very poor traveler. For God's sake, George, get Sarah out here to attend to her."

"Well, you haven't changed much, Vyvyan. You always were a queer one, and now you've got a queer wife."

"George! Go and get Sarah."

"No, St. Just," Pamela interposed. "Do not expose Hetty to the servants while she is in this condition. Let me try to see if I can revive her."

As Pamela snatched up the vinaigrette she had been using during the journey, she saw the faint nod of approval George gave. Placidly, he came closer, knelt down, and began to chafe the countess's hands. Hetty's blue eyes fluttered open, fell on his quietly smiling face, and remained fixed.

"Hallo," he said gently. "Feeling more the thing?"

"Who . . . who are you?"

"Cousin George, at your sevrice, ma'am. Honored to make your acquaintance. Bow to you if I wasn't kneeling down already."

Hetty giggled faintly and asked, "What happened?"

"Don't know m'self. Came out of the house. Saw you faint away. Asked what was wrong. Vyvyan said you was travel sick."

"Oh, yes," Hetty faltered, losing some of the color which had come back into her face. Pamela leaned forward with the vinaigrette again, but Hetty turned away from it so that St. Just's face and Tremaire came into view. She shuddered.

"Don't like his face, eh?" George remarked

cheerfully. "Can't blame you. Don't like it m'self. Looks even worse burned black like that. Not his fault, y'know," he added apologetically. "Nice enough fellow. At least, used to be. Here, old bean," he said to St. Just, "you'd better let me take the lady. Face like yours is a dreadful shock to someone who don't feel well to begin with."

Hetty giggled more strongly. "That's silly, Cousin George. Vyvyan is my husband."

"Oh, yes. Used to his face, I guess. Still, might be a shock after a faint. Would be to me."

He rose to his feet, dusted his breeches carefully, and helped Hetty to stand, enabling St. Just to rise. Pamela had been biting her lips in an agony of mirth. All that kept her sober was the feeling that her laughter might sever the last strand of St. Just's self-restraint, and Hetty was in no condition to endure a quarrel raging around her. Besides, nothing could be better for Hetty than George, even if her diversion was at her husband's expense. Only Pamela found that she had underestimated the bond between the two men.

"What is wrong with my face?" the earl asked mildly.

"Cornish," George replied, as if that explained everything.

"It was not Vyvyan," Hetty said a little pettishly, resenting the fact that attention had wandered from her. "It was the house." She shuddered again, dramatically. "It is so forbidding."

"No, no," George comforted, patting her hand. "Just Cornish. Does look queer — everything in Cornwall is queer. You'll find it is better inside than out." He laughed merrily. "Just like Vyvyan — better inside than out."

Pamela had turned away to hide her laughter. It was not that George was unusual. Really he was a typical London dandy, from the carefully brushed burnished blond of his waving hair to the brilliantly polished tips of his white-topped boots. He was merely out of place. In London or a fashionable country house near the city, Pamela would have felt no amusement at the clipped yet drawling speech with its carefully ungrammatical affectations, at the deliberately uttered idiocies. She might have been bored, or wearied, or mildly pleased, depending upon the situation. Here, however, she was almost in hilarious laughter, only . . . Could there be a purpose in those idiocies? Was George trying to warn Hetty of something?

Sobered by the idea, Pamela looked seriously at the place St. Just had married Hetty to save. It was built on a natural plateau of the northern cliff that rose above the valley in which the village of St. Just lay. To the south, the land fell away gently into grazing land, and below that the strange luxuriant arable valley of Cornwall. To the east and north, there was more grazing land, which rose until it melted into the arid, hilly Cornish backbone. To the west, a quarter-mile away and far below, the sea moved restlessly.

The house faced southwest, its drive snaking away from the main road across a lawn that was more field than park. There were no ancient oaks or limes to line the drive. The Cornish wind would not let them grow. Thus the house stood naked, presenting its many-windowed blue-gray front defiantly to the sea. The central portion was three stories high, with four windows to each side of the door on the first level, ten on the second, and ten, much smaller, in the servants' quarters on the third. It would have been a hard, grim front except for two wings that protruded slightly. These were topped by graceful, frivolous cupolas with round windows — obviously accretions of a later date than the main structure.

All in all, the house was not typical in any sense. The building was constructed of Cornish granite rather than the customary brick, and its cornerstones were of a strange, exquisitely colored rock that drew the eye.

24

Moreover, every window had heavy, solid shutters. These were now open to admit the light, but their presence hinted of the need to be armored against some fierce onslaught.

Possibly the combination of stonework and shutters on an essentially Jacobean house did have what George called a queer effect; possibly with the eyes of the house blinded by closed shutters it would look forbidding. Possibly; but Pamela knew that to her it looked right; it belonged here in Cornwall, made of native rock and adapted to its surroundings.

The others were moving in now, and Pamela followed hastily through the large door that opened into the central hall. She drew her breath with pleasure at the sight of the warm afternoon light falling upon the well-polished furniture. That, too, was Jacobean in style, old and heavy but lovingly cared for.

"Oh," Hetty's voice rose in protest, "this is Gothic — quite Gothic."

"No," St. Just replied dryly, "it is Jacobean. My — I-don't-know-how-many-back — grandfather was old-fashioned. The house was built in the 1670's, I believe, but the furniture either was already in the family or was built to match an earlier style."

"Don't be dense, Vyvyan," George said in his light, amused tone. "Lady St. Just was describing the aura of the place, not its period. Must agree with her. Gothic it is. Always after your father to get rid of this stuff. Family tradition's fine, but not when it's uncomfortable."

"Hetty," Pamela interposed softly as she saw little muscles bunch in St. Just's jaw, "do you not think you had better go through the formality of inspecting the servants before you continue this discussion? It is, after all, none of their affair what you decide to do about the furniture."

The countess glanced toward the east end of the hall, where the butler, housekeeper, footmen, and maids stood in a long line waiting their attention. She shrank back a little, and George, who misunderstood her distaste and took it for alarm, took her hand gracefully in his.

"Won't bite you," he murmured. "Very good sort of people. Better let me," he added more loudly to St. Just as the master of the house stepped forward. "Been away a long time, you know. Lot of changes. You'll make a mull of it."

Pamela closed her eyes for a moment, sure that this last piece of tactlessness would break St. Just's so-far admirable control over his usually hasty temper. She was even more alarmed, a half-second later, at the expression which flickered over Hetty's face. That Hetty disliked her husband was nothing unusual in this day and age when marriages were made to ally families and bolster dwindling fortunes. However, if Hetty was going to be attracted to George and show it, the situation, which was now merely uncomfortable, might become explosive. St. Just had not seen Hetty's expression, fortunately, and there was no anger in his voice. He sounded mildly exasperated by George's interference, but rather indulgent.

"Now, George," he remonstrated, "how could I forget Hayle or Mrs. Helston? Tremaire would not be Tremaire without them. And Sarah . . ."

Pamela was amazed when St. Just went forward and took the hand of a middle-aged woman, kissed her cheek, and said a few words too low to be heard.

"Nathan," he continued, smiling at the oldest of the footmen, "I remember, and Benjamin also. Some of these people are new," he added, gesturing to Hetty to walk down the line with him, "but I have their names from our agent, and I am sure I know who is who."

Of course, he got every name and face — down to the boot boy and second scullery maid — correctly matched. It was not really difficult. Since place in line was rigidly fixed by household position, St. Just could hardly err. Nonetheless, few masters bothered to learn the names of the lower servants. Watching the faces light with pleasure, Pamela thought the effort well worthwhile. St. Just's control over his household had doubtless been improved by this little scene.

"And this," he added when he had said a personal word to each, "is Lady St. Just and my wife's friend and guest, Lady Pamela Hervey."

A wave of movement stirred the rigid line, the menservants bowing, the women curtsying. For a moment Pamela could not see distinctly through the mist of tears that rose in her eyes. By the choice of words in his introduction, a very deliberate choice, Pamela was sure, St. Just had saved her a world of petty humiliations. If he had said "companion" instead of "guest," every servant would have resented attending to her; her bell would have been answered late, her dresses carelessly pressed, her orders ignored or responded to with insolence. When her vision cleared, Pamela smiled at the row of servants, giving a little more particular attention to the woman called Sarah.

St. Just had mentioned her as his mother's maid, but he had kissed her with affection in public and spoken to her in the low tones of intimacy. She did not look much like a lady's maid to Pamela's experienced eyes, either. Her hair was drawn back into a tight bun, and her dress was that of a local countrywoman, but she was examining Hetty with an assurance that augured a privileged position.

"Would you like to see the rest of the house now, Hetty," St. Just asked his wife after he dismissed the servants, "or would you like to go upstairs and rest awhile?"

"Just because you think Tremaire is the beginning and the end of the world, Master Vyvyan, don't you be believing everyone else thinks the same," the woman called Sarah said in the blighting tones of a nurse to a small, inconsiderate charge. She had taken no notice of St. Just's dismissal of the other servants, confirming Pamela's impression of her position in the household. "I've readied madam's room for her ladyship. She can see the house after she's put aside her pelisse and freshened her face and hair."

Although it was plain that Hetty was affronted by Sarah's presumption and found little to recommend her in her address, she was willing to follow her suggestion. She wanted to see her bedchamber and was eager also to change her dusty and soiled clothing. They filed out through the northeast corner of the hall, through a short corridor, and up a handsomely carved staircase. Sarah took the lead, which made Hetty purse her lips, but Pamela could not see what else the maid could have done, and in spite of her frown, Hetty followed, trailed by Pamela, with St. Just bringing up the rear. Sarah turned right and walked down a central corridor.

"That is my suite," St. Just commented, gesturing to a room that was above the hall. "It was my father's, of course." A shadow crossed his face, but he continued steadily, "There is another door, which opens in the cross-corridor. It is a convenient pair of rooms."

They bypassed another equally handsome stairway, which St. Just said led down to the dining room, billiards room, and breakfast room, through which one could get to the large drawing room. Sarah then turned right again and opened a heavy door.

Sunlight flooded through wide-open windows facing south and west, giving jewel tones to the rich Turkish carpet on the floor and making the emerald green curtains that draped the bed almost painful to the eye.

"How beautiful," Pamela breathed.

"Oh, do you think so?" Hetty asked doubtfully. "It is not very . . . very feminine."

"Madam was a strong woman," Sarah said

dourly. "She liked it so."

"Well," Hetty remarked as if she had not heard the maid speak, "it does not signify. I will get it furnished anew."

Pamela glanced at St. Just, saw the blank, withdrawn expression he wore, and looked away. She knew he was being very foolish. Hetty was quite right. However lovely the furnishings, they would not suit her. Nonetheless, her heart was wrung for him. His homecoming had been spoiled. The things he loved had been sneered at as worthless. It was very tactless of Hetty to criticize a house she must have known he adored and had longed for.

It was worse than tactless, it was deliberately cruel, to speak so casually about discarding his mother's possessions. He must have been happy in this room, for it was plain he had loved his mother. The room, the furniture, must hold memory upon memory for him. Could Hetty not have waited until those memories were overlaid with new ones before suggesting a change? Impulsively Pamela sprang to the defense of a precious memory.

"But see how conveniently everything is arranged, Hetty," Pamela suggested.

"Conveniently!" the countess exclaimed. "Why, the sun glares from those windows right into your face when you sit at the dressing table. And whoever heard of a lady's bedchamber that had no dressing room attached."

"No, no," Pamela urged, sorry that she had not let well enough alone, but forced to continue her defense. "It is too early now," she pointed out, going and sitting down at the dressing table, "but a little later the sunshine would go above one's head and cast the most excellent light. And in the morning, you know, the sun is not on this side, and the light would be clear and soft. Then, look, right to hand is the wardrobe. You could choose which dress you wanted without even turning around."

"Yes, indeed, I see. I said I thought it disgraceful that the mistress of the house should not have a dressing room. A wardrobe in the bedchamber! How paltry! What is a maid for but to carry dresses for me to choose."

Both had found it necessary to raise their voices a trifle, because a rising murmur was coming from the windows. Hetty turned her head irritably in the direction of the sound, then, as it began to fade, walked to the wardrobe and opened the doors. She pursed her lips discontentedly and looked toward the inner wall, where a fireplace was flanked by two comfortable Queen Anne chairs, each with a small table and a branch of shaded candles beside it. The murmur of sound began again and increased in volume. Hetty looked toward the windows once more.

"Whatever is that noise, Vyvyan?"

He had been looking out, and turned toward his wife. "The sea. Come here, Hetty. You can see it. My mother would stand at these windows for hours at a time when the wind was strong, watching the whitecaps. She said one could never be dull in this room, because the waves told her stories in pictures — never the same. The tide is going out now, but when it comes in on a gale, you can almost feel the breakers under your feet in this room. My mother loved the sea."

"Well, I do not," Hetty said sharply. "If you are telling me that that noise becomes louder, I can say right now that this room is not suitable. Why, I could not sleep a wink with all that howling and growling."

There was a tense silence. Pamela caught a single twist of St Just's lips before he turned back to the window. He did it on purpose, she thought with a quiver of unease, now watching Hetty stand stubbornly in the middle of the floor, refusing even to approach the window or look at the view. He does not want Hetty in his mother's room.

"There is the other Lady St. Just's suite," Sarah said flatly. "That was prepared for her ladyship's guest. Perhaps her ladyship would like to look at that. It is on the most sheltered side of the house, northwest, it is. The other lady was a little shaken in her nerves. She didn't like the sea neither. If you will come this way, my lady."

They passed out into the corridor again and immediately into a small dressing room. Here Hetty paused, her eyes brightening. The delicate writing desk and chair were white and gilt, the curtains of gold brocade, and a small Aubusson carpet of roses and ivy covered the floor. There was also a chaise longue of the same gold brocade as the curtains, with a white-and-gilt table bearing a branch of candles.

"Pretty," Hetty purred, and stepped lightly through an open doorway into the bed-chamber.

This was more of the same, dainty and delicate, breathing the spirit of a gentle woman who wished to be ensconced and cherished. Pamela agreed heartily that it was pretty and in excellent taste. However, when Hetty said grudgingly that she could not deprive her "guest" of so lovely a pair of rooms, Pamela replied quite sincerely that she would feel like a bull — or rather a cow — in a china shop there.

"It is much more suitable to you, Hetty,"

she agreed. "A great blundering creature like myself would make these delicate chairs creak."

"Very well," the countess said happily. "See that my things are moved, uh . . . uh . . ."

"Sarah, my lady."

"Yes, Sarah, of course. Well, now, what room will you have, Pam? I declare, this is very amusing. I am feeling much better."

"That is a problem, my lady," the maid said stolidly. "Most of Tremaire is very shabby. The two countess's rooms were kept up because the late earl desired it. Master Arthur's and Charles's room would not be at all suitable, being arranged for gentlemen."

"Why do you not simply exchange rooms?" St. Just asked. "Will the sound of the sea disturb you, Lady Pamela?"

Pamela was both flattered and mildly alarmed. She had come to like and admire St. Just in the time they had traveled together, and it was pleasant to know that he would not mind her using his mother's things. On the other hand, she had no desire to make Hetty jealous.

"No," Pamela said hesitantly, "I love the sea, and I think the room is beautiful, but if it was the late countess's perhaps I had better not."

"Oh, do, Pam — if you would not mind

dreadfully," Hetty urged. "Then you will be right next to me, and that would be so convenient."

I will also be closer to your husband than you will, Pamela thought uneasily, but she could not say that, nor even protest again without placing a totally unwarrantable emphasis on the subject. Besides, it was only her own suspicious mind that had raised the problem. She accepted the offer quietly.

CHAPTER 3

After the inauspicious beginning of the journey, life in Tremaire settled into a very pleasant pattern. Pamela generally woke early and rode before breakfast. She tried all of the ladles' horses and settled on a strong but rather skittish black mare as her favorite. George, when he discovered Pamela was riding Velvet, protested that the animal was not safe, but St. Just laughed. It was his opinion, he said, that Lady Pamela could manage anything, and he would back her against a mere mare any day.

Breakfast was eaten with Hetty in the small breakfast parlor adjoining the large drawing room. Often George, who was not an early riser, joined them. Pamela liked George. He was amusing and thoughtful, and he never teased Hetty the way he teased St. Just. In fact, Pamela found him of the greatest use in remolding the countess's manners and habits as soon as he discovered her real purpose. His gentle, "No, m'dear, bad ton," was more effective than all Pamela's explanations. The fact that he was able and eager to discuss the follies and foibles of the set Hetty wished to join also helped. Almost more important than his help was the fact that George accepted Pamela as a paid companion without the slightest change in manner toward her. She was so struck by this unusual forbearance that she once thanked him for it.

George uttered his light laugh. "No, no, no credit to me," he disclaimed with a sudden shrewd twinkle breaking his usual fishlike stare. "Th'only difference between you and me, Lady Pam, is that you do something for your allowance. Glad to be of assistance. Servant, any time."

After breakfast Hetty customarily walked through the large drawing room and went to sit in the morning room or small drawing room beyond it. If George accompanied her, as he often did, Pamela knew she would be free for several hours to deal with household matters. She had been shocked when Hetty refused to examine the menus that Mrs. Helston submitted for her approval, or to discuss the proper punishment for a laundry maid who quarreled with a scullery maid. On this subject, however, Hetty was adamant.

"I would scarcely need to employ a housekeeper if I am to be troubled with this nonsense," she said to Pamela, "and you may tell Mrs. Helston so."

What Hetty was to do in the future, if she would not attend to running Tremaire, Pamela could not guess. At present the countess was very much occupied in looking through catalogs of furnishings and examining cloth samples sent from Plymouth, Bristol, and even London. St. Just had agreed to refurnishing part of the house. The hall, his suite of rooms, and Pamela's bedchamber were not to be touched. For the rest of the house Hetty had a free hand, subject to George's and Pamela's corrective taste. But Pamela soon found herself *de trop* in these discussions, and since she had perfect reliance on George's knowledge of such matters, she was happy to leave the affair completely in his hands.

Pamela herself picked up the reins of the household. She could not repeat to Mrs. Helston what Hetty had said. That would merely set the housekeeper against her to no purpose. Mrs. Helston was an employee of long standing and could not be summarily discharged. Hetty really knew this, for she had had a furious battle with St. Just over Sarah, whom she disliked intensely. What Hetty did not seem to understand was that offending the upper servants would merely result in disrupting the staff to the discomfort of everyone involved. Pamela told Mrs. Helston, therefore, that Lady St. Just was unaccustomed to running a household — which was true — and that she did not like to interfere for fear of making trouble — which was not.

"Then what am I to do, my lady?" the woman had asked stolidly. "There are things I can't do on my own responsibility."

That this remark was merely a sign of resentment, Pamela knew. Mrs. Helston fully intended to run the house in her own way, but she expected verbal appreciation for her efforts and approval of her plans. This was her due, and Pamela promptly said she would undertake to obtain decisions from Lady St. Just if Mrs. Helston would bring the problems to her. This fiction lasted about a week. At the end of that time, she and Mrs. Helston were working together so smoothly that neither felt it necessary to pretend the decisions Pamela made came from Hetty.

Of St. Just, Pamela saw almost nothing. He was generally out of the house before she came down, and he rarely returned before dinnertime. At table he was abstracted and curt, his mind plainly on things unrelated to the company in which he found himself. When George and Hetty remonstrated with him, he snarled, and both soon found it more comfortable to ignore the silent figure at the head of the table. After dinner he either rode out again or retired to his own rooms. Precisely what he was doing, no one seemed to know, although George seemed certain it had to do with the estate.

"Mad about the place, you know," he remarked when Hetty complained bitterly that if Vyvyan would join them they could play whist. "Probably riding all over it examining every blade of grass to be certain it's growing just where it was when he left. Got some notion about making the place pay better, too. Swears there's tin and copper on his land. Might be. Owns miles of that useless ridge stuff. Good thing if he found it. Very profitable stuff, tin."

"Well, really," Hetty exclaimed, "that is the silliest thing I have heard yet. Vyvyan does not need money. He has all of mine, and since my brother died he could buy the whole county if he wanted to."

George's rather protuberant eyes regarded Hetty thoughtfully. "True enough, but better not to speak of it, m'dear. Bad ton to talk of money at all. Besides, Vyvyan's a plaguey proud devil. Don't like to owe anyone anything."

"I don't care," said Hetty, flushing. "It is

41

only my money that has permitted him to keep this God-forsaken desert of a place. He might show a little consideration for me, under the circumstances."

"Perhaps that is just what he is trying to do, Hetty," Pamela suggested. "I am sure he does not like to think that Tremaire is a drain upon your fortune. If he could make the estate pay for itself, his conscience would be less troubled. Anyway, there is no sense in teasing ourselves over his freaks of behavior. We cannot make four for whist, but if George would not mind, we could play at loo."

"Delighted. Very good practice for you too, Hetty. Ladies all play loo in town. Lose a lot of money at it, some of them."

As the weather grew warmer, Hetty began to drive out on pleasant afternoons. She would take no part in the housekeeping, and condemned English servants roundly, but apparently she delighted in at least one aspect of country life. Being the great lady of the estate and village appealed to her. She visited both the town and the cottages on the estate and enjoyed the condescension with which she was able to treat these people. The expeditions were made in a pretty little pony cart drawn by a surefooted white mule. The equipage had been made for the same Lady St. Just whose room Hetty had approved. The mule was her own idea. Pamela was appalled and George revolted, but Hetty had her own way. She had driven a mule on the islands, she said, and understood their temperament. Horses were too nervous for her. She had, in fact, purchased the mule herself and had brought back with it a young man from the village to be her groom and care specifically for the animal.

Pamela had been concerned, fearing resentment among the already established stable hands, but George told her there would be no trouble.

"Wouldn't mention it to Vyvyan, though." George laughed. "Joke on him. Bigger joke on Hetty. Shouldn't wonder if it worked out for the best."

"Of course I shan't say anything to St. Just. It is Hetty's affair, but —"

"Oh, no harm in it, since the boy was willing. He's a son of one of the People. Funny thing him being willing to take the place. Probably want to keep an eye on Vyvyan. Silly thing."

"What do you mean, he's a son of one of the people? And if anyone wants to 'keep an eye' on St. Just, shouldn't he know?"

George shrugged. "People — with a big P — are the witches. Leave them alone — better that way. Lot of bad feeling here once.

43

M'grandmother got an odd disease — wasted away. M'grandfather got the notion that his wife had been hexed. Believed that then. Set out to clean up the covens. Couldn't, of course. Hanged one old devil, though. She cursed the family. Odd sort of curse, too. Eldest son would never inherit until the earl married a witch. Damned funny thing. The eldest son drowned, and m'uncle — Vyvyan's father — inherited. Damned funny thing."

"But . . . but did not St. Just's father and his two elder brothers drown also?" Pamela asked, horrified in spite of the common sense that told her these things were the merest coincidence and that drowning was scarcely an uncommon fate for people who lived on the coast and had sailing for an amusement. But four in one family!

"Said it was a damned funny thing," George remarked, his eyes more fishlike than ever as they stared past Pamela into the distance.

"Part of a witch's power is to bring on storms — is it not?"

"The locals believe it. Reason no one can touch the covens. Make their living at fishing, a lot of them — and they're wreckers too, y'know. None of 'em would dare cross a witch. When the fleets go out, they hex good weather. When a fat merchantman sails by, they sing up a storm."

"What!"

"Bad coast — all rocks. Ship founders, locals go out, pick up what they can. Know the rocks, you see. Caves for storage too. Who's to say where the stuff came from a couple of months later?"

"But the crew . . . the passengers!"

"Oh, they don't kill 'em. This coast ain't as bad as some others. Not enough wrecks really to make murder profitable. Pick up the passengers for the 'reward.' More like ransom, but it's legal."

"George!" Pamela exclaimed. "Can nothing be done?"

"Done about what — the weather?"

Pamela flushed slightly. It was hard to tell what George thought, since his voice held only its usual cool indifference and his expression its habitual placidity. In fact, she did not believe that a witch could sing a storm, and, indeed, nothing could be done about the weather or the coastline. As long as the local fishermen did not actively cause wrecks by moving warning beacons — and she devoutly hoped this was so, although she feared to ask — they could not be blamed for making what profit they could out of wrecks. Certainly if they rescued the crews and passengers, it was better for them to act than to remain ashore.

"You did not answer my other question," Pamela said, changing the subject. "If Hetty's groom is spying on St. Just, should he not know of it? And why *should* he be spied upon?"

"Not sure, of course. Don't deal with the People m'self. Imagine they want to know whether he blames them for what happened. Fond of his father, y'know. Quarreled over the West Indies business, but . . . Fond of his half-brothers, too. Got along well. Damned funny thing. Freak storm. Late earl didn't like sailing either. Got a distaste for it when *his* brother drowned. Odd all around."

"But then . . . Does he blame them, George?"

The blank eyes focused on her. "Known Vyvyan all my life. Never understood him. Like his mother. Cornish — queer. Locals said she was one of the People, y'know. Said she bewitched m'uncle or that he married her to break the curse. Doubt it m'self. Damn fine woman. Lot like you, come to think of it — not in looks, but big and graceful. . . . Except her eyes were like Vyvyan's — green as glass, clear."

"What happened to her, George?"

His face closed. "Ask Vyvyan."

It was only later that Pamela realized she had never had an answer to why it was wise to keep the identity of Hetty's groom from St. Just. She worried at the idea for several days and finally decided to hold her tongue. It was very unlikely that Hetty knew — or if she were told, would care — about the groom's association with the coven. She had indicated her contempt of witchcraft clearly enough. In addition, Pamela was reasonably certain that St. Just harbored no ill intentions toward the People. In the discussion they had had at the inn he had seemed on the favorable side of neutral. In that case, Hetty's groom could learn nothing that would harm St. Just. There was a last consideration, which clinched Pamela's decision. The tension between Hetty and her husband was not easing. If St. Just were told, decided he did not want a spy on the estate, and dismissed the groom, Hetty would have still another cause to feel ill-used.

A few days later it was Pamela's turn to feel ill-used, or at least irritable. The morning had poured rain, so that she was deprived of her customary exercise. George had left the day before to visit friends in Penzance, and his absence had made Hetty extremely fractious. Now, here was Mrs. Helston with an involved tale of woe. One of the gardeners — a married man — had made one of the maids pregnant. The man, Mrs. Helston said furiously, should be dismissed. He was insolent and a poor workman. And what was she to do with the maid? The girl was a foundling. To dismiss her would mean the workhouse or starvation. To keep her would set a bad example for the other maids. If such transgressions were not punished, there would be a flood of such incidents.

"Oh, dear," Pamela sighed, acutely aware of the powerlessness of her position. It was one thing to approve menus and agree to Mrs. Helston's minor disciplinary actions. To dismiss servants who were not her own was another matter. "Are you certain that the man is guilty?"

"Oh, he admits it, bold as brass, my lady. Lays the blame on the girl, saying she's a hussy and he just took what was freely offered."

In spirit Pamela groaned even more dismally. She could see the signs. Mrs. Helston would stand up for her subordinate; the head gardener would stand up for his subordinate. Neither of them actually cared for the rights or wrongs of the situation. Had they been her servants, she would have had them all up before her and thrashed the matter out. It was the only way to bring Mrs. Helston and the head gardener to agree and save years of resentment, backbiting, and cross-accusations. Unfortunately, to do that, one also had to administer the punishment at once. To delay meant time for the upper servants to reconsider, think of new arguments, and begin all over.

"Very well, Mrs. Helston. I will take the matter up with Lady St. Just."

Pamela rose and shook the creases from her Indian muslin dress, thinking that Hetty was the oddest mixture and as unpredictable as a child. It would be just like her to decide to handle this affair herself and make a mull of it. St. Just really should deal with it, since the outside servants were not Hetty's responsibility; but St. Just — as usual — was out, and the longer action was delayed, the more firmly set Mrs. Helston and the gardener would become in their opinions. Pamela opened the door to the morning room, and had she been less disciplined, would have burst into tears of frustration. Hetty was not immersed in her catalogs and swatches. She was sitting and tapping her fingers on the small table by her chair to show her impatience and need of company.

"Where have you been, Pam? I declare, you take longer over breakfast than anyone I know."

"I've been speaking with Mrs. Helston, Hetty. She is having trouble with one of the maids."

"That woman is incompetent. Why, at home our housekeeper handled five times the number of servants with less fuss."

"Perhaps, but they were slaves, and those methods cannot be used on our people," Pamela said coldly.

"More's the pity. Really, Pam, you worry more about offending the servants than about offending me."

That was probably meant to be a warning. Pamela, enraged still further, felt like saying that the servants were more necessary to her comfort, but she took a grip on her temper and recounted the situation. "Will you speak to them, Hetty, or give me leave to dismiss one or both as I see fit after finding out the truth?"

"Speak to them? About their sordid . . . Certainly not! I told you before that if Mrs. Helston could not do her work, she must be replaced with someone who can."

At least the worst had not happened, Pamela thought. Hetty had not decided to stick her finger in the pie. "Be reasonable," Pamela suggested, still hoping to get authority to deal with the situation herself. "Mrs. Helston has no power to dismiss the gardener's man, and if he lied to the girl and seduced her, to dismiss the maid would not solve the problem. In a month or two another maid would be pregnant. Naturally, Mrs. Helston places the blame on the man, but the gardener seems to think it was the girl's fault. This must be settled by outside authority, or there will be a feud between the inner and outer servants — and that will make *us* uncomfortable."

"I cannot see how it could. By the by, I saw a very likely girl in the village the other day, and she is coming here to be my maid. I will not have that loathsome creature Sarah pressing and mending my gowns. Will you be a sweet love and teach the girl to do my hair? Dear Pam, you have been so kind, letting me make use of you in ways that are not fitting, but I cannot take advantage of you forever."

"A raw girl from the town, Hetty? But —"

"Oh, no. She has been in service before, but she was looking out for a mistress who would not remain fixed in this wilderness."

"Of course I will teach her," Pamela said slowly.

It would be a relief to be free of the personal services she had performed for Hetty, although Pamela had not minded much, because Hetty was always very pleasant and grateful. There was also nothing unusual in a new mistress adding to the staff of a household. Still, there was something odd here. If the girl had been in service, how had Hetty seen her or made her an offer? If she was at home in the village, why was she there? One did not look for a new place in even a large village like St. Just if one's aim was the one Hetty stated.

"How did you find this girl, Hetty? Are you sure —"

"Quite sure. I have seen her, and I like her. I . . . I heard about her family from Alice, and on one of my drives, I inquired," Hetty said with heightened color.

That might be true, although Pamela knew that Hetty and her sister-in-law did not get along well. "But was she dismissed from her place? Has she any other recommendation?"

"Are you my friend or my jailer, Pamela? Am I to have no one around me but old women who hate me?"

"Hetty! I was only concerned that the girl might steal your jewels, or . . ."

The countess cocked her head, and her pale eyes gleamed. "Oh, she won't do that. This is not London, with a market for such things."

Pamela's lips parted to say that there must be takers for unaccountable property in the neighborhood because of the wrecking activities, but she realized that Hetty probably did not know about that. It would be foolish in the extreme to tell her and give her another reason to dislike the locality. In any case, it was unlikely that a local girl would steal jewelry or cause any other major trouble. Even if she could get away, her family would bear the brunt of her misdeeds, and these people were closely knit in their family groups. It occurred to Pamela that Hetty had not told her who the girl was, but after the turn the conversation had taken, she was not going to ask. Anyway, she had issued her warning. Whatever happened was Hetty's responsibility.

"You must do as you like, of course, Hetty. About the other matter, Mrs. Helston was very upset. Would you mind if I mentioned it to St. Just?"

Hetty began to laugh. "If you can get speech of him," she chortled. "It is just the sort of thing to hold his interest. Really, Pam, you are as bad as he. All you seem to think of is servants and the estate. One would think you had some personal interest in Tremaire."

"I like a well-run house," Pamela said stiffly. She had a momentary fear that Hetty thought there was something more than friendship between St. Just and herself, then dismissed the idea. They had scarcely exchanged a dozen words a day, and his manner was no more or less civil to Pamela than to his wife.

"Don't let us quarrel, Pam," Hetty said, putting out her hand. "See, all these new journals have come. Do help me pick some pretty gowns. George says there are some very fashionable assemblies at Plymouth and that Torquay is becoming quite favored as a seaside resort. Perhaps we will go there for a few weeks."

The state of the roads and Hetty's difficulty in traveling, not to mention St. Just's probable reluctance to tear himself away from his estate, raised questions in Pamela's mind, but she did not voice them. She carried the journals to the sofa and sat down beside Hetty. Usually Pamela found dress an absorbing subject, but somehow today it was difficult to concentrate on the relative merits of Belgian lace over French or to conceive of a particular gown trimmed with bows of ribbon instead of tucks. Still, it was a source of satisfaction to her that Hetty had learned so quickly. The models she chose for morning dresses were entirely appropriate — simple and elegant. Even her choice of evening dress was restrained, showing no indication of the tendency to overdressing she had originally displayed.

"I shall have these four made up," Hetty said finally. "That will be sufficient. Now you must choose some for yourself."

"You are very kind, Hetty, but since we do not entertain, it seems useless." Pamela laughed at Hetty's frown. "When we get to London, I will sing quite another tune. That is when I shall become an expensive luxury. I will remind you then of my present restraint."

"You make me sound so cheese-paring, as if I would grudge you a dress or two. I can buy what I like for people who please me."

"I am sure that is true, Hetty, and that you mean to be generous, but you must not throw your wealth in people's faces." Pamela mitigated the criticism with a smile, although her pride was stung, because she believed Hetty meant well.

The countess tossed her head. "Oh, look," she said, ignoring Pamela's reprimand, "the rain has stopped. I am glad of that. I think I will go out driving this afternoon." She hesitated, then said, "Would you like to come?"

Pamela also hesitated. She had no desire at all to remain in Hetty's company, but she did not wish her to think she was still annoyed about the offer of a dress. "Will you be offended if I say no? I am really pining for some exercise, and that carriage you have, chartering as it is, rather cramps me. Shall I accompany you on horseback?"

"No, indeed," Hetty said, but with a very sunny smile. "It will make you cross as two sticks to be held to a walk when you wish to gallop. Vyvyan could never *abide* it. I don't mind going alone. I will have my groom, of course."

It was only with the brightening of Hetty's eyes and the relaxation of her expression that Pamela realized how reluctant the invitation had been. Hetty did not want her to come. All the irritability she had displayed must be connected with some plan with which the rain had interfered. Pamela wondered idly what purpose Hetty could have. By mutual consent they walked through the corridor to the saloon that fronted on the gardens. Here there was a sheltered porch, and, having stepped outside, they could see that the sky was clearing and the weather promising fair. With a lift of spirits, Pamela followed Hetty upstairs to change to her riding habit.

Usually she rode along the cliffs to watch the sea. The scene was fantastic in its variability. On a clear, soft day, the water was as green as St. Just's eyes, translucent, with the wavelets sparkling like light laughter on it. When the sky was bright but the wind high, there would be bands of whitecaps, like lace, on the swelling bosom of the waters as far as the eye could see. And sometimes it was true witch-water, a ghostly gray shimmering substance that looked as if you could walk into it, still breathing, and be wafted away into some mysterious otherwhere.

Today, however, Pamela soon turned Velvet's head inland toward the arid hills. The sea was sullen and merely reinforced her bad mood. Following a well-marked track, which led northeast, she came to a low ridge. Above her the ground grew more and more tortured, rising in sharper ridges that were broken by steep gullies. Pamela knew that if she did not soon turn back she would be late for dinner, but she could not yet bring herself to face the querulous complaints about the cooking, the service, and everything else that Hetty, no matter what her earlier mood, never failed to utter in St. Just's presence. If she were tired enough physically, Pamela knew, she would not have so difficult a task in keeping her temper.

She went down into another dip, and up another ridge. Just as she was heading into still another hollow, a rider came around an outcrop of rock farther up, perhaps a half-mile away. It was too far to see the horseman's face, which was hidden by his hat in any case, but it was impossible to mistake the action of St. Just's big gray or the way his powerful body seemed almost a part of his mount. Pamela stopped and waited, conscious of an easing of her tension. They could ride home together, and she could tell him of Mrs. Helston's problem. She knew she was on the easiest and most direct path to the house, and St. Just was riding quickly, obviously anxious to get home. He would certainly come that way. There was another outcrop of rock between them. Suddenly St. Just's horse swerved as if he had intended to go around and then decided to come down on the near side of it; and horse and rider disappeared.

For a few minutes Pamela continued to wait, assuming that the faint scrambling she heard was the horse making its way down and up a hidden gully. She even smiled. St. Just must have seen her and decided to take the shorter, though harder path. The horse appeared. Pamela took an expectant breath, ready to call a greeting, then cried out in fear. The big gray had no rider.

CHAPTER 4

He was lying in the gully with blood on his face. "St. Just," Pamela shrieked, conscious of a tearing sense of loss she could not explain. He did not stir, and Pamela bit her lips when she saw how deep and precipitous the gully was. It was impossible to leave him there, not knowing whether he was dead or badly hurt, and Pamela did not lack courage. She looped Velvet's reins around her arm and slid and scrambled toward him. An eternity passed before she knelt and saw he was still breathing, that his eyelids were already fluttering open. The green eyes were dazed, unfocused.

"Thank God," Pamela breathed.

St. Just's hand twitched, moved uncertainly toward his head. Pamela caught it, bent to lift him, and stopped. It was better not to touch someone who had taken a bad fall until the damage done was known.

"Don't move, my lord. Can you hear me?"

"Pam?"

"Yes, don't move. Where are you hurt?"

"Sergeant? Where's Sergeant?"

"He's all right. Gone off home. St. Just, where are you hurt?"

He closed his eyes again, and Pamela could see him fighting sickness. He moved slightly, bit his lips. "My head. I must have hit it. I think that's all."

"I'm going to lift you up. If I hurt you, tell me."

His eyes snapped open, focused this time, and an expression of incredulity mixed with the pain on his face. "Don't be silly. It takes a winch to lift me."

Pamela smiled. "I'm as good as a winch any day. Strong as a horse." She released his hand and put her arms around him. St. Just went rigid, put out a hand to push her away, and groaned softly. "Where does it hurt?" Pamela asked anxiously.

St. Just ignored her hesitation, drew convulsively away from her, and sat upright. "It's all right," he said, struggling to steady his breath. "I've only sprained my wrist." He lifted the hand to look at it. There was a jagged cut in the palm, which made Pamela wince, and the wrist was already swollen. "I suppose I broke my fall with it," St. Just continued indifferently. "I cut it on a rock, I daresay. I'm lucky it's no worse." He reached out toward the side of the gully with his good

60

hand and rose to his feet, wincing. "All right and tight," he announced.

The next minute, however, he would have fallen, had not Pamela leaped to support him. She eased him to a sitting position, troubled by the set look of misery he wore. It was plain that his expression had little to do with his physical condition and that he was not much hurt, for his color had come back to normal, and his eyes were perfectly clear. A mixture of relief and an inexplicable feeling that she must ward off something made Pamela furious.

"Whatever made you think you could careen down a gully like this at the pace you were going?" she snapped.

St. Just started to shake his head, groaned again, and touched his scalp gingerly. "I didn't. I saw you, and maybe I touched Sergeant up a bit, but I intended to go around by the path. I swear I didn't move the reins. I don't know what happened. I was looking at you, damn it. Maybe there was a shadow or something, but I've ridden this way a dozen times, and Sergeant never shyed before. He's not a nervous horse. Are you sure he's all right?"

"There couldn't be much wrong with him at the rate he was making off for the stables. Perhaps he cut his knees. I was not worrying about the horse."

"Just like a woman," the earl said with mock disapproval. "After all, a broken leg or a couple of marks on my hide would scarcely be a tragedy, whereas a horse . . ."

Pamela chuckled, although she was still much shaken. "I was thinking more along the lines of a broken neck or mashed brains, although I suppose I should not have worried. The latter certainly wouldn't have done you any harm, my lord."

He uttered the little choke of laughter so characteristic of him, and Pamela's heart contracted. "That is no way to talk to your employer," he said, but there was a caressing note in his teasing that made Pamela climb hastily to her feet and move away.

"I am very sorry," she said stiffly; and then, bitterly regretting her coldness because of his suddenly stricken expression, she added, "How can you tease me when you are bleeding like a stuck pig?"

"But I'm not." St. Just held up the blood-clotted hand as evidence. His tone was light, but his eyes were wary.

Pamela shook her head impatiently. "Bleeding or not, you should be attended to. There is not even any water here to wash the dirt from those cuts. We will be dreadfully late for dinner, too, and Hetty will be frantic."

At the mention of his wife's name, the life

drained out of St. Just's face. "Very well," he said dully. "Ride back and let them know what has happened. One of the grooms can come back with a horse for me."

"Leave you here alone?"

"I shall be perfectly safe. There are no fierce wild animals to attack me. After all, I suppose I deserve an hour or so of discomfort and boredom for being such a fool as to look at a pretty girl instead of my path, not to mention being so careless as to part company with my saddle and then commit the greater sin of leaving go the rein."

An inexplicable and wholly unreasonable reluctance to part from him clutched at Pamela. "No!" she exclaimed, and then, seeking a reason for what she could not explain, she added, "I am afraid I would never find you again. There are thousands of gullies like this."

St. Just frowned consideringly. "I suppose if you don't know the land, all of these sheep tracks look about the same." He hesitated, glanced sidelong at her. "Were you looking for me, Pam? Is something wrong?"

"Nothing is really wrong, just a household problem that is beyond my authority to solve." Pamela's color rose slightly in spite of the innocent words. "I was not looking for you," she said with a little too much emphasis.

St. Just made no reply, merely dropped his head into his unhurt hand. He had been unhappy for years, ever since need had tied him to Hetty, but he had learned not to chafe too much in his bonds. When he had come to England, he had thought life was offering him an escape, that his love for his home and lands could fill his emptiness. On the ship, during the long weeks of voyage, he had tried to make up his differences with his wife. She would never be a woman he could love, but they could live at peace. And now he wanted children. He needed a son to inherit Tremaire.

He knew now that he would not have even that — not out of Hetty. And in his first reckless rush of despair, to make his misery complete, he had hired Pamela to be Hetty's companion. With his eyes closed, he could see her — her rich warm body, her generous mouth and kind eyes. He could no longer bear to be in the house with her. He dared not open his lips at his own dinner table for fear his desire would show. And Hetty stood in the way. If he could be rid of Hetty! But he could not give up Tremaire — not even for Pamela; and it was Hetty's money that kept Tremaire from being swallowed by those who held the mortgages on it.

"My lord," Pamela said softly, coming back

toward him, "do you feel worse?"

She had a softness for him, she did! St. Just raised his head and smiled. "No, no worse than could be expected." When she was thoroughly trapped, perhaps . . .

"Come, St. Just, try your legs again and let us see if we can clamber out of here. I cannot leave you down here alone."

She stretched a hand to help him, as if defying a private fear. St. Just, afraid of the reaction even so casual a touch might set off, ignored the gesture and got to his feet unaided. He stood steadily, although his brows contracted against the suddenly increased pangs of headache.

"Very well," he said, taking himself firmly in hand, "I will push you up as far as I can. Then you can reach down and help pull Velvet up."

"But you will still be down, St. Just, and with a bad hand and a bad head, I cannot see how you will manage. You go first. I think I am strong enough to give you a boost."

Every word she spoke made him love her more. This was what a woman should be, forthright and strong. In self-defense St. Just burst out laughing.

"You certainly don't suffer from die-away-missish airs, do you? Do you propose to lift me in your arms like a baby, or to put your

65

shoulder under my . . . er . . . bottom?"

"Missish airs would suit me about as well as an ostrich feather stuck up my . . . Oh, dear!" Pamela exclaimed in embarrassment as she realized what she had been about to say.

St. Just, who realized too, roared.

"My father always said that. I wish I could remember to guard my tongue," she said desperately.

"You simply must stop making me laugh," St. Just reproved weakly. "It is most unkind in you, knowing the headache I have. Now, I know you are a strapping big wench, Lady Pam, but not quite big enough to have me sit on you. Up now. No more argument."

The climb was not as bad as it looked except that the rocky earth had a disconcerting tendency to slip away from under Pamela's feet. With St. Just supporting her from behind, however, she soon had a grip on the bracken at the lip of the gully. She struggled up and over, lying breathlessly on the level ground for a few minutes. Velvet was then urged to put her forefeet as high as she could, and Pamela, after some straining, grasped the end of the rein. When she heard St. Just strike the mare, she tugged and crawled backward. Once she was nearly jerked down, but a shout and another blow startled the horse into frantic activity, and

Pam leaped to her feet, still pulling, as Velvet made a convulsive effort that took her over the lip.

She had to spend some time soothing the frightened animal, and even when Velvet stopped rearing, she dared not let go of the rein. St. Just had still not appeared.

"My lord," she called. "Are you all right?"

"Yes, I'm coming."

"Wait a minute. I'll find something to tie Velvet to. Then I can reach down and help."

There was nothing large enough to hook the reins on where Pamela was, and she moved around the irregular outcrop of rock. On the other side, where the path bypassed the gully, a stunted tree grew in the shelter of the boulders. With a sigh of relief, Pamela tugged the mare over and bent to fasten the reins to one of the lower branches, which were stronger than those at eye level. On the ground a decorative fob glittered against the dull earth. Pamela picked it up and slipped it into a pocket of her habit. She went back and lay down on the edge of the gully again.

Now Pamela had cause to bless her size and strength. Halfway up, St. Just went dizzy. Pamela's arm was nearly wrenched from her shoulder, but her grip on his wrist never faltered, and she drew him up. He was white with pain, and the cut on his hand had started to bleed again.

"Oh, I am so sorry," she murmured, kneeling down beside him as he rolled over and lay flat on his back in the bracken. "I should have ridden home and left you. I don't know why I was such an idiot as to think this was better."

"It is better," he gasped. "I could have made you go if I wanted to. Just let me catch my breath." He opened his eyes to gleaming slits and saw Pamela's anxious face. To remain silent or to thank her for her concern would only increase his torment. "I'll never say you aren't as good as a winch again," St. Just said, laughing. "God forbid I should ever give you cause to be angry with me. You could knock me endwise, I daresay."

"If you are going to make fun of me — and after nearly tearing my arm off, too — I shall just roll you over and drop you down there again."

"Did I hurt you, Pam?" the earl asked quickly, lifting himself on an elbow.

Pamela felt acutely uncomfortable again, but she pushed him down gently, wiggled her fingers, and thrust both hands in her pockets with an exaggerated gesture to show she could move her arms. Her fingers touched the fob. "Oh, here, St. Just, before I forget to give this to you. You must have lost it when Sergeant reared."

"An honest woman, too." He smiled and held out his hand. Then, just as he was about to thrust the trinket into his pocket, he sat up and looked at it. "This is not a coin, it's a fob. It isn't mine, Pam. I wouldn't wear a fob with these clothes. Who the devil . . . ?" The mystery was all too easily solved. Chased in elaborate tracery on the fob were the initials G.G.T. "George Gillespie Tremaire," St. Just muttered.

"George? But George went to Penzance yesterday. I thought he would be away for a week. Why do you look so troubled, my lord? The fob could have been here for a long time."

"Show me where you found it."

She took him around and pointed to the spot. St. Just knelt and examined the earth. Nothing grew under the scraggy tree, and the morning's rain had washed loose dirt and pebbles from the rocks down around its roots.

"Did you clean it, Pam?"

"No, I only noticed it because it shone. I was tying the horse, not looking for treasure."

"Then it cannot have been here before the rain. It would have been covered, you see, or at least there would have been a dry spot on the ground. And Sergeant was badly startled. He's not a shy horse, you know."

"St. Just" — Pamela's voice was little more

than a horrified whisper — "you cannot mean that George intended to harm you."

"He knew the gully was there. He did not go sailing with my father and brothers. . . ." The earl's voice quivered. "Nonsense," he said with sudden passion. "One does not die from a fall from a horse, and he was ill the day my father drowned. Mrs. Helston told me so, and she would not lie. And the rain stopped at least an hour before I rode by here. We really must start home now, Pam, or it will be dark before we arrive. Mount up; I will hang onto your stirrup."

"No, you cannot walk so far. You ride. I love to walk."

Her concern for him after the shock he had just had nearly overset him, and St. Just again took refuge in laughter. "Ride?" he asked, his eyes twinkling. "On a lady's saddle? How?"

Pamela yielded but would not permit St. Just to lift her. Instead she climbed a rock and mounted, only to find with the first few steps the mare took that she was lamed. "Oh," she cried between laughter and exasperation as she slid down, "and we were arguing about who should ride. And I am so hungry, too."

It was full dark when they finally arrived at Tremaire. The servants were in an uproar, Hayle providing lanterns for the grooms and footmen who were to search the grounds and surrounding territory, and Mrs. Helston trying to quiet the maids who were running about and getting in the way, shrieking with excitement. One, in fact, was keening with ghoulish relish that the family was doomed, that one death would follow another until there were no Tremaires left.

"Good God," the earl said under his breath to Pamela after he had patiently assured everyone several times that he was quite safe. "We have had our troubles, I admit, but that girl makes us sound like something out of the *Castle of Otranto*. That is what comes of teaching servants to read."

"No," Pamela replied, echoing his amusement, "that is what you get for making yourself so well-liked by them and then coming in the servants' entrance."

St. Just again urged everyone to calm down, then shrugged as this produced more tears and good wishes, and turned toward the back stairs. Hayle, seeing the movement, neatly freed himself from the men whom he was dismissing, and followed.

"Mr. Tremaire and Lady St. Just are in the morning room, my lord — in case you wished to step in and let them know you are safe."

With one foot on the stair, St Just turned. "What!"

"I thought perhaps you would . . . wish to

see them now," the butler repeated in a color-less voice.

Pamela could feel her complexion change. Hayle was a good servant. Hayle knew his place. It was not a servant's place to tell his master that his cousin and his wife were . . . Were what? Rejoicing over his demise? Supporting each other's spirits in a time of crisis a little too warmly? Which? Or both? The first sentence could have been foolishness or officiousness. The second could not be misunderstood. St. Just's hand tightened on the stair rail, but after his first startled expletive, his face had become expressionless.

"Thank you, Hayle. I think, however, the shock to my wife and cousin would be less if you brought them the happy tidings."

"Very good, my lord."

"And will you send up some dinner or supper or what-have-you for Lady Pamela and myself? We have had nothing to eat in hours."

"At once, my lord."

"To my sitting room, if you please. Will that suit you, Lady Pamela? It will make less trouble for the servants than serving two separate meals."

"Certainly, my lord," Pamela replied, her voice as colorless as Hayle's. "Oh, Hayle, you had better send someone for a surgeon. I am

72

afraid that his lordship's hand will have to be stitched."

"It's all right. Sarah will do that. Never mind, Hayle, just dinner."

They were silent as they mounted the stairs and until St. Just reached for the door handle. "Hetty and George," he muttered in a stunned voice.

"I am sure Hayle misunderstood," Pamela said with dry lips. "George is very kind about amusing Hetty, and Hetty is fond of him, it is true. She depends upon him, but she has never flirted with him. Indeed, she has not."

"Do you think I am jealous? Do you think I care what Hetty does?" he burst out. "It is George! I cannot believe that George would use me so. But this is too pat. Not only the title, but the money too."

Pamela knew that St. Just should not be speaking to her about such things, but he had been badly shaken up. And to whom could he speak?

"It is all a mistake, I am sure," she insisted. "You cannot be afraid of George."

"Afraid of George? Don't be silly. I could break him in two between my hands — even with a sprained wrist. I'm not worried, I'm sick. Why should he? I have always been fond of him, and he of me. I have said some things, it is true, but not because I believed them.

Only because my pain was such that I needed to lash out against someone, and George was all that was left who was dear to me. Good God, Pam, I am speaking of this, but I cannot believe it."

"We should not be speaking out in the corridor at all. Please go in, my lord."

Sarah was waiting for them, grim and silent, her hands clasped before her. She did not cry out or exclaim at her master's appearance as the maids and Mrs. Helston had done. In fact she scarcely glanced at him, and then her eyes moved to Pamela.

"Is he hurt, my lady?"

"You might ask me, I can still talk," St. Just said, amusement in his voice.

"Why should I? You never spoke the truth about such things to me or to your mother. I remember you had a broken collarbone for three days before we found out. I'm no fool, whatever you are, Master Vyvyan, and I learn from experience. I'll ask where I'll get an answer I can trust. Your man's waiting in your room. Go get those dirty, wet things off you."

Pamela's lips twitched. Sarah may have been the late Lady St. Just's maid, but she had also, obviously, been the present earl's nurse. The sullen pout of his lips was that of a resentful child told to do something he knew was right but did not wish to do. Pamela felt a spurt of tenderness, which she pushed resolutely out of her mind.

"He has a cut on his hand — a bad one, I'm afraid, a sprained wrist, and a knock on the head," she said to Sarah, striving to keep her voice steady and ignoring St. Just's outraged gasp and accusing glance.

"Conspiracy," he muttered.

"That's enough of your funning, Master Vyvyan," Sarah said sharply, and then she nodded at Pamela. "You don't need to look so worried. It's not the first time I've sewed him up. All in all, I've done more stitching on his hide than on his clothes. The clothes were usually beyond help. The wrist will mend itself, and the knock on the head will do no harm. His head's the thickest part of him." She paused, turned to cast a dispassionate glance at her erstwhile charge, and shrugged. "Won't do him no good, either," she added, clearly to the ambient air. "Even splitting his head open never let any sense into it. Are you going to stand there all night, Master Vyvyan, or are you going to let the rest of us do our work and get some sleep?"

The strictures at least had the effect of restoring St. Just's good humor. He chuckled and went into his bedchamber, carefully not looking at Pamela, who now had her lower lip between her teeth.

"And as for you," Sarah said, turning suddenly on Pamela, "I can see you aren't much better than he is. What do you mean by coming in here in all that dirt, grinding grit into the floors and carpets? Go and change. Come here, I'll unhook you, now. He won't come out yet."

Pamela was startled at the change in tone from stolid respect to maternal scolding. Her eyes flew to Sarah's face. Then, meekly, she advanced and turned her back to be unhooked. To be berated in this particular way could only mean that Sarah had accepted her as a member of the household on a level beyond that of mistress and servant. The maid's hands were deft, and the riding habit hung loose in seconds. Then Sarah seized Pamela's arm, turned her about again like a child, and unbuttoned her sleeves.

"Quick now," Sarah said, "so you'll be back before he's ready. I'll want some help with patching him. He won't act up with you here. Send that dress down to me. I'll have it fresh for you by tomorrow. Are you hurt too?"

"No, only a few scrapes on my hands and knees."

"You'll hold till I have him abed. I'll come to you then. Go now."

"Thank you, Sarah."

The remark, though formal, was deeply heartfelt, and Pamela hoped that Sarah understood the depth of her appreciation. She realized that Sarah had just volunteered to become her personal maid. One girl or another had waited on her and cleaned her room since she had come to Tremaire, and all had been respectful and obedient. A personal maid, devoted to one's private service, was an entirely different matter; and Sarah was someone special.

In ten minutes Pamela had donned her shabbiest gown. First St. Just, then supper, then Sergeant and Velvet. The grooms would see to the horses, of course, but someone had to check their work and praise them for doing it; then bed. Pamela sighed, then smiled. It had been a long time since she had felt tired enough to want to go to bed. A lady's companion had little opportunity for physical exercise, since the type of lady who wanted or needed a companion was either too old or not the type to enjoy exertion. Pamela had opened the door to St. Just's suite and stepped inside before she realized what she had been thinking. But not to be tired this way again, she thought, the smile wiped out. Let it have been an accident. Hetty enjoyed George's company; that was all. Surely Hayle had merely misinterpreted what he saw.

Surely a mountain of accusation was being built upon a molehill of coincidental, unrelated fact.

"You don't look to be the type to be squeamish. What's wrong with you?"

Sarah's sharp voice awakened Pamela to the fact that, having entered St. Just's room enveloped in her unpleasant thoughts, she was standing stock still and staring at a small table laid out with lint, salves, scissors, a curved needle, and silk thread. Her expression had doubtless been one of horror. She raised her eyes to the maid's face.

"No, I'm not squeamish."

"There was something funny about that fall Master Vyvyan took. Well, I knew that. He wouldn't be jumping back on the ridges — there's nothing to jump there. And for all I say he has a thick head, that's stubbornness, not foolishness. You tell me later."

That was a stunner. Old and privileged servants often took advantage, but not to this degree. Pamela, however, trod warily. "Has Lady St. Just been here?" she asked as an appropriate change of subject.

"I sent her right-about, and Master George too." There was a swift smile on the grim mouth. "No trouble. Asked if they wanted to watch or help me cut and sew. Master George never could abide the sight of blood, and that

78

other one pretended to shiver — but that was to impress him. She don't care a pin either for blood or for Master Vyvyan."

The conversation was growing more embarrassing by the minute. Sarah never seemed much in evidence around the house, but apparently she saw and heard everything — and guessed too much. Fortunately, Pamela was spared needing to answer, because St. Just came out, his man following with the soiled garments. The valet was an old acquaintance of Sarah's, it appeared, for he merely nodded at her as if to say it was her turn now.

"Ah, the two torturers await," St. Just remarked, his eyes gleaming.

CHAPTER 5

"You must get rid of that woman — you must!" Hetty shrilled, rushing into St. Just's sitting room.

He winced slightly at the sound of her voice, and put down the wineglass he had started to lift to his lips. "Don't you wish to inquire how I am, Hetty?" he asked quietly.

"I can see quite well there's nothing wrong with you. Nothing ever happens to you."

Considering the fact that the left side of St. Just's face was scraped raw, already bluing with bruises, that his hair was cut away from a nasty scalp wound, and that his left arm was in a sling, that hand swollen to twice the size of the other, the statement seemed inaccurate as well as unfeeling. No doubt Hetty resented Sarah's manner. Pamela, even though she was beginning to feel an affection for the woman, felt the resentment to be justified. But something more than a servant's insolence was behind this outburst of fury. The countess's voice had been bitterer when she spoke the second time than the first.

"Hetty, m'dear," George protested, having followed her into the room and shut the door, "I've told you that Sarah was a bit odd. She don't mean any harm. Fond of Vyvyan. Upset when he was hurt. Anyhow, Vyvyan don't look too chipper. Talk it over tomorrow."

"Tomorrow! Do you expect to see him tomorrow? I do not."

"Don't look that bad," George remarked soothingly, and then, as Pamela bit back a spurt of laughter and Hetty turned eyes that were fairly bulging with rage on him, "Oh, see what you mean. Been a bit exclusive, I agree, but bound to be about for a day or two now. Don't look fit to go out. Mess."

This time Pamela heard a nervous titter pass her lips. She had never tittered before in her life, but the contrast between the fears she had conjured up around George and the real person was extreme. In addition, his manner of speech somehow made the whole situation ridiculous. St. Just was a mess, but the way George said it made something that had been frightening into something ludicrous. What was more, the casual display of the intimacy George and Hetty shared almost obviated any guilty passion between them. It must have been this which had misled Hayle. Pamela, so accustomed to it, forgot how it might appear to an outsider's eyes. St. Just thought so too.

Pamela could see some of the tension go out of him.

"Thank you for trying to explain Sarah," he said to George, and then to Hetty, "If you don't like her, she need not wait on you, but she is attached to me, as George said, and I cannot dismiss her."

"She's attached to you and that gives her license to be freely insolent to me? Is that it?"

"No, of course not, Hetty. I will speak to her about her behavior."

Pamela thought of the probable effect any remonstrance of St. Just's would have on Sarah and choked, but when she saw Hetty's furious eyes turn to her, she made an effort at control.

"I don't think she can help it. Really, Hetty, you should hear what she said to St. Just. Very nearly called him a nasty, dirty, little boy. I shouldn't have been surprised if he was a few inches shorter, to have seen her turn him over her knee."

"No, and it wouldn't have been the first time, either," St. Just said, seizing gratefully on this evidence of Sarah's general application of her sharp tongue.

"No, by God, and when Sarah spanked, she spanked," George remarked reminiscently.

"You didn't get as much of it as I did." St.

Just's tired eyes brightened with shared memory. "She took a hairbrush to me, bristles down."

"I didn't try to ride dangerous bulls and nearly get gored, not to mention shooting sheep with a bow and arrow. You were a hellion, Vyvyan. Gave us all some frightful turns. Which reminds me. How did you get into this scrape? Could swear you knew every inch of ground."

"If these revelations of a happy childhood were supposed to divert me, they have failed of their purpose," Hetty said coldly. "I may be quite ignorant of the proper thing, but among my people servants did not strike the children of their betters."

"Perhaps it had been wiser if they did," St. Just snapped.

"Now, now, Vyvyan," George remarked, as if his cousin had been making a philosophical comment rather than a personal one. "Different thing, y'know. Alice was never spanked. She used —"

"Thank you for trying to hide the fact that my husband was deliberately insulting me, George," Hetty interrupted, "but it was not necessary. Since he has become an earl, I have become quite accustomed to swallowing insults."

This time even George's address could not

cover the situation. A dead silence ensued. Pamela was furious with Hetty for quarreling with her husband, who was in no condition to bear it, but she could see Hetty's point of view, too. Bred in a family which obviously regarded servants as something to be used and thrown away, it was impossible for her to understand the bond between master and servant in a family that retained an old feudal relationship. It must have seemed as if St. Just was deliberately trying to hurt her when he persisted in supporting Sarah. And about things like this, Hetty was stupid; explanations were useless. Hetty did not belong in the country; she would be much more comfortable in town, where servants were hired and dismissed, sometimes before their employers knew their names.

St. Just had dropped his head into his good hand. "I do not like to hear Sarah abused, Hetty," he said, "but I did not mean . . . Perhaps I did. I have the most abominable headache. If you wish me to say I am sorry, I will, but I will not dismiss Sarah, no matter what she says or does. I will hire another maid for you, and tell Sarah to keep out of your way."

"You are all kindness, Vyvyan. But do not, I pray you, go to so much trouble for me." Venom dripped from Hetty's tone. "I have already hired another maid, *and* told that . . .

that thing to stay out of my way. Pamela, I wish to speak to you."

Pamela rose at once and followed her from the room, ignoring the fact that St. Just had lifted his head and was clearly about to protest. The very worst thing that could happen was for him to try to protect her. If she, as well as the other servants, became a bone of contention, she would be unable to endure it.

As the door closed, George emitted a low whistle. "Hetty's got a temper, hasn't she? Well, old man, you'd better totter off to bed. Had a hard day."

"Just a minute, George. Did you realize that you lost your fob?"

"Found it, did you? Too bad. Yes, I knew."

"Knew where you lost it, did you?"

" 'Course I knew," George said with slight irritability. "Value that fob. Present from your father on m'last birthday. Sentimental about it. Would have picked it up tomorrow. No one out there to take it, and besides, everyone on the estate knows it's mine."

St. Just reached for his wine, saw his hand was trembling, and rested it on the table. "Why, George?" he asked, his voice shaking. "God in heaven, why?"

"What the devil's wrong with you, Vyvyan? It should be clear enough why I made myself scarce and why I didn't go back to pick up the fob." His affectations had dropped away, and his distaste for what he was saying was plain. "It is no affair of mine if you want to bring your mistress out here as Hetty's companion. I must say you have both been decent enough about it. I would not have guessed if I had not seen your face when you spotted her." He shrugged, and the mask of a London dandy dropped back into place. "Embarrassment all around. Least seen, soonest forgotten."

"Lady Pamela is not my mistress, nor did we meet by assignation."

"No? Well, sorry. Mistook your expression. Light in my eyes, perhaps. Where's the fob? I'll take it, if I may."

"God damn it, George, you cannot pass it off like that. Do you mean to pretend you didn't know I had gone over into the gully?"

"What? Good God, no, I didn't know. No wonder you asked me why. Thought I'd tried to ease myself into the succession, eh? Damn it, Vyvyan, that's a stupid way to do it. I could find a dozen better ways of polishing you off if I wanted to. Besides, you should know better than that. First of all, what's there to succeed to? You die, off goes Hetty, loan sharks swallow the place. Better off as I am. What's more, fond of you. Said so before."

"But you must have heard the noise when Sergeant went down."

George's protuberant eyes narrowed. "Don't know what's eating you, Vyvyan. Don't want to know, but you're coming over quite nasty. I'll tell you, because you've had a shaking up and maybe you aren't quite clear in your head. I didn't hear you. Did you hear me riding away? I was coming from the other direction, the shortcut from the Penzance road and I saw Lady Pamela. She didn't see me because of the rocks there. I was about to give her a hail when I saw you coming. You wasn't looking at the path or at me, Vyvyan, you was looking at her. Maybe I was wrong in what I thought, but all I wanted was to get clear of there before I heard something I shouldn't. If I'd never seen you, we wouldn't have to talk about it — or specially not talk about it — would we? Anyhow, I took off the way I'd come. Felt the fob catch on that tree, but I guessed you'd be too busy to notice it. Path drops a bit there. Pretty sure you wouldn't notice me, either. Rode straight back to the road and came up the long way through the village. I did hear Lady Pam call, 'St. Just,' but I thought she was hailing you. So help me, I didn't hear you fall. Sorry. Could have helped."

"No, I'm sorry, George. I never believed it. I don't know why I asked. I suppose you are right about my being shaken up. But you really must believe that Pam isn't my mistress."

"Your affair, old bean. Nothing to do with me. Don't fancy her type. Won't cut you out."

St. Just burst out laughing and held out his hand. "Bless you, George. You'll make me laugh on my deathbed."

"Doubt it. Got a few years on you. Natural course of events, I'll go first. Not but what you look like death warmed over right now. Go to bed, Vyvyan."

"Yes, I will. Send Sarah up here, will you, George?"

"Right. You might say a word to her. Don't like Hetty. Shows it."

St. Just nodded, but in fact he said nothing to Sarah about his wife. He told her instead to fetch Pamela to him as soon as she was free of Hetty.

"Laying in trouble for yourself, that's what you're doing, Master Vyvyan. And I'd like to know how you came to fall. I'll get it out of the lady if you don't tell me."

St. Just made no attempt to convince Sarah that he was indifferent to Pamela. He had failed signally with George; and Sarah, if anything, knew him even better. "The fall was an accident. That was what I wanted to tell Lady Pamela. Both of us thought my horse might have been startled deliberately, but that was not the case."

"No? Well, I'll fetch her."

"Not out of Hetty's room," he said with belated caution.

Sarah looked at him with the pitying expression one might assume over the witless remarks of an idiot child, and left without answering. Almost immediately, Pamela entered.

"Hetty did not keep you long. Was she unpleasant?" St. Just asked in a rather constricted voice.

"No. You look dreadful, my lord."

"Do I? I feel much better, in my mind, at least." He recounted what George had told him, except for George's suspicion about their relationship. A specious excuse for George's decision to return by the main road contented Pamela for the moment. She liked George, and she was tired and worried about St. Just's physical condition."

"Thank God," she sighed. "It was too dreadful. It could not be real. The shock made us both imagine things."

"Yes," he agreed. "I had to tell you tonight. I did not want you to cast repulsive glances at poor George tomorrow. Now I will drag my aching bones to bed."

"One minute more, my lord. I did have

something to tell you — or rather, ask — but in the excitement I forgot." Pamela then described the situation of the pregnant maid and the gardener. "Shall I tell Mrs. Helston that you will set matters right yourself, St. Just, or shall I try to get to the bottom of it?"

"My head is muzzy, Pam, but not that muzzy," St. Just said with a wry smile. "You are deliberately killing time. Why?" And then, before she could answer, Sarah came in bearing a nauseous-looking liquid in a glass. "Oh, no!"

"Oh, yes," Pamela said. "Sarah guessed you would protest. Now, drink it."

"A conspiracy," he complained. "I wish you would both remember you are in my employ. Conspiracy is an adequate reason for dismissal."

"Drink it, my lord. Your hand looks frightening, and your head must feel like something better not discussed." She took the glass and offered it to him. "I shall hold your nose, and Sarah will tip it down your throat," she threatened laughingly. "I am quite strong enough, you know."

He drank, made an agonized face, and said, "Discretion is the better part of valor — but you won't trap me again."

"No," Pamela replied smugly, "we will design another ruse." She did not notice the glance St. Just and Sarah exchanged, but went on, "Good night, my lord. Oh, what shall I tell Mrs. Helston?"

"To go to the devil," St. Just replied with a beatific smile. He controlled himself with an effort. "No, don't frown. You handle the maid. Find out if she is worth saving and whether this is likely to be her only slip. I'll speak to the gardener. I'd send them both off like a shot, but if she is a foundling, it would be like murder to do that. And the man's wife and children must be considered, too. God, my head hurts. Good night, Lady Pam, I'll see you in the morning."

Without expression, Sarah tugged the bell cord that would summon St. Just's valet and then held open the door for Pamela, whom she followed into her room. Surely, Pamela thought, as she submitted gratefully to Sarah's deft ministrations, I am approved. It was very pleasant to have an experienced maid caring for her wants. It was also pleasant to know she could count on St. Just's authority to back her decision about the maid, but was it fair or right? She was usurping Hetty's position in the household. Hetty did not want it; nonetheless, it was an injustice to her, to the servants, and even to St. Just. The house would be run better now, and everyone would be happier, but when she left, the contrast would increase the difficulties and further embitter the situation.

Sarah turned back the bed covers and waited for Pamela to slide in so that she could cover her. "Oh, Lord," Pamela cried, "I forgot the horses. Sarah, I must dress again and go to see to them."

The maid looked at her with approving eyes. This was the mistress Tremaire should have, a woman who understood responsibility and would sacrifice her own comfort to fulfill a duty. She shook her head.

"No, you won't do that. Master George will take care of what's needed in the stables. And don't you fret about Master Vyvyan either," she said, her eyes and mouth a little softer than usual. "I'll look in on him during the night. He's had worse knocks."

"Do not hesitate to call me if you need me. Thank you, Sarah. Good night."

The maid snuffed the candles and closed the door behind her. Pamela expected to go out like the candles, but for all her aching fatigue, sleep would not come. St. Just had asked if Hetty had been unpleasant, and she had denied it. On a personal level she had told the truth, but the scene she had been involved in had been far from enjoyable. Poor Lord St. Just, Hetty did hate him — and not completely without cause.

Far from being angry or scolding Pamela, Hetty had asked if she were hurt, had apologized for her husband's lack of consideration in making her eat in his room to save the servants trouble. She had asked, of course, how Pamela happened to be involved in St. Just's accident, but had accepted the explanation without a flicker of any concern beyond that for Pamela's fright and exhaustion. Finally she had said, "Oh, dear, how unkind of me to be asking questions when you must be worn to the bone. I only called you away from Vyvyan's room so that you could rest. He is never tired and never thinks anyone else could be — no, nor would he care if he did think it. He is a beast."

"No, Hetty," Pamela had replied, automatically soothing a constant plaint. "You think he has disobliged you, but there are certain situations in which servants become . . . well, just as he could not send George away if George offended him, he cannot dismiss Sarah for offending you."

"I was not thinking of that," the countess said. "Stay away from him, Pam." And before Pamela could make an angry protest, she continued, "I could see you felt sorry that he was hurt. You should not. He is evil. Oh, you do not believe me, but you will see. He killed my brother to inherit my father's entire fortune through me . . . and he plans to kill me too."

"You must not say things like that, Hetty. You are upset. St. Just may not always be as considerate a husband as he should be, but he means you no harm."

The pale blue eyes bored at her like gimlets. "I cannot prove it, but I know. You know what Vyvyan is — the finest swordsman, the finest shot, the most bruising rider, the best whip — well, I had a brother not twenty years old, and he idolized Vyvyan. He had to do everything Vyvyan did. And Vyvyan encouraged him. Taught him to fence, encouraged him to shoot and ride — encouraged him and laughed at him. He was a wild boy, and Vyvyan . . . Oh, it was easy. Vyvyan had a horse, a big red devil as mean as he. He let Harry ride his other horses, but he kept at him all the time about that one. Harry must not touch that stallion, must not try him. It took a man to ride that horse, Vyvyan would say . . . and laugh."

"But surely it was right to warn your brother that the animal was dangerous."

"Warn! You did not hear him or see him. He was daring Harry, not warning him. Oh, it was easy. Harry rode the horse . . . and Harry died."

"How dreadful!" Tears filled Pamela's eyes, not for the foolish dead boy but for the

94

man who bore the burden of that memory and for the woman whose marriage — whatever it had originally been — was now beyond hope of repair. "When did this happen, Hetty?"

"A year ago. We had been married four years. He was angry because he had found out something about our marriage contract he did not know was in it."

"Hetty, people do not commit murder because of disagreements over a marriage contract. I understand your grief, but do not take it out upon your husband. He must feel even worse."

"He made restitution," Hetty said dully. "He shot the horse. There were tears in his eyes when he did so. There had been none when he had the news of my brother's death."

"I am so sorry, Hetty, but I am sure St. Just blames himself as much as you can. It is horrible, but men do tease boys unthinkingly. To say that St. Just intended murder is not reasonable. It merely increases your unhappiness."

That Hetty heard her was improbable. And Pamela had not spoken with any intention of mitigating Hetty's grief or suspicion. Hetty wanted to feel those things, and Pamela knew that nothing could reconcile Hetty to her husband. Yet it was impossible to stand in silence and seem to agree. As long as Hetty accused, Pamela was forced to offer mitigating platitudes.

"You think I hate him," the countess said after a short silence. "Indeed, Pam, I do not. I am so consumed by fear that there is no room left for hate. Cannot you see why I am afraid of people like that Sarah, who is so devoted, fanatically devoted? Do you think she would not slip poison into my morning chocolate? Do you think the grooms, who worship the ground Vyvyan walks on, would not do something to the horse I drove, or to my carriage? Do you wonder why I surround myself with my own people?"

"Hetty, Hetty, this is hysteria. Even if St. Just were what you said, for practical considerations alone he would not harm you. Suspicion would fall upon him directly. You will make yourself ill with such thoughts. You do not believe this yourself. Why would you remain with him if you did?"

"Why? Have you never wondered why, if the money is mine, Vyvyan pays your wages, pays the bills, hands me my pin money?"

Naturally Pamela had not wondered, since in England husbands regularly controlled their wives' fortunes. She had no time to say this, however, since Hetty had continued to speak with a half-mad intensity.

"Why? Because when I was utterly beside myself with grief over my brother's and father's deaths, before I realized what had really happened — one does not, as you say, believe such things easily — Vyvyan induced me to sign some papers that put my entire fortune into his hands. Did you not notice how quickly I was hustled out of London? How seldom Vyvyan was away from my side? He does not dare let me come in contact with a solicitor who might advise me on how to free myself from this coil."

"No, really, Hetty, this cannot be true."

"Do not argue with me. I know what I know. He is planning something or doing something away all day in the hills. Watch him; you will see."

Of course, Pamela knew what St. Just was doing in the hills, but she made no attempt to tell Hetty. George had done so several times already, and had apparently made no impression. Instead Pamela had said that she was tired and left.

Now Pamela shifted her aching body in the bed and sighed. The man she had left a short time ago was not the sort who could plan and carry out the murder Hetty described, although if Hetty drove him much further he might throttle her in a fit of rage. If Hetty, who must know her husband after five years of marriage, concluded that her brother's riding accident was murder, it was because she wanted to believe that. No one in his right mind would choose so unlikely and unsure a method. Broken arms and legs, broken collarbones, and bruises were frequent results of riding accidents, but deaths were unusual. They did occur, but were certainly not a thing one could plan on.

As far as keeping Hetty from a solicitor, that was another fiction of her mind. What had there been to stop her from excusing herself on one of their shopping expeditions and seeing one, or even taking Pamela to his office? In addition, Hetty drove to the village of St. Just almost every day. What could prevent her from posting off a letter from there and asking a solicitor to meet her at the inn?

Although she could have wept with fatigue, ideas continued to squirrel around in Pamela's head. She was sorry for Hetty, who insisted upon being blind and making herself miserable, and sorry for St. Just, who was trapped by circumstances. At least she did not need to be sorry for George, and he was the best one to help with Hetty. The connection brought Hayle's suspicions to mind, and that led her thoughts back to St. Just's accident. Quite clearly Pamela perceived that the reason George had given for riding off was ridiculous. A wave of fear enveloped her and was swiftly rejected. If St. Just accepted George's explanation, it was doubtless her own thick-headedness that caused doubt. That thought eased her tension, and at last Pamela felt sleep coming.

It was snatched away by the sound of foot-steps in the uncarpeted corridor. Pamela pulled on her dressing gown. If St. Just had taken a turn for the worse, she could help. She opened her door, stepped out, and the corner of her eye caught Sarah, standing quite still and staring at Hetty's door.

"St. Just . . ." Pamela said softly. "Is he all right?"

Sarah turned, and Pamela's breath caught. The maid's eyes were . . . were like the earl's. They were not so large nor so well-lashed, but wide open now, in the pale moonlight, they had the same long shape and were of the same weird green. And like St. Just's when he was intense, Sarah's eyes also glowed. Her face, however, was expressionless.

"That woman is a fool to think she can be rid of me and so be free to play her game." She spoke softly, not to Pamela, but not excluding her, either. "She has brought evil to this house. There has been great trouble here before, but that was trouble born of love. She has brought hate into Tremaire, where hate never lived before. There is a death wish in this house — a threat of death-singing — and the dark of the moon is coming." A single convulsive shudder shook her body, while her face remained unmoved. "Master Vyvyan must be free of her." Sarah's glance shifted up and down Pamela swiftly. "Tremaire needs a better mistress," she added in a flat, practical voice.

Before Pamela could speak or move, Sarah had turned away from the patch of moonlight and disappeared down the black stairwell, her feet unfaltering in the dark.

CHAPTER 6

Incredibly, Sarah woke Pamela the next morning, smiling her grim smile as if there had been no meeting in the dim corridor. Pamela accepted the cup of chocolate and watched Sarah hang the cleaned riding habit in the wardrobe, lay out a morning gown and suitable underclothing, and pour hot water into her washing basin. Beyond a "Good morning, my lady," the maid said nothing, and Pamela found the strangest reluctance in herself to bring up the subject.

"How is Lord St. Just this morning?" she asked at last.

"Sour as bad wine, but much better. Swelling's nearly gone from his hand. He's feeling his bumps and bruises now."

"He will not ride out today, will he?"

"Not even Master Vyvyan's fool enough to try to handle his horses with a bad wrist. He'll find mischief enough to be up to around the house."

Pamela was washed and half-dressed when she turned suddenly on Sarah. "What did you mean by what you said in the corridor last night?"

The woman was unabashed. "I meant what I said. I can smell evil, and the death wish is so strong it chokes me."

"You are not a witch, are you, Sarah?" Pamela tried to make her voice light, as if she were joking, but the words fell heavily.

"No, my lady, I am not, but my mother . . . That's neither here nor there. Anyhow, I feel such things."

Absurdly, Pamela was relieved. She realized it would not have mattered what Sarah replied. The calm acceptance in her voice and manner turned the remark into a statement of ordinary fact rather than a hideous confession. Pamela found herself saying, "Oh, yes," in a faintly disapproving voice, as if Sarah had said she was a Methodist, and then passing on to some instructions about her clothing. Sarah handed her her reticule and handkerchief, and she went down to breakfast.

"Not riding today? Don't blame you."

"Oh, good morning, George. No, I am rather stiff. How is Velvet's fetlock?"

"Stiff too. Be right as rain in a fortnight. Ride Blue Lady until then, if you take my advice."

"Yes, I will. I found it hard to choose

between them in the first place. I settled on Velvet because she was more of a goer, and perhaps because she was a bit unpredictable."

"Hmmm, yes, you would, m'dear. Late Lady St. Just's favorite, too. Remarkable how much you two are alike. Velvet will be all right. More worried about Sergeant. Cut his knees up."

"Oh, dear. St. Just will be livid."

George laughed. "Good word, 'livid.' Used to go just that color before he burned so black. Bad temper Vyvyan's got. Stopped in to see him this morning. Take my word — don't. Be down to bedevil us all soon enough."

"Will you ride down to the village and have the farrier up to look at Sergeant, George?"

"No need. I've applied fomentations, and we'll keep the knees dressed with a spermaceti ointment. Might keep them from scarring. Farrier couldn't do more."

"No. I didn't know you were interested in horses."

"Must be interested in something to make living out here endurable. Land's not mine. Horses and sailing." A shadow marred his bland expression. "No sailing now. Yacht's gone, and . . ." He pushed his cup away. "I'd best be off to the stable again. Infuriating horse, that Velvet. Likes to eat the poultice off her leg. Grooms don't watch her close enough."

He started to slide back his chair, but the legs caught in the rug behind it and kept him bent over the table awkwardly. Pamela had reached for another slice of bread and was applying butter to it. There was a scream, a clatter, a loud thump, another scream, and loud sobbing. George tipped his chair over backward; Pamela flung down bread and butter and leaped to her feet. Their eagerness undid them. They reached the doorway at the same moment and became entangled. George drew back, and Pamela burst through, rounded the corner of the corridor, and flung herself to her knees beside Hetty, who was lying at the foot of the stairs.

"Hetty," she cried, lifting the countess into her arms like a doll. "Are you hurt? How did you come to fall?"

"I was pushed," Hetty whimpered, trembling and clinging to Pamela. "I was halfway down, and someone pushed me."

Her eyes were turned to the head of the stairs and held an expression of horror. Instinctively George and Pamela looked up too. St. Just stood at the top of the stairwell, his body half-turned so that it was impossible to say whether he was mounting or descending. Now he turned fully and came down slowly. Hetty screamed again.

"Stop your nonsense, Hetty," he said sharply. "Who the devil would want to push you down the stairs? And don't say it was I, because you'd never let me get behind you on the stairs."

"Now, m'dear," George said, "can't have been Vyvyan. You'd have heard him. Wearing boots. No carpet in the corridor."

"Do you think I don't know whether I trip or am pushed?" Hetty screamed. "Someone put his hands on my back. I felt it."

"Tell me first whether you are hurt," Pamela urged. "That is most important. Can you stand, Hetty?"

George lifted Hetty out of Pamela's arms and set her on her feet, and Pamela rose too. Quite obviously the countess was not hurt, except that her palms were reddened by their sharp contact with the floor. She was helped into the drawing room and laid upon the sofa. Pamela rang for a maid, sent her to the house-keeper for restoratives. George chafed Hetty's hands and murmured soothingly. St. Just propped his broad shoulders against the mantelpiece and glowered.

"If you would slap her face," he recommended coldly, "she would come around quicker."

Frankly, Pamela held the same opinion, since Hetty seemed to grow more hysterical the more attention she received. Another thing Pamela noticed was that all George's attempts to assure Hetty that she had not been pushed merely increased her terror. At last she half-forced a large glass of brandy down the countess's throat, and while Hetty was gasping and silenced by the fiery liquor, she changed the tack of their argument.

"I have just thought that it is very likely Hetty was pushed," she said thoughtfully.

St. Just, who had been looking fixedly at an ornament on the fire screen, jerked his head up and stared.

"Now, now, Lady Pam," George protested.

"Oh, not on purpose, but just think: if one of the maids, who has no business on that staircase, was coming down quickly and looking around to make sure no one would see her, she might well have run into Hetty."

"And then she disappeared into thin air?" St. Just asked dryly.

"Please, my lord," Pamela snapped, casting a monitory glance at him over Hetty's head. "Hetty is not such a fool that she does not know whether or not she has been pushed."

His lips parted, but the Hervey eyes shot sparks, and he closed his mouth. Whatever caustic comment was on the tip of his tongue remained there.

"Well, but would a maid just leave Hetty lying there?"

Now it was George's turn to receive a stabbing glance from the green-and-gold glinting eyes. "What undermaid in this house would you expect to confess she had just knocked her mistress down a flight of stairs she had no business to be on in the first place?" Pamela asked.

George had the grace to look slightly abashed. He realized now what Pamela was doing and realized that she was succeeding, too. Hetty was interested in this discussion. Her sobs were diminishing noticeably.

"Stupid of me," he murmured. "Of course, she would nip up the stairs like a shot. Sure she'd lose her place if she were caught."

"And run right into me," St. Just said. Both George and Pamela glared at him, but there was a twinkle of amusement in his eyes now, and they realized he was deliberately playing the heavy to give them an excuse to continue talking.

"No, she wouldn't do that," George pointed out. "You had to come around from the front of the house. Wouldn't move too fast, either, because you're bound to be sore. All she had to do was turn the corner of the stairs, gallop down past my room, and there she is at the backstairs, where she belonged."

"That sounds very likely to me," Pamela approved, wondering how Hetty could swallow it when even in the excitement no one could possibly miss the sound of a maid's clogs running in the uncarpeted corridor. It would have been easier for St. Just to creep up behind her.

"Does it not sound to you as if that is what occurred, Hetty?" she asked cajolingly.

The countess stared resentfully at her husband's booted feet. He was wearing breeches and top boots, and there could be no doubt that it would take him several minutes to get the boots on, even with his valet's help. He could not have pushed her, run back to his room to don his boots, and got to the head of the stairs again in time. He could not even have placed the boots near the stairs and put them on there, because with his sprained wrist he would need his valet's help to get them on. If he had been wearing pantaloons and hessians, it would have been barely possible, but not with top boots. It was just like Vyvyan to wear boots when you would expect him to put on proper morning dress.

"I suppose it must have been so," she said grudgingly. "And what is to be done about it."

"Nothing," St. Just replied. "What can be done?"

"Now, now," George protested. "Can't have the girls gaily toppling us down the stairs. Set an inquiry afoot."

Pamela drew breath sharply, having suddenly realized that Sarah did not wear clogs — Sarah, who moved so silently and knew the house so well. The ugly notion was gone in a moment, not because Pamela believed Sarah incapable of removing what she believed was an obstacle to her nursling's happiness, but because Sarah — Pamela had a vision of the grim mouth and hard eyes — would never do anything so haphazard. If Sarah decided to harm Hetty, there would be no chance involved. Of pushing Hetty down a wide, unencumbered flight of stairs, Sarah was innocent.

"Well, but how can we investigate?" Pamela asked, knowing that George had said what was necessary and now needed someone to argue him out of his position. The servants all know what has happened by now, and you know how they all stand together. Probably they would hold their tongues even if the girl had burst into the servants' quarters all unnerved. After all, it was an accident, and Hetty was not hurt. Besides, the maid may well have run upstairs instead of down. This is the hour when no one really is in a fixed place. The rooms are being done, breakfast is on the sideboard, and no other meal yet being prepared. Why, even cook and the scullery maids may have been upstairs."

"Then we are just to forget the whole thing? My father would have whipped the whole staff and turned them out to field labor."

"Possibly, but I am not likely to do that. For God's sake, Hetty, be reasonable. The girl — if anyone did push you — must be more terrified than you were. You may rest assured she will never use that staircase again."

"No, you would not like an inquiry, would you, Vyvyan?" Hetty spat. "It might turn out to be no accident after all. You should look rather nowhere if someone confessed she had been told to push me."

St. Just burst out laughing, and George, with staring eyes, bleated, "Now, now, Hetty, no!" in an agonized voice.

"Why not?" St. Just choked. "What is there unreasonable in it? Surely I would have made a general announcement to the servants at large that any and all attempts to maim or murder my wife were to be encouraged and would be deeply appreciated. I wonder what inducement I'd have offered them — not only to do the deed, of course, but to keep silent about it during the ensuing investigations?"

"Vyvyan," George cried, quite put out, "go away, for God's sake. Go look at Sergeant and see if the fomentations should be removed."

Pamela was bent over Hetty, who had thrown herself back on the sofa, weeping noisily again. She wondered wearily, as she administered hartshorn and water, whether every meeting between St. Just and his wife would be this wearing. Up until the previous night, both had maintained the appearance of civility to each other most of the time. The violence that had taken place, unrelated though it might be to the differences between them, and clearly in neither case anything more than an accident, had broken some thin barrier of reserve. There could be no solution now except a separation.

In the background, Pamela could hear George saying, "That's enough, Vyvyan, you are being objectionable. Can't you see the girl's shaken out of her wits?"

"Do you want me to listen to her accuse me of attempted murder — such a clumsy attempt, too — and smile? You didn't think it was just the thing last night."

"No. Didn't make any stupid, sarcastic cracks, either. Reasoned with you. Worked. And you ain't the most reasonable person in the world, Vyvyan."

"Is Hetty?"

"Woman. Bound to be unreasonable. If you were kinder, Vyvyan, showed her a little more attention, she wouldn't get this way."

"You would show her more attention, wouldn't you?"

"Well, I would. Save a lot of argument. Come on, Vyvyan, come out of here."

George drew his still-glowering cousin from the room, and Hetty soon quieted. Pamela found herself wondering whether it was the removal of the irritation that St. Just applied to her nerves or the simple removal of her audience that calmed her. In any event, Hetty soon stopped sobbing and even agreed that it was probably useless to pursue an investigation of which maid had pushed her.

"Oh, I know Vyvyan would not do such a thing," she sighed finally. "He is far too clever."

"Have you thought of separating from him, Hetty?" Pamela asked. "I am sure you are wrong with regard to his intentions toward you, but if you feel this way, would you not be better apart? If it is only the money, some binding arrangement might be made so that he would free you. I am sure he only desires enough to keep Tremaire running. He is not expensive in other ways. Surely you could let him have that, and enough would remain for you to be very comfortable in London or . . . or even to go back to the Indies, if that is what you desire."

"Leave St. Just?" Hetty exclaimed in a shocked voice. "You mean live alone? I could not. I have never done so. It would be most improper."

"Improper? But, Hetty, surely you cannot value propriety more than your life."

There was malice in Pamela's voice, for her temper had been worn thin by fright and what she considered histrionics on Hetty's part. She was tired of hearing Hetty scream murder every time a glance was thrown at her. If she could make Hetty see how ridiculous her pretense of fear was, perhaps St. Just would be spared the constant reminders of his brother-in-law's death. The point went right over Hetty's head.

"Well, I do value propriety more," the countess rejoined with a sullen pout. "For what is life if one cannot move in the best circles and go to balls and card parties and suchlike? I may be very ignorant of certain things, but I do know the value of being a countess, and I know, too, that, situated as I am — a stranger — the worst possible construction would be placed upon my separation."

"But that might be got around, Hetty. If

Lord St. Just's sister would support you —"

"Lady Boscawen? She hates me! She would sooner poison me than support me."

Pamela could no more imagine Lady Alice Boscawen dancing nude in the street than exhibiting sufficient passion to be called hatred, and the reference to poison seemed to prove that Hetty was not rational on this subject. She abandoned the question of Hetty living separately in England.

"If you went home, Hetty, none of these problems would arise. You would be safe and among all your own friends."

"Oh, I shall not do that. Good heavens, the islands were well enough when I knew no better, but they are a paltry place compared to London." She looked at Pamela with her head cocked to one side. "One would almost think, dear Pam, that you *wished* me to leave Vyvyan." Color rushed into Pamela's face, and Hetty laughed merrily. "I assure you I would not care. Moreover, it is all nonsense. If I went, you could not stay, so if you were . . . er . . . friendly with Vyvyan, you would never urge me to leave him. I do not suspect you. Besides, Vyvyan does not seem to care much for women. He is attractive — to a certain type, of course — and has had opportunities among the less elegant ladies we knew. I never cast the slightest impediment in his way, but nothing ever came of it. He likes only the filth one purchases with money. *That* is a 'gentleman's' taste."

The flush receded slowly from Pamela's face, but her eyes blazed her indignation. Hetty had the grace to look down uneasily.

"Dear Pam," she said after a short unpleasant silence, "do not be cross for my little joke. I promise I will not fun in that silly way again. My dependence for entrance into society is all upon you and Lady Boscawen."

After that Pamela could only wonder if Hetty was quite right in the head. One moment she said Lady Boscawen hated her and insulted Pamela grossly, the next she acted as if a single sentence wiped out everything that had gone before. In a moment Pamela sighed. It was she who was silly, not Hetty. Hetty was perfectly in character — a spoiled child. If she did not get what she wanted, the world was against her. All the accusations and hysteria about her brother's death were simply a method of bedeviling her husband, turning the knife in the wound in his conscience, because he had not given in to her demands. Certainly Hetty did not fear for her own life. If further proof than their conversation was necessary, Hetty promptly furnished it by making an excellent breakfast and setting about her normal morning pursuits.

Pamela was thoroughly sickened. She would write to her friends in London and ask them to find another position for her as soon as possible.

If she had the money, Pamela told herself, she would have gone to her room, packed her things, and left that very day. The countess's insinuation about her relationship with St. Just lay like a shadow on her mind in spite of the apology, yet she did not go to her bedchamber or to the library to write her letters. I must settle the business about the maid with Mrs. Helston, Pamela decided, and went off to the kitchen to interrogate the girl.

She found that Mrs. Helston had given a very fair picture of the pregnant maid, and concluded that it was most unlikely that she had seduced the gardener. Whether or not she would be a source of trouble in the future was more doubtful. The girl was rather simpleminded and, deplorably, pretty. It seemed only too likely that in a large household such as theirs she would fall into the same error again. In a small place where no menservants were kept and she could be closely watched, she might do better. They could not find a place for her before the child was born, however, and what to do with the child, who would make finding another place for her after her delivery very difficult, was another problem. Pamela went upstairs to the house-keeper's room and was discussing the matter with Mrs. Helston when a footman came to summon her to Hetty. Callers had arrived.

Casting an anxious glance at her dress, Pamela hurried down the stairs. She had not paid any attention when Sarah laid out her clothing, and she was surprised to find herself suitably arrayed in an Indian muslin morning dress with a flounced hem and a rather severe tucked bodice. Usually she wore rather worn merino garments around the house, because clothing was becoming an expensive burden to her. Sarah may not have been a witch, but she seemed to have precognition. Quick fingers twitched her sash straight, felt to be sure that her heavy loops of hair were neat; she opened the door of the small drawing room to hear Hetty in the final stages of description of her morning's accident. Hetty had not done herself any good, Pamela thought, reading the expressions of the guests. Sometimes Hetty seemed to have a quick, sly mind, but she was a fool about people.

"Oh, Pam," the countess said, a trifle sullenly, "here are Sir Harold and Lady Harold come to pay a call. This is my companion, Lady Pamela Hervey."

The introduction was not properly made, even the naming was wrong, and Pamela did not miss the touch of spite that had called her "companion" instead of "friend." That did not bother her, because one glance told her that Sir Harold and his lady would judge by what a person was. In fact, as annoyed as Pamela had been with Hetty earlier, she was sorry for her now. She made a mental note to drill Hetty in the correct forms of introductions before she left, and came forward smiling to greet the heavyset, grizzled gentleman and plump, cheerful lady of middle years. Civilities were exchanged, and Lady Allenby turned to Pamela with the faintest flicker of relief.

"It is most shocking to hear of Lady St. Just's experience, but I have been telling her that, in general, our local people make most excellent servants."

"Indeed, I have found that so," Pamela agreed smoothly.

The set around Lady Allenby's mouth softened slightly. She recognized that she now had a skillful partner in small talk. "And it may have come about because there has not been a mistress at Tremaire for so long. When was it, my dear," she asked her husband, "that the late Lady St. Just died?"

"All of seven years ago, Caroline. I thought young Arthur would marry, but . . ." His wife cast her eyes up at him, and his speech ended in an abrupt "harumph."

"You know how it is when there is no lady in the house," Lady Allenby covered swiftly. "The maids take all sorts of advantage. I am sure now that you are here, Lady St. Just, all will be restored to order."

"I am not very well used to dealing with this type of servant, and I do not think I care to adjust to insolence," Hetty said loftily.

Pamela bit her lip. There was no way she could excuse what Hetty had said without calling further attention to it. She tried to catch Hetty's eye to warn her, but failed.

Lady Allenby's lips had tightened again, but her well-bred voice was unchanged when she spoke. "You will learn, my dear. It takes more than a few weeks. I remember when I first came to Cornwall — I am from Kent — that I was appalled at the freedom of the servants. But they are very attached and faithful and, I think, far more honest than the usual run. Oh, I am the most scatterbrained thing," she said, trying once more to change the subject. "I have been meaning to apologize for not calling sooner."

"We thought it best," her husband put in, "to wait until the first shock wore off. The tragedy, you know — terrible thing, that."

"But Vyvyan has known about his father's and brothers' deaths for months," Hetty said.

"It could scarcely be a shock any longer. Besides, I was very surprised that, even when we first heard, he did not seem to be much distressed by the news."

A startled glance passed between husband and wife, and Pamela bit her lip again. Hetty should not have said such a thing, whether or not it was true. And, from the very chilly glance Sir Harold was now turning on her as his lady skillfully brought the subject around to servant problems again, Pamela had reason to believe he did not credit the allegation against St. Just. In fact, Hetty had probably made an enemy.

"I think Lady St. Just phrased what she meant awkwardly and did not quite understand that you meant the shock of revived memories upon coming back to his home," Pamela murmured to him. "Lord St. Just has great command over his feelings and would not wish to distress his wife by displaying them openly. I think Lady St. Just meant to praise his self-control."

Disconcertingly keen eyes stared at her approvingly, although a twinkle of amusement in them told her that Sir Harold knew as well as she did that if St. Just had learned to control his feelings, it was an entirely new thing. "Oh, certainly," Sir Harold replied, but a flashing glance at Hetty showed no softening. "Vyvyan . . . I mean St. Just of course. Keep thinking of him as a boy. He was quiet when his mother died. Sad thing, that. She was a fine woman, and very young."

"The family has certainly had its share of troubles," Pamela agreed noncommittally.

"Hmm, yes. Odd family, the St. Justs. I'm a bit interested in families, you know. Very old family myself. We can trace ourselves back to the Conqueror. The St. Justs are Cornish, though, and very proud of it. Given to marrying locally — the heir, I mean. They were country people who came up under the Stuarts. Very common practice among them for the younger sons to marry well. Now, let me see. Hmmm. Lady Pamela Hervey. That would make you one of Bristol's daughters."

"No, sir, I do not have that honor." Pamela smiled, not in the least offended by the effort to place her. People interested in genealogy were often totally unaware that their searching personal questions might be embarrassing.

"No? Married one of his younger sons?"

"No, sir." Pamela smiled more broadly. "I am the daughter of his youngest brother."

"Can't be. You would be Miss Pamela, then, not Lady Pamela."

"I am afraid I am teasing you, sir. I am the Baroness Oxted in my own right through my mother. We have not used the title for several generations, however, since we have no property or influence in the area, not even a house. I am afraid my several-times-removed great-grandmother was a creation of the merry monarch's."

Sir Harold's lips twitched. "Very good king, Charles, for all his odd creations. Only fault was too soft a heart toward that Portuguese wife of his and his silly brother."

"Yes, indeed. But my mother's family became very proper under Queen Anne, I believe, and since there was no son, the lady who married Lord Hoo and Hastings simply did not use the title. We do, however, continue to call ourselves Lady this or that."

"Very proper. Shows — Good God, Vyvyan, whatever has happened to you?"

"How do you do, Sir Harold," St. Just said, coming forward to shake his hand and bow to his wife. "Lady Allenby, how kind of you to call." He glanced around the room. "George, ring for Hayle. Let us have some refreshments up here. I hope you will forgive me, sir, for not coming as soon as my wife's message reached me. I stopped to wash my hands. I have been in the stables."

"And so your boots show, Vyvyan," Hetty said.

"Sorry, Hetty. If I had stopped to change

those, I might never have got here in time at all."

"But my dear St. Just, how did you come to be hurt?" Lady Allenby asked, rising and looking more closely at him. "Do sit down, my poor boy; you are quite pale. Let me see your hand and your head, and your poor face too. If I were you, Lady St. Just, I would apply —"

"I do not know how you can tell I am pale under this sunburn, ma'am," St. Just put in, stemming the tide, but in decidedly affectionate tones, "but Sarah would be furious if poor Hetty tried to interfere with her ministrations. I am sure she has done what was right, too, because I feel quite well. As for how it came about, I was so foolish as to tumble off my horse into a gully."

"Tumble off your horse!" Sir Harold exclaimed unbelievingly. "You?"

St. Just laughed. "It happens to the best of us, sir. I was distracted by . . . by something, and not attending properly. The worse of it is that Sergeant cut his knees."

"That *is* too bad. Will they scar, do you think?"

"Horses!" Hetty exclaimed. "I do declare that if both Vyvyan and the horse had broken a leg, there would be more concern shown for the horse."

Lady Allenby smiled, and George, who had been shaking hands with Sir Harold, turned toward Hetty. " 'Course, m'dear. Wouldn't have to shoot Vyvyan, y'know."

"Well, it is a very fortunate thing that Vyvyan did fall," Hetty said after the laughter at George's remark died down, "for if he had not, you would not have seen him. He is out from dawn to dinner every day, as an ordinary thing. One would think he had a distaste for . . . for the house."

There was a second's silence during which another significant glance was exchanged between the Allenbys. Then Sir Harold harumphed again. "Very proper, though a bit hard on you, Lady St. Just. Looking over your lands, eh, St. Just?"

"Yes, sir. I have been away over five years. I wish," he added with a slight unevenness in his voice, "that you would call me Vyvyan."

Sir Harold came across to him and took his hand again, saying softly, "Sorry. You know that. Well . . . Least said, you know. . . ." His voice regained its briskness. "Shouldn't think you would have any trouble. There haven't been many changes. But any help I can extend, my boy, you have only to ask."

"Thank you, you are very kind. I shall ride over. I had hoped to see William. Will he come and spend a night or two with us? We

124

do not need to stand on ceremony with him. As soon as my wife has her bearings, we shall try to begin entertaining formally at Tremaire, as we used to do, but I hope my friends will not wait for that."

"William is too busy!" George laughed, turning from the decanters Hayle had placed on a table. "You don't have pansy-brown eyes, Vyvyan. Lack certain other attractions too."

St. Just lifted his brows, and Lady Allenby smiled. "Yes, it is not public yet, because Elinor is not out, but I believe we will be able to announce William's betrothal very soon."

"I am very happy for him, if you mean Miss Elinor Austell. I only remember her as a child, but —"

"Will see him, though," George interrupted. "Bound to be looking for distraction. Forgot. Measles. That's why I came back. Rode over to visit the Austells, but couldn't trouble them when there was sickness in the house. Daresay William will be home by now."

"Oh, dear," Lady Allenby cried, "I wonder if perhaps we should drive over. If I could be of help to Mrs. Austell, I would not like to think I had not offered. And we could take the other road, Harold, and come around by Penzance, so if there is anything she has ordered in the town, we could bring it."

Sir Harold hastily finished the glass of wine George had put into his hand. "Very well, my dear," he said resignedly. Then, with a rather stiff smile at Hetty, who was protesting against endangering oneself by going into a house of sickness, "Illness is to Caroline as a trumpet to an old war horse. You will have to pardon her, Lady St. Just. She will fret herself into a spasm if she cannot recommend remedies and have a look at the invalids."

Good-byes were murmured and an invitation extended to return the visit. Pamela thought it might have been given more warmly, and was sorry, for Hetty looked hurt. Nonetheless, she had to admit that Hetty had brought it upon herself by her spitefulness. These people had obviously known St. Just since he was a boy and were fond of him. Sir Harold's reminder to St. Just that he had promised to ride over was a good deal more cordial than his invitation to Hetty.

As they reached the door, the older man paused uneasily. "By the way, Vyvyan, meant to mention, there's something in the wind. You haven't been stirring up the coven, have you? What I mean," he added in a lower voice, "I hope you don't believe they were involved in . . . Harumph. Your father and brothers never had any trouble with them,

126

you know. Sorry. It's an awkward thing to say, but there has been an unusual activity since you came home. My people are all uneasy about the meetings."

"No, sir, at least I haven't stirred them intentionally," St. Just replied, frowning.

"It's the thing now to laugh at them, but I've seen too much," Sir Harold continued. "Didn't think much of it at first, but you people seem to be having a rash of accidents here, what with your wife falling down the stairs and you being thrown from your horse. Made me wonder."

CHAPTER 7

The next day, St. Just found Pamela in the still room with Sarah, who was explaining to her the use and preparation of a number of herbs and simples she had never come across before. He stood watching them for a few minutes, the gray head and glossy brown bent together. A list in Mrs. Helston's writing lay on the dresser. Doubtless Pamela had been checking the stores of preserves. Very likely she had come across his mother's medicinals and had asked Sarah to explain. His throat contracted with pain as the inevitable comparison with Hetty came to mind.

"Pam."

She turned smoothly, unstartled, a woman in her rightful place. "Yes, my lord?"

"I have been speaking to that gardener, and we have a problem. His wife . . . She's a witch, is she not, Sarah?"

"Ned Potten's wife? Yes. And nasty with it, too."

"I thought I saw the signs on her."

"I don't think the girl knows anything

about that," Pamela remarked. "She is simple, and it is most difficult to get a clear tale from her. She knew the man was married, which led me to believe at first that she was not as innocent as she pretended. Later, however, she said the oddest things — that it was most fortunate her baby would be born in June, because that would assure it of fulfilling some high purpose. Yet, when I tried to interest her in arrangements for raising the child, she was completely indifferent. She said that Potten would take it."

"That woman raise a brat not her own?" St. Just asked incredulously.

"Unfortunately not, although that was my first reaction. I felt relief, for, indeed, if the man were responsible enough to suggest that expedient, and his wife willing, it seemed to me that the whole might be easily settled. When I continued to question her, however, I . . ." Pamela hesitated. "I know very little about this man," she then said quickly, "and I do not like to cast suspicion, but I began to have the most dreadful ideas. Does Potten have relatives or connections in some distant place?"

"Not that I know of. Do you know, Sarah, whether his wife might have a connection through the coven? She is a local woman. I seem to remember my father was not best pleased when Ned married her, and said something about her grandmother. Good Lord! She could not have been the woman my grandfather hanged, could she?"

"I wouldn't know that, Master Vyvyan. Once Maud took the coven, that trouble was ended."

"I shall have to look through my grandfather's papers. I hope she is not, because it will complicate getting rid of Potten, which I would like to do. I would not like anyone to think I dismissed him because of an old prejudice. Well, there is no use in worrying about a crossing until I come to it. Why did you ask about Potten's relations, Pam?"

"Because the girl said something about the child being transported to a far-distant land to serve a great purpose. I could not believe . . . I hoped that another village or county might seem to her . . ." Pamela's voice faded.

Sarah had sat down suddenly, her face gray with shock and St. Just stood staring at Pamela, his green eyes wide with horror.

"Oh, heavens, then he did mean to kill the poor little thing," Pamela whispered.

"Oh, God," St. Just muttered. "Oh, God, no! Not here!"

It was immediately apparent that there was more behind the violent distress Sarah and St. Just felt than simple revulsion at the intention of child murder. That, once known, could be prevented. The idea might cause anger or disgust, but not this almost despairing horror. Pamela glanced from one face to the other and found no comfort in either.

"My lord," she said sharply, "you are frightening me. Tell me what is wrong."

"There are some things it is better not to know."

"Tell her, Master Vyvyan," Sarah said. "You need not hide evil from this one. She will not be tainted, and she will fight."

St. Just veiled his eyes, hiding what was in them. "I remember saying to you that witchcraft was mostly harmless, but there are old, ugly things in it which I did not mention. Sacrifice — black cocks, black goats — one turns one's eyes away. There can be worse."

He wiped his hand across his mouth as if there were filth on it, and Pamela swallowed sickly. She knew the old tales about the witches' sabbat. Sacrifice . . . a newborn baby . . . a great purpose . . . What purpose? She asked that aloud, her rich voice turned thin.

"What purpose?"

"Death," Sarah said flatly. "One would not use such strong magic for any other purpose than a deathsinging. Midsummer eve falls in the dark of the moon."

"Would they desecrate a rite of fruition

with such foulness?" St. Just grabbed at a thin hope with the flung question.

"When once the mind becomes twisted in that path, it is not thought to be a desecration." Sarah did not cling to forlorn hopes.

"Then that will be the time," he muttered. "But who?"

"The moon will be dark on Sunday," Sarah replied. "Before that week is out, we will know surely . . . or never know."

"No!" Pamela cried, and both pairs of eyes turned to her. She could feel her cheeks flush with rage. "I will not stand here and listen to you speak as if this is inevitable. You must do something. You cannot permit this to happen. Turn your eyes away from a black cock if you will, but not from a baby."

"Of course not," St. Just soothed. "We will do everything we possibly can."

Pamela fought an impulse to burst into tears. Instead of being comforted, she had been further frightened by the defeated tone in which he spoke.

"I will take care of the baby myself," she cried.

"No! You will not meddle in what you do not understand. I am not condoning this," he added angrily in answer to her expression, "but I will not permit you to involve yourself in what will certainly be dangerous."

"Master Vyvyan is right," Sarah put in. "You might do more harm than good, not knowing their ways. Just watch and be ready to help if we need you."

"Just watch!" She looked wildly from one to the other, but Sarah's face was closed, and St. Just had again veiled his eyes. "In God's name, my lord, at least send the girl away."

"Where to? You said she was simple, and convinced Potten would do well by her. Would she be willing to go?"

"Then send Potten and his wife away."

"Pamela, don't talk like a fool or begin to think like Hetty. I could drive them off my land, yes, but I do not own the county. What is to prevent them from taking shelter with friends or staying in the village? I am better off, if what we suspect is true, with them under my eye."

"Then what will you do?"

He looked goaded and uncertain and made no reply, but Sarah, who had been staring at him, nodded her head as if some message had passed between them. The maid's eyes were fixed upon her master with compelling intensity.

"Perhaps if she were called, Maud might come again. The cottage below the house at the edge of the coomb is empty still. No one would take old Maud's cottage, nor would

133

the People let it fall into disrepair. It is ready and waiting. And you need not appear in this at all."

"Who is Maud?" Pamela asked.

She was instantly sorry she had drawn St. Just's attention. His expression grew even more uncertain, and then his mouth set in a determined line.

"You had better go," he said.

A flush of rage colored Pamela's face, making her eyes so bright they glittered. "Do you mean to dismiss me, my lord, so that you can better allow a child to be sacrificed in some foul rite in order not to inconvenience yourself? Do you think I will go without taking precautions, warning a justice!"

"Don't you go vaporish on me, Pam," St. Just snapped impatiently. "I have worries enough without you acting the fool. I did not mean to dismiss you. I simply feel that the less you know about this whole affair, the less danger there will be in it for you."

What he said was reasonable, but Pamela could not be content with the explanation. "My lord, Mrs. Helston brought this problem to me, and I brought it to you. There can be no secret that I am involved." She still suspected that St. Just and Sarah might agree to do nothing. "Whether or not I know of the action you take, I will be held responsible for it, at least in part. If there is danger here, I had rather know what I am getting into. In any case, what must I think of myself if I should desert in the face of danger? I will not go."

They faced each other, Pamela stubbornly determined and St. Just gnawing his lips in an agony of desire. He had only once known a woman of such strength, such beauty, such courage. He would have her. With a strangled sound, St. Just rushed from the room, slamming the door behind him. Pamela stared, openmouthed, and Sarah clucked her tongue irritably.

"Now you've overset the fat into the fire," the maid said sharply.

"What is it? What happened?"

Sarah shrugged. "He's gone to run his head into more trouble. Never had patience to wait, not Master Vyvyan. Well, who knows what's for the best? I told you, that wife of his doesn't belong here. You do, and Master Vyvyan knows it. You think about it."

"You don't know what you are saying!" Pamela recoiled from knowledge and reached for the door to escape.

"I know Master Vyvyan. I know what he wants before he knows it himself. I didn't think you were the kind to lie to yourself, Miss Pam."

Without waiting for a reply, Sarah walked out of the still room, leaving Pamela gazing blankly after her. Lie to herself? Had she? Promptly the memory of the sense of loss when she had thought St. Just dead, her reluctance to leave this place, came to answer the question. Pamela blushed, but not with shame at her love for another woman's husband. In this day of marriages made for name or money, such a love was so common as scarcely to be a matter for shame. She was appalled at what she considered her deliberate blindness to her own motives.

There was no help for it. Now she must leave at once. But how? She had about ten shillings, scarcely enough to hire a carriage to take her to the village, certainly not enough to pay her fare to London, not to mention paying for food and lodging on the way. To whom could she appeal for money? St. Just owed her two months' wages, but it was impossible to ask him now. Besides, what excuse could she give Hetty for wanting to leave? And that wretched girl and her baby . . . How dreadful to be driven away now!

George, she thought, I can ask George. She walked slowly to the small drawing room, wondering how to get George alone. Finesse was not necessary, however, for George was the room's sole occupant. Before she could broach the topic, George raised a quizzical brow and laid aside the newspaper he had been idly perusing.

"Too late," he said with an ironic twist of the lips. "Took her off upstairs. Vyvyan's a fool sometimes. Put Hetty into a pet, dragging her off like that. Whatever he wants, he won't get it now. Hetty's not a bad sort. Vyvyan handles her wrong."

Pamela went white. She had not understood what Sarah meant when she said St. Just had gone to run his head into more trouble. Rage replaced every other emotion. There was no need to say anything to George. Doubtless her wages would be forthcoming from Hetty. St. Just was a fool.

The earl had goaded Hetty into a fury quite deliberately, however. First he had told her in the voice one uses to an erring servant that he had something private to say to her. When she, naturally enough, protested against his manner and replied that she would be happy to speak to him when he was more civil, he had grasped her by the arm and dragged her roughly up the stairs. In the process, St. Just had collected several nasty scratches and a number of painful kicks on the shins, but considered that a small price to pay for Hetty's nearly incoherent rage.

"Damn you, you're my wife. When I want a

word with you, you come with me. You don't tell me to be civil."

"Get out!" Hetty screamed. "I shan't speak to you. I shan't listen to you. I shan't."

"You'll do as I tell you — whatever I tell you. I'm tired of your airs and your graces, and I'm tired of having you throw your money in my face."

"But you aren't tired of using it, are you? You greedy filthy beast, you —"

"Yes, I am! I don't even want the money any more if I've got to have you along with it. I want a divorce. I'll give you cause — any cause you name — and you can divorce me."

St. Just was not certain what his wife's reaction to this would be. He was prepared for hysterics, for counting accusations, for instant relief and acceptance. The only reaction he did not expect was the one he got. Hetty stopped gasping with rage. Her empurpled face faded slowly to its natural color. And she smiled — sweetly.

"No, Vyvyan, oh, no. Don't you remember why I married you? Did you think I was ever taken in by those high-and-mighty manners of yours? Did you think I ever wanted any part of you? You are ten years younger than I, Vyvyan — did you know that? Did you know how many men there were before you? You and your infantile sense of importance — you made me laugh. At least, I would have laughed had I not found you so revolting. A big, clumsy animal — you even smell like an animal, because you never use scent like a civilized man. But I married you anyway. And what I married you for, you've still got." She laughed lightly. "You've got more of it, in fact. I'm not the wife of an honorable, I'm a countess — Lady St. Just — and a countess I'll stay. Oh, no, Vyvyan, I'll never divorce you."

He stood speechless, glaring, and Hetty laughed again.

"And I'll never give you any reason to divorce me, either. I've had all the men I've ever wanted. Don't waste your time spying on me."

"I'll kill you," he choked.

The laughter disappeared from Hetty's face, and she took a step backward, away from her husband. There was caution overlying a weary contempt in her voice.

"Be reasonable, Vyvyan. To divorce you would ruin me. Women don't divorce their husbands, not nice women. I'll behave better. I won't interfere with your . . . pleasure. I'll be blind and deaf and mute too. Let us call a truce."

The color drained from St. Just's complexion as he looked at his wife. Hetty watched him keenly; she needed time. Her examination told her nothing, however. All play of emotion on his face had stopped, and his queer green eyes were hidden behind their heavy lashes. Without another word, he turned and left the room. As soon as the door closed behind him, Hetty sank onto the chaise longue, trembling and whimpering, and a young woman with a dark, sullen face came out of the shadows behind the door of the bedchamber.

"You heard, Mary?" Hetty quavered. "Did you hear him?"

"Yes, my lady. Your ladyship should take care." The words were more than a servant's practiced agreement with her mistress's whim.

"Oh, yes, I will have to, won't I?"

"Yes, my lady. You lie back and rest now. I'll bring your ladyship's drops."

The clatter of booted feet on the stairs gave George and Pamela a moment's warning. They had been seated in uneasy silence, straining to hear. George, half-smiling, did not try to conceal his interest, and Pamela was too furious and at the same time too worried to consider the implications of hers.

"Told you," George said mildly as St. Just erupted into the room. "Wrong way to go about asking a lady for something. Best thing to do now —"

"Get out!" the earl snarled.

Unable to think of anything else, and hoping that even a few seconds' delay would give St. Just a chance to regain his control, Pamela rose to her feet as if the remark had been addressed to her.

"Not you," St. Just snapped. "You, George, get out."

George's eyes, normally fishlike in their round expressionlessness, narrowed, giving a singularly wicked look to his face. "Sometimes you go beyond the bounds of what is permissible even between relations, Vyvyan."

"Will you get out, or must I throw you out?"

"St. Just!"

Unheeding, the earl advanced on his cousin. George rose, and Pamela leaped forward to interpose herself between the two men.

"George, please," she cried, "please do not quarrel with him. He will hurt himself."

Even with an injured hand and a sprained wrist, there was about as much chance of St. Just being hurt in a set-to between him and George as a lion being seriously mauled by a rabbit. It was excuse enough, however, to permit George to retreat with some remnant of dignity.

"That was disgusting, St. Just," Pamela gasped. "How could you!"

"I asked Hetty for a divorce. She refused."

For the moment the lesser but more immediate outrage blanked Pamela's mind to what St. Just had said. "I don't care what Hetty did," she cried. "You have no right to treat George that way."

St. Just's hands shot out, seized on Pamela's shoulders with bruising force, and shook her until her teeth rattled. "Did you hear what I said?" he bellowed.

Exerting all her not inconsiderable strength, Pamela wrenched herself free and landed a resounding slap on the earl's distorted face. He gasped and brought a hand up to his maltreated cheek.

"You are perfectly correct," Pamela said coldly. "A slap in the face is an excellent remedy for hysterics. Will you stop acting like a spoiled child instead of a grown man! I must assume, since you are telling me this, that I am the reason you broached this topic to your wife. You should have consulted me first. I could have saved you the trouble on two counts. First of all, I could have told you Hetty would not consent to a divorce. How you could have thought she would is utterly beyond me. And as for myself —"

He did not allow her to finish, but sneered bitterly, "It does not matter. I have permission to take my pleasure when and where I will."

Instead of being insulted, Pamela had to suppress an urge to laugh. If St. Just thought he was proposing an illicit relationship to her, she could not conceive of a more inept way to do it. "You are an inconsiderate beast, St. Just," she remarked dispassionately. "Does it not occur to you that, even if I were so lost to the world for love of you as you think, the present circumstances might make it awkward for me to make light conversation with Hetty?"

The sneer was gone, and there was only a gray, blind look to his face. "You know I did not mean that. I can buy amusement, and I do," he said bleakly. "I do not need to offend a woman like yourself to obtain that." Then the full meaning of what she said penetrated his duped senses. "For God's sake, I said nothing of my feeling for you. I am sure Hetty does not suspect that. There are troubles enough between us to account for my request without implicating any woman. Pamela, you will not leave us? Hetty will go mad here alone. In common mercy . . ."

"I will not leave this afternoon or tomorrow," Pamela said slowly. "If Hetty does not connect me with this sudden desire of yours for freedom, I should not like to add that to the other causes of friction between you."

"Curse me for a stupid lout," he burst out.

"You liked me before this. You were willing to be my friend, and I had to try for more. Well, what are your terms? Am I merely never to exchange a word with you in private, or will it be necessary for me not even to speak or look at you in company?"

This was the moment to ask for her money and set a definite date for her departure in a week or two. Pamela could not do it. St. Just's situation was heartbreaking. His wife hated him; there must still be a seed of doubt in his mind as to whether his cousin had tried to kill him. Pamela longed to take him in her arms and assure him that someone cared. She could not do that, but she could not leave him either.

"You are entirely too given to overdramatizing a situation, St. Just. I make no terms. I merely remind you that I will not be Hetty's companion for very long. I will stay a little while because I do not see what excuse I can give Hetty for leaving without ruining myself as well as hurting her." Pity and rage brought tears to her eyes. "Why did you do such an insane thing?"

"I'm like a trapped animal," he said softly. "I endured it quietly when there was no way out. Then someone came, and I thought I saw an escape, so I struggled. The worst of it is that I cannot blame Hetty. She has her faults,

144

but a clear bargain was made, and she has kept her part of it. I have the money. For the rest, probably I made most of the trouble between us. I did not enter into our relationship in the proper spirit. I was young and resentful."

"And knowing yourself to be in the wrong makes you even more unpleasant and unreasonable. How well I know it. It has a similar effect upon me. What a very lovely, pleasant house this is going to be to live in. And now you have even alienated George! I declare, if I were not backed into an impossible situation, I would take to my heels."

St. Just did not seem to have heard. He had walked to the window and was staring out at the rising ground. "I threatened to kill her," he said suddenly.

Pamela's breath caught. She knew how often a man with a violent temper would say those words, but St. Just sounded as if he were surprised, as if he had suddenly realized that he meant them. He had called himself a trapped animal, and desperation could unhinge a man's mind. Her father had been a trapped animal too, and he had killed himself — for all they covered it with nonsense about an accident. Would he have killed someone else if it could have saved him? A vicious man, but very kind to me . . . That was what

Johnson had said about a Hervey, but perhaps it did not apply only to the Herveys. Any man, tried far enough, could turn vicious. St. Just must be diverted from this particular line of thought at once.

"Do you intend to use the same method to pacify George?" Pamela asked acidly.

"George?" he asked vaguely. "Why should I need to pacify George? Oh, lord! Well, it's no matter. George is used to me."

"Nonetheless, I doubt that he finds it enjoyable to be made to look nohow in front of a comparative stranger. That really was a revolting exhibition, my lord. A man of your size had no right to threaten someone like George."

"Oh, all right, all right! I will make my peace with George."

"Yes, but you must beg his pardon as publicly as you insulted him — and not in such a way that it is a further insult — and you must thank him for his consideration in not pressing the point, too."

St. Just turned from the window and leaned back against its frame. He was smiling, as if he had realized why Pamela was baiting him about George. "Will you call me Vy?" he asked softly. "My mother used to call me that. No one else ever did."

Cautiously Pamela shook her head. It

would be dangerous to yield an inch. "It would be too hard to explain."

"Not even that?"

She bit her lip but would not answer. However clumsy St. Just might be in dealing with Hetty, his touch with her was sure.

"I have succeeded in making us both thoroughly miserable, have I not? That is reasonable enough. It is an art with me. Everything I touch, I destroy."

With a sense of desperation, Pamela laughed aloud. She had to stop this scene before she ended up in St. Just's arms. "Surely not," she gasped. "I suspect we will both survive."

Fury distorted his expression as the notion that she had been laughing at him all along sprang to his mind. An instant later, he was laughing himself. "Damn you, Pam. Don't you know better than to laugh at a man when he has been blighted in love and is wallowing in self-pity? If I don't come to wring Hetty's neck, I shall certainly wring yours."

CHAPTER 8

"You can say what you like about the advantages of English servants," Hetty remarked with a playful shake of the head, "but I cannot discover a thing to recommend them."

George lifted his eyes from the two swatches of cloth he had been comparing. "Why, m'dear? Thought you had everything settled all right and tight between that new groom and new maid of yours. Not working out?"

"The maid is a treasure, but the groom, for whom I had the highest hopes, has disappointed me sadly."

"In what way, Hetty?" Pamela asked without hesitating over the beading she was sewing onto the bodice of an evening dress.

"I don't precisely know," Hetty said merrily. "That's the trouble. I have the feeling that I have been taken in by a Banbury tale, but if I have not, then I am a good, kind mistress instead of a silly fool."

"Hetty," George said with mock severity,

"you are trying to make a May-game of us again. Declare, I don't know what has happened to put you into such spirits."

It was true. Pamela thought, that Hetty was in the most delightful temper, and had been for days. About an hour after the discussion she had had with St. Just about the divorce, Pamela had gone into the garden hoping the air would clear her head. There she had met Hetty and her maid obviously coming back from a walk. Hetty had been so sunny and cheerful that Pamela had scarcely recognized her, and the mood had persisted. It was a most welcome proof that St. Just had indeed concealed the reason he had asked for a divorce and that Hetty did not relate his desire to be free with Pamela. Perhaps the shock had made Hetty realize that she could not go on tormenting her husband without some dangerous reaction. In any case, Hetty's good humor made life so much more pleasant that Pamela had temporarily reconsidered her decision to leave Tremaire.

"No, really," Hetty giggled. "He told me this farrago about being a witch's son and having to go away for a few days because of that. Well, Vyvyan told me most specifically that I must not annoy the witches — and you warned me too, George — so I told him to go. The more I think of it, though, the less likely it sounds. I am sure I have been taken advantage of sadly."

"He's a witch's son, all right," George said, his staring eyes quite expressionless. "Don't know why he should need to take off work, though."

"Really!" Hetty exclaimed. "How . . . how interesting. I suppose I have done just right, then, in giving him time off. Do you think he would tell me what he was about? I did not wish to ask him, you know, but now that I have shown myself to be sympathetic and obliging, perhaps it would be safe."

"Wouldn't have anything to do with the thing m'self. Fact is, don't like it. Something going on. Noticed . . . Never mind."

Pamela's lips felt dry. She had noticed too. There was a growing tension in the house among the servants, and there had been other odd goings and comings. Sarah had not come to wake her yesterday morning, and when Pamela questioned her, the maid had replied enigmatically that she had been away for the night. Mrs. Helston had been distressed too, because on Sunday night, the first night of moon-dark, the pregnant maid had been found trying to open the kitchen door to go out. The girl had seemed dazed and offered as explanation only that she had heard someone calling her. None of the menservants would leave the house during the dark of the moon, and Mrs. Helston would not consider waking George or St. Just to investigate, so it was impossible to discover the truth of the matter.

"Oh, George," Hetty protested, laughing, "you are as bad as Vyvyan. I daresay you believe this nonsense too."

"Don't know what I believe. Seen some pretty odd things." George laid the swatches he was still holding down on the table. "Use the yellow and grey if you take my advice, m'dear. Brighten up the northern aspect. Very pretty, yellow. Don't soil quickly out here. Gray rug, yellow chairs, striped curtains. Smart." He rose from his chair. "Ride out, I think. Got a thought."

Pamela's lips parted, and she clamped them firmly together, repressing the pang of fear that stabbed her. She wished she could forget the accident in the gully and the ridiculous reason she had been given for George's actions. St. Just had been out since early morning. If George had wanted to follow him, he could have done so less obviously before Pamela and Hetty came down to breakfast.

"Will you pass through the town, George?" Hetty asked.

"Don't mean to be disobliging, but if it's

fish or something else smelly, I won't bring it back for you."

Hetty looked horrified. "As if I would ask! Pam is the one whose mind is full of fish and other housewifely things. I have ordered some gloves and stockings from the draper. Now, do not frown at me," she added, smiling. "I know they will probably be ill-made, but I wished to seem to give my custom in the town. It is the best way to get on good terms with these people."

"Good thought," George approved. "Not but what the draper here has obtained excellent goods. M'aunt, the late Lady St. Just, bought everything from him. Never left Cornwall. M'uncle went to London. Took us all with him. M'aunt wouldn't go. Bring the things back. Gladly."

"George is most obliging and very much the gentleman," Hetty said when the door had closed behind him.

Pamela murmured an absentminded agreement. She was thinking that Hetty was really trying to adjust at last. Vaguely she heard Hetty continue to praise George, while her mind drifted to her own situation and whether it would be possible for her to stay at Tremaire. She loved the place and running the house, and Hetty was very pleasant now, and St. Just stayed out of her way. . . .

"Pam, you are woolgathering," Hetty said sharply. "I asked why you think George is not married."

"Most likely because he cannot afford it. He has no money at all. Perhaps if the late earl had lived, a suitable girl with money would have been found. In fact, it does not seem to be a marrying family. Even St. Just's eldest brother was not married, and one would have thought as the heir he would have married young."

Hetty giggled, but the sound had unpleasant undertones. "Oh, that was my papa's doing. There was something in our contract, and it cost a great deal of money. Vyvyan did not know about the agreement, and when he found out, he said he'd see the title go to George before it went to my child." Suddenly, irrelevantly, Hetty laughed aloud, a single, almost hysterical peal, but she controlled it at once. "He thought that would hurt me, but I did not care in the least. It . . . er" — Hetty tried to look roguish and only managed a rather obscene leer — "relieved me of a burden I was most unwilling to bear."

"Are you going to order the yellow chairs that George suggested?" Pamela asked stiffly.

"Have I said something improper, Pam?" Hetty purred. "I thought it would be safe to confide in you. You must have wondered why

Vyvyan and I had no children."

"It is best for a companion to know as little as possible about the relationship between the people she is employed by," Pamela replied coldly.

Hetty burst out laughing. "But you are my friend, Pam dear," she protested merrily. "Oh, very well, I never knew you were such a prude. You seem to be free enough in joking with the men."

Jesting was one thing, but revolting revelations about private life were another, and Hetty could never see it. Once more Pamela explained, but she despaired of teaching Hetty where the line between fun and vulgarity must be drawn. They went back to a discussion of the chairs, but Hetty seemed to find the subject less absorbing now that George was gone, and Pamela too found it difficult to concentrate. Hetty threw the swatches down.

"We both need diversion, Pam. Tremaire doesn't provide much, but I think I will take you visiting around the estate with me today. You must wonder what I do there."

Pamela accepted placidly. She had wondered how Hetty got on with the independent yeomen and their wives. The little outing was very revealing. Hetty played the lady bountiful with good grace, but the cottagers were apparently divided as to their reactions. Some accepted her advice and her little gifts placidly; among others there were uneasy glances, not of resentment, Pamela thought, but of suspicion. What was more surprising was the avid curiosity with which Pamela herself was examined by all. They see few strangers, Pamela decided, and dismissed the matter. All in all, Pamela enjoyed herself. If it would not have infringed further on Hetty's territory, she would have done some visiting herself. They were on their way home, both pleasantly refreshed, when Hetty pulled her mule up suddenly.

"Look, Pam, there's smoke coming from that chimney."

"Smoke comes from every cottage chimney all year round, Hetty. Why should you be surprised?"

"But that cottage was empty only yesterday. I am sure of it. I walked in the garden, and you can see its roof from there. Yesterday there was no smoke at all. It is the strangest thing. I asked about it, because it is odd to have a cottage so close to the house empty, but no one could — or would — tell me anything. One woman said it was old Maud's cottage. Only, when I asked who old Maud was, she gave me the strangest look and would say no more."

The name old Maud brought back, vivid and frightening, the scene in the still room. There was a tight feeling in Pamela's throat, but she managed to speak with a trace of boredom. "And quite right of her, I daresay. I cannot feel that I care much who she might be. It is nearly time for dinner, Hetty. We had better get back."

"Oh, no, we must stop in and see who is there. After all, we cannot have people moving into the cottages without permission."

She tethered the mule, and they walked toward the door. Hetty had no chance to knock on it or to walk straight in, however, because it opened when they were about five feet away. The entrance was blocked by a figure so obviously hostile that Hetty's assurance faltered a little.

"I am Lady St. Just," she said. "Who are you, and by what right do you occupy this cottage?"

"It's my cottage," the woman replied.

Pamela's heart sank. If this was the old Maud whom Sarah believed could help them, there was reason for St. Just's defeated attitude. The woman was totally unprepossessing. She was so gross that she literally blocked the doorway. Her eyes, nearly obscured by the fat that bloated her cheeks and pushed them upward, were muddy and expressionless. Her mouth was sunken and toothless, giving an impression of senility to the whole face. The remark she had made, in a dull, flat voice, could have been taken for insolence. Hetty took it so. Pamela could see the way she stiffened, but Pamela herself thought it might be stupidity.

"You are mistaken," Hetty said disdainfully. "The cottage belongs to my husband. Do you have his permission to be here? If you do not, he will evict you at once."

"Master Vyvyan? He'll have naught to say to me." The fat fingers seemed to make a sign, and then interlocked upon the woman's paunch. "He knows best when not to meddle, being born to it. Witch-born and witch-bred, he is, and knows enough to come to old Maud only when he's asked."

"Hetty, come away," Pamela said.

Her original opinion of the woman was undergoing a change. She liked her no better than at first sight, but something emanated from her that could be felt almost as a physical force. That Hetty felt it too, there could be little doubt. The countess was pale, and her breath was coming quickly. Nonetheless, she shook Pamela's hand off her arm.

"So you are a witch," she said with an effort at pleasantness, although her pale eyes were

157

bright with anger. "I would like to come in and see a witch's cottage. Perhaps I will buy a . . . a love philter from you."

Old Maud remained unmoving and immovable in the doorway. Some effort depressed the fat-swollen cheeks so that her eyes became larger. Pamela now saw that they were of that changeable shade of hazel that could, according to the light, become almost any color. At present they were green, possibly reflecting the woman's dress; not the clear green of St. Just's eyes, though, but a color that reminded Pamela of the slime she had seen floating on a stagnant pool.

"I have nothing to sell."

All pretense of civility left Hetty. "I said I wished to come in. Move aside. As a matter of fact, do not bother. I do not want you here at all. Get out."

"When I am ready, I will go. But you will go before then. I do not sell, but I give advice. Go away. You are meddling with what you do not understand. Evil sent against one who is protected returns threefold upon the sender."

"If you are not out of here in two hours," Hetty blazed, "I will set the men on the estate to drive you out by force."

The sausagelike fingers unlaced. One hand traced a complicated sign in the air. "This threshhold is forbidden you — you and your

158

creatures." And with a movement so swift that it was incredible in someone so fat, old Maud twisted inside the door and shut it in Hetty's face.

Hetty gasped with rage, her face purple. "I will get her out if I have to burn the cottage down," she spat. "I will give orders at once that she be driven out — naked."

"Don't Hetty."

"What!"

"Listen to me," Pamela pleaded. "I don't like her any more than you do, but from what I have heard, ordering the men to drive her away would be useless. They will not do so."

"Then I will see that not one of them remains on this land. I'll sell them."

"Hetty! These people are not slaves. They have leases on their land. They are protected by law."

"I need not renew leases, however. And they will soon know it."

Pamela said no more. If Hetty was so enraged that she forgot that only St. Just could make or break leases, it would certainly do no good to remind her of it. They mounted the pony cart and drove toward the house. When they had passed through the park gates, Pamela sighed. Hetty was still furious, but it was impossible to let the matter rest. To have the countess threaten what she could not perform would make her ridiculous, set the people against her, and deprive her of the only real pleasure she had here — that of playing the lady bountiful.

"Hetty," Pamela said softly, "should you not discuss this with St. Just before you do anything? It is barely possible that he has some use for this woman. Also, you know how defensive he is about his people. Most of the tenants have farmed the same land for generations. It might not be easy for him to break leases or refuse renewals, even if he wished to."

There was no reply until the countess halted her mule at the front steps and cast Pamela a venomous look. "Tell them to hold dinner back until I come." She barely waited for Pamela to step down before she slapped the reins on the mule's back to start it up again.

To remain looking after the pony cart would be unwise, Pamela decided, and she hurried into the house. In the hall, she almost ran into George, who had apparently just come in himself. His hat, gloves, and whip were on the table, and he was beating a rapid tattoo on it with the fingers of one hand. His expression was as bland and meaningless as ever, but the restless fingers indicated some tension of the nerves. Pamela's fears for St.

Just, which had been pushed into the background, returned in a flood.

"Have you seen St. Just?" she asked anxiously. "Has he come back yet?"

George turned his head and blinked as if he had just noticed her. "Didn't see him. Not back yet, either — at least, his horse isn't."

The remark had no special significance. George had just come from the stable and had given Pamela the best evidence he had that St. Just had not returned. Nonetheless, Pamela could not help being reminded of the last time St. Just's horse had come back without him. Could George have said it that way to prove he had forgotten the incident? What a farfetched idea, Pamela thought. Soon I'll be like that kitchen maid, moaning about a cursed household.

"Dinner will be a little late," Pamela said, striving for some semblance of normality.

George's protuberant eyes, which had drifted away to stare at nothing, returned to her. "Oh?"

"Hetty . . ." Pamela bit her lip. If she told anyone of Hetty's wild intentions, it must be St. Just. "She had an errand that she forgot. I must go and tell cook to hold back dinner."

An eyebrow lifted in response to the obvious lack of truth in Pamela's statement. Hetty never ran errands. But George remarked blandly, "Good. Give me time to dress without rushing."

Having given her message to the cook and summoned Sarah, Pamela dressed for dinner with one eye on the road and one ear cocked for footsteps in the corridor. She did not know whether she was more worried about Hetty or St. Just. Visions of Hetty in the middle of a riot of angry farmers made her wish she had followed her, whatever the result, and these alternated with visions of St. Just as the victim of another "accident." A man's booted feet in the corridor made her start nervously, but she did not want to rush out and then discover it was George. When the steps stopped at St. Just's door, Pamela flung herself out of her room. She wanted to explain about Hetty and Maud, but she wanted to catch St. Just in the corridor so that she would not have to enter his room.

Lord St. Just, however, was in no hurry. He had not gone to the entrance of his sitting room, as was his usual habit, but had paused outside the little-used door of his bedchamber to stare hungrily at Pamela's. As a result, her precipitous exit from her room flung Pamela right into his arms. St. Just maintained his balance with commendable agility and uttered no more than a faint "oof" under the impact.

"I am glad to see you safe and sound,"

Pamela said, withdrawing herself from his embrace with what dignity she could muster.

His arms had opened very reluctantly, and his eyes lit at Pamela's remark. She blushed, realizing how completely she had given herself away, and she prepared for a rapid retreat. St. Just made no attempt to take advantage of either the involuntary embrace or the inadvertent confession, however.

"Well, I was," he said in response, "before you hit me like a cannonball. Is there some reason you should think I was not?"

"No, only that you are so late."

"I met William Allenby. There *was* measles at the Austell house, and that was why George left. And why were you waiting my return so anxiously that you noticed I was late?"

There was the tiniest note of teasing malice in his voice, the faintest hint of a smile curving the corners of his well-shaped lips. St. Just did not expect Pamela to confess that she had worried because she loved him, but he wanted her to know that he was sure. Resentful, Pamela squashed his confidence with a statement that she was afraid that Hetty was in trouble. She then described their meeting with Maud, and Hetty's decision to have her evicted by the men of the estate. As St. Just's expression grew blacker and blacker, Pamela softened the tale as much as possible, but she was not sorry about telling it, because with each passing minute she grew more and more worried about Hetty.

"Please go after her, St. Just. If the men will not obey her orders, heaven alone knows what threats she will make. If she should strike one of the men . . . These people are not accustomed to being used in such a fashion. She might be hurt."

St. Just merely shook his head. His eyes were veiled, his expression withdrawn. "No one on this land would raise hand or voice to my wife."

"But they will be angry and be unpleasant when she visits them. She has so few pleasures here."

"I do not care what trouble Hetty mixes for herself," he said in a bitter voice. "The more miserable she is at Tremaire, the less likely she will be to return to it. After a taste of London, and you may rest assured I will do my best to have her accepted by society, I plan to make a permanent residence at Tremaire the condition of our continued union. Perhaps that will change her mind about divorce."

"So she may," Pamela retorted furiously, "but why you should continue to think the matter of any interest to me after what I have already said, I do not know."

"I am perfectly sure you love me as much as I love you." But he was not sure; his voice was uncertain, and his eyes held pain. "By hook or by crook, I shall have you, Pam, even if I must drag you to the altar by the hair."

"That does it! I cannot remain as Hetty's companion after this."

St. Just's lips curled back from his teeth in a feral snarl. "If you leave here — if you kill my hope — I'll kill Hetty!"

He would not kill her in cold blood; Pamela knew that, but as she stared at his distorted face, she feared he might well carry out his threat in some blind fit of rage. They backed away from each other as Hetty's voice came up the stairwell to them. St. Just muttered an oath and disappeared into his room, while Pamela leaned against the wall, trying to still her trembling. Steadying herself with an effort, she rounded the corner of the corridor as if she were coming out of her own bed-chamber to greet Hetty.

All of the countess's good humor seemed miraculously restored. She smiled at Pamela, apologized for her bad temper, and told her contritely that she had reconsidered. A little drive had cleared her head, she admitted. The beneficent mood held, to Pamela's amazement, even after Hetty had complained of Maud's insolence to St. Just and had been told it was merely the old woman's normal manner. Perhaps the way he explained was what had the good effect. He was subdued and genuinely apologetic. Hetty did not press the point; she laughed and said she had expected nothing more conciliatory from her husband.

The evening would have been perfectly pleasant, had not George, the mainstay of light conversation, seemed oppressed. He was obviously very much surprised both at the mention of Maud's name and at the attitude St. Just displayed. His expression grew blanker by the moment, but his eyes moved uneasily from Hetty to St. Just over and over. The more silent George grew, the merrier the earl became. He began to twit George on, of all things, his innocence. A flush of color lent a rich glow to his sun-browned skin, and his eyes sparkled dangerously.

"It is very warm for May," St. Just said with a laugh, as general conversation faltered, and he flung open one of the long double windows.

"Don't act the fool, Vyvyan," George snapped. "It's moon-dark," he said, and for the first time since she had known him, Pamela heard a nervous quiver in his voice. "If you must open the window, at least don't stand in it outlined against the light that way."

"Why?" St. Just asked tauntingly. "There is no one on this land who wants to harm me — is there, George?"

"Listen to the birds," Pamela interposed. "Whatever is wrong with them?"

There was always some sound of sea-bird cries at Tremaire, but it quieted toward evening as the marine hunters and scavengers, who depended upon their sight, came to rest. Tonight it seemed as if every gull and osprey in the heavens had gathered above the house to wail and shriek. Part of the answer Pamela guessed. The wind was almost still, and the surf was also gentler than usual, so that the bird cries were not masked by other sounds. But why were they flying and crying at all in the dark? she asked.

"Storm coming," St. Just said. "A bad one." His nostrils were flared and his head raised like a questing beast sniffing a scent.

"Witch blood," George murmured. "Always know, don't you, Vyvyan? When?"

"Not tonight."

"Are the witches singing a storm, Vyvyan?"

"I don't know." St. Just answered his wife with a strange glinting smile. "They are singing something tonight. I should imagine it is something big and bad."

He seemed amused rather than disturbed, however, and for some reason the attitude

167

annoyed Hetty. She lost a little of the sunny sparkle in her eyes and told him, rather crossly, to shut the window, because the candles were flickering. Although there was scarcely a breath of wind, St. Just did not argue. He did as he was told, then yawned hugely and said he would go to bed. The others soon followed.

Pamela rang for Sarah and then stood at her window puzzling over the unaccountable actions of the others in the house. Loving St. Just could not blind her to the contradictions in his behavior. In the light of that, Hetty's determined cheerfulness took on frightening undertones. And what was dreadful enough to discompose George?

"You rang, Miss Pam?"

"Is there going to be a storm, Sarah?" Pamela asked without turning.

"Yes, tomorrow night, or the day after. Looks too calm to storm, but it's coming."

"How do you know? Lord St. Just knew too."

Sarah laughed. "Making himself mysterious, is he? Don't let Master Vyvyan tease you. It's the birds. There's no witchcraft in knowing when this kind of sea storm is coming. The fish swim ahead of it, you see, and the schools are so thick that the birds can get them even in the dark. No matter where

168

they dive, they hit fish. The whole fishing fleet is out too. Everyone knows."

"George did not seem to know."

"Oh, Master George." Sarah dismissed him. "He doesn't want to know. You go to bed now, and don't worry your head."

This time Pamela did not find Sarah's practicality particularly soothing, but there was nothing she could do except go to bed. She slept at last, to dream of the screaming birds, a dream in which storm-driven fish played no part. And the screams mounted in meaning and intensity until she sat bolt upright, gasping with fear. Even then it was a few sleep-dazed minutes before she realized that the screams were real and human, not dream bird calls.

"Hetty!" Pamela cried, and leaped for the door.

CHAPTER 9

The shrieks rose in volume as Pamela burst into Hetty's room, still struggling into her dressing gown. She barely restrained herself from adding to the countess's cries when a darker shadow in the dark straightened abruptly from bending over the bed. In the faint glow of Hetty's dying fire — the countess kept her room stiflingly hot — Pamela could see the dull sheen of a long-barreled pistol trained upon her. Before she really had time to feel afraid, however, the weapon dropped.

"Pam?"

"St. Just! What is the matter?"

"I'm damned if I know. Can you quiet her, or shall I?"

"No, don't hit her."

They had both been nearly shouting themselves to hear each other over Hetty's hysterical screams. Now St. Just stepped back, and Pamela bent over Hetty, begging her to be calm and tell them what had happened.

"Good God, what now?" George's

170

resigned voice asked from the doorway.

He had recovered his aplomb and came in carrying a large branch of candles, which he lifted so that the room was partly illuminated. Under the influence either of the light or of George's calm presence, Hetty's shrieks began to diminish. She screamed again, however, as St. Just approached the bed, her eyes fixed on his pistol, but when Pamela waved him away, her renewed hysteria quieted quickly.

"There was a face, a face at the window," she sobbed, then began to whimper again as St. Just thrust back the curtains with the barrel of his pistol.

"Will you put that gun away, Vyvyan?" George said in a disgusted voice. "Hetty must have had a nightmare. Easy enough thing to do with the racket those birds are making. How could she see a face at the window when the curtains are drawn?"

"Cousin, there is no gainsaying your logic," St. Just replied dryly.

He thrust the pistol into the pocket of his dressing gown and moved toward the other window, stepping very softly. Less occupied now with Hetty, Pamela noticed how swiftly and silently the earl could move in spite of his bulk. Before George could make another remark, St. Just had opened his long arms

171

wide and then closed them in a snatch, sweeping the entire area behind the curtains and the curtains themselves into his grasp. George stared openmouthed. St. Just threw the curtains aside and revealed the wide-open window.

"Good God!" George repeated in a shocked tone. "Do you sleep with your windows open, Hetty?"

"No, no, of course not," she whimpered.

"But, Hetty," Pamela began, then bit her lip. She had realized it would be impossible for the countess to have seen a face at that window because of the angle, even if her bed curtains and the window curtains had been pulled back — which neither of them were. This, however, was no time to raise difficulties.

St. Just had latched the window and dropped the curtains back into place. He stood with his back to them, staring at his wife, his mobile face very still. "You saw this face at the window, Hetty, not in the room?"

"In my room?" Hetty quavered. "I don't know. I was asleep. I don't know what woke me. I saw a face and I screamed, and the face disappeared. The window was not open when I went to sleep. I know it was not."

"Who has been in the room besides yourself?"

"No one. My maid, but she could not have opened the window. She knows I am always cold. Anyhow, she did not go near it."

"Could you have felt too warm and opened it when you were half-asleep, so that you did not remember?"

"Don't be foolish, Pam," Hetty replied sharply. "I just told you I am always cold. I have not felt warm since I came to this country."

George brought the candles to the window and was examining the way they fit. After a while he reopened them and peered out at the frame. "Hang on to me, Vyvyan," he said, and leaned out until he was almost upside down, his cousin's powerful hands on his hips alone keeping him from falling. "Pull me back," he gasped, and the earl helped him upright again. His face was encarmined from his position, but his expression was blank. "No way for anyone to climb up now, Hetty. Window's locked securely, too. Let me ring for your maid? See if you can sleep?"

It seemed a reasonable suggestion, but Hetty resisted wildly. Nearly half an hour was spent in soothing and reassuring her before she would agree. Her maid was summoned at last, however, and her drops administered. St. Just took no part in this activity. He merely watched his wife with a calculating expression, as if he wished to guess how much distress she really felt. He preceded the others into the corridor when they finally left, but turned on George as soon as the door was safely shut.

"What did all that nonsense at the window mean, George?"

"No one came in that window, Vyvyan. No one opened it from the outside. *And* no one went out it, either. No ladder, no rope, no marks on the house, either."

"Yes, I assumed that from the beginning. There couldn't be much purpose to trying to enter or leave an occupied bedchamber when there are so many empty ones."

"Don't you *care*, Vyvyan?" George asked, seeming shaken again.

"Could we not discuss this in a better place?" Pamela asked softly. "Our voices will keep Hetty awake." St. Just seemed about to shrug the whole thing off, but then he led the way to his sitting room, opened the door for them, and lit all the candles. "I don't see what there is to discuss or care about. Hetty sleeps like the dead. She says not, but she does. Someone in the house entered her room and somehow startled her awake, then opened the window to make us think it was not a member of the household."

"Very nice," George said coldly, "except

174

who would do it, and why? Our people have been with us a long time, and the lower servants ain't allowed to roam. Trying to tell me Hayle or Helston is turning thief now?" The remark held an unspoken warning, which St. Just chose to ignore.

"Thieves? Nonsense!" He opened his mouth to say something more, and sneezed sharply instead. St. Just then looked down at his bare feet, picked up a branch of candles, and headed for the inner door that led to his bedchamber, obviously intending to put on slippers. There was no reason for him to close the door, and both George and Pamela watched him approach the bed, stop short.

"Good God! No!"

Pamela was the first to reach him. "St. Just, what is it?"

Wordless, he set the candles down and pointed at what looked like a scrap of yellowish paper covered with some sort of crude diagram lying on his pillow. Pamela moved forward and stretched out a hand. "Don't touch it," St. Just snapped. His voice was firm, but his face showed revulsion and an angry pain, as if he had been betrayed by someone he liked and trusted.

"What is it?" Pamela repeated.

"A Saturn pentacle designed to bring about the destruction of the recipient," George said dryly. "For God's sake, Vyvyan, how could you let things go so far?"

Fury mixed now with impotence in St. Just's face. "I thought I had stopped it," he said. He reached toward the crude drawing, but George caught his wrist.

"Leave it alone."

"Why? That I have seen it is enough — is it not?" The blazing green eyes narrowed, and Pamela felt relief at the display. Whether or not St. Just believed in witchcraft, there was no despair in his face now. "If this is a declaration of war, I will give them a fight they will not forget," he added grimly, confirming Pamela's opinion. "But you are quite right, George, about not touching that thing. Pam, ring for Sarah. One must fight with fire. We will have to spread the news that the spell has been countered, because everyone will know that it was laid on me." A smile without humor twisted St. Just's lips. "This is part of the operative principle," he said to Pamela. "Everyone looks at you with pity and fear until you begin to pity yourself and fear everything."

Pamela's well-trained face had been expressionless since George had explained the meaning of the scrap on St. Just's pillow, and now she curved her lips into a smile. "It must be very effective with the ignorant," she said, hoping her voice really held the slightly contemptuous note she had tried for.

Then she said she would fetch Sarah. It was ridiculous that her heart should be pounding so hard she could feel it in her throat. The thing was nothing but a dirty scrap of old paper with a few ill-drawn scrawls on it. This was the nineteenth century, not the Middle Ages. She could not fear witches; she simply could not. She rang and waited, her throat constricting as she wondered whether Sarah could have gone out again that night. The cries of the birds, still flying, came to her faintly, and she turned sharply toward the windows.

Had the curtains bellied? Pamela swallowed sickly and took a noiseless step backward. Then her generous mouth set hard. She was a big, strong woman, the equal of most men. The green draperies that curtained the windows were still now. Well-measured, their ends swept the floor, so that anything might be hidden behind them. Pamela advanced soundlessly on the nearest, arms spread wide, about to use St. Just's technique. If there was an intruder, she could grapple him and pull the curtains down on him.

"Hide-and-seek, Miss Pam?"

Sarah's harsh voice made Pamela whirl, her cheeks flaming. Too embarrassed to explain what she had been doing, she plunged into the story of what had been found in St. Just's room. Sarah's face set like stone.

"Go back and stay with him. I'll get Maud."

Half an hour later the gross creature waddled in. Her insolent, muddy eyes wandered over George without pausing. To St. Just she sketched a curtsy so slight as to make it mockery, and then her gaze fastened on Pamela.

"Give me your hand," she said.

Reluctantly Pamela rose from her chair. St. Just stood also. "No. She is not to be involved in this."

The old woman moved her head slowly. "Tha wert alwey one to set thysen ayen t'tide. For t'blud 'tween us, I ha come wha I list na be. Send she hen, tha, na and alwey. Tha canst na bi wi lif an na liv."

Pamela could not understand what had been said, but St. Just did. He made no move when Maud's eyes moved back to Pamela.

"Are you afraid?" the old woman asked in perfectly clear English.

"Yes," Pamela replied truthfully.

Maud smiled grimly. "You are wise. Will you give me your hand?"

"Yes."

"You have courage." Maud took Pamela's

proffered hand and held it for a moment. She nodded as if satisfied. "Good, then. Come." Hand-in-hand they walked toward the bed-chamber, leaving St. Just to stare after them, fists clenched and teeth set in his lower lip. "Keep handfast," Maud said quietly. "Take a taper and light the fire. When that flares, throw it" — she gestured at the pentacle — "into the fire. It must land in the flames; they must touch it at once, so be careful where you throw."

The whole thing was silly, Pamela told herself, utterly and completely ridiculous. Yet her hand clutched Maud's as if it were a life-line, and somehow the fat figure seemed solid and reassuring rather than flabby and repulsive. The ready-laid fire caught, and Pamela watched the flames crackle. More frightened than ever, and more irritated with her own irrationality, she moved toward the bed. When she seized the drawing, she gasped with surprise and nearly dropped it. The thing was not paper at all. Slightly damp, warm, and flexible, it was like . . . like fresh-flayed skin.

Maud's hand tightened on Pamela's until her nails bit into the flesh. She was muttering softly, but no language that Pamela could understand, nor were the words addressed to her. I am a fool, Pamela thought desperately, and she thought the words over and over as if they were a charm that could insulate her against her unreasoning fear. She held the pentacle fast now, but by a corner not covered by the drawing. Fool or not, Pamela could not bring herself to touch the diagram. The two women walked to the fire, and Pamela made a casting motion, but she did not let go. Tugging Maud's hand, she knelt on the hearth and put the pentacle directly into the heart of the flames. She drew breath sharply as the fire scorched her, but the drawing was exactly over the reddest embers when she released it.

Still it did not burst into flame. It browned and shriveled, and a revolting odor of burning flesh came from the fireplace. Maud watched, still muttering, and Pamela, feeling nauseated with revulsion, stared at the withering thing until, quite suddenly, it crumpled into black ash. For one instant before it disintegrated completely, the design returned to view, a startling white against the now-black background. Pamela drew in her breath sharply again at the manifestation, but Maud broke off her muttering and chuckled glutinously.

"I have won this round," she said, "and you have played your part well, my lady. When you want a favor — if this does not bring you your heart's desire — come to old Maud. Or if I do not last out your time" — she chuckled again — "and I may, I may, the coven will remember."

The crisis over, Pamela found her distaste for the old woman returning. She rubbed her scorched fingers with the hand she had freed from Maud's grip. "Whatever I did, I did for Lord St. Just."

The glutinous chuckle mocked her. "So you did, but not in the way you thought. Master Vyvyan has been protected against such spells from birth. The son of my own . . ." Maud stopped abruptly, and some emotion flickered behind the muddy eyes. "My own mistress," she continued with twisted lips, "would not be left naked to the shafts of envy which might be aimed against him."

"Would it not be helpful to him to know that?" Pamela asked coolly. "He was much shocked by seeing that . . . that thing in here."

The old woman was fumbling in a pouch suspended from the cord that served her as a belt. "He knows," she replied briefly, and extracted a dirty twist of leather. This she undid, and from it scooped a fingerful of brownish grease. Without warning, she seized Pamela's burned hand and smeared it with the unguent.

By the time Pamela's surprise at the swift action receded enough to make it possible to protest, the salve was already taking effect.

The smart of the burn was considerably reduced. She uttered a rather resentful, "Thank you." Maud did not answer, although she laughed unpleasantly again, and with another movement, incredibly quick for one so fat, disappeared out of the bedchamber into the corridor. Pamela stood staring stupidly at the closed door. Too many things had happened too suddenly. Her brain felt numbed by the quick successions of fear and relief. She did open the door but there was no sign of Maud in the corridor. Now, in the backwash of her emotions, she was desperately tired. If it had not been for the memory of St. Just's anxiety, she would have slipped through that back door herself and gone to bed. As it was, she closed it gently and returned to the sitting room.

"Maud?" St. Just asked.

"Gone." Pamela described the suddenness of the old woman's departure. St. Just's lips tightened, but he made no comment, and then Pamela noticed that George, too, was absent. A question elicited only a shrug at first. "Was he not interested?" Pamela asked then.

"He said it was silly to lose sleep over what he could not help. He left as soon as you and Maud went in."

"Your anxiety seems to be considerably

182

reduced also," Pamela commented caustically.

St. Just looked at her sharply, then dropped his eyes. "I don't know that I really was anxious. 'Shocked' expresses my feelings better. I thought I had settled it, and then this!" He rose from his chair and came toward her. "I am sorry, Pam. I am a fool to keep you talking. You are quite white with exhaustion. And I was worse than a fool in the corridor before dinner," he added in a soft, defeated voice. "I still beg you not to leave Hetty, but there is no reason why both of you should stay here. Go with her to Plymouth or Torquay."

It was possible that embarrassment at the memory of that scene made him keep his eyes fixed on the carpet, but Pamela had never noticed the smallest sign that emotional scenes embarrassed St. Just, either at the time or later. The fear that had left her after the pentacle was destroyed returned to tighten Pamela's throat. Hetty was in no danger; St. Just would scream at her, might even strike her when she tried him too high. He would do no more than that, ever. But he was in danger. And I love him, Pamela thought defiantly. I love him. I will not leave him until he is safe.

"I will suggest it to Hetty," she said, "but I do not think she will agree to go without you. She has the greatest aversion to being thought

183

unprotected. Will you come?"

"I cannot, until the business with the witches is settled," St. Just replied with a peculiar grimace.

"I am relieved to hear you say that. Truthfully, until I am sure that girl and her baby are safe, I have the greatest reluctance to leave here myself."

"They are safe," St. Just said impatiently. "She is being watched, and she has made no further attempt to leave the house. I know I should make you go, Pam, even if Hetty will not leave."

"But can you? You cannot dismiss me, you know, because Hetty could pay my salary from her pin money. Surely you would not be so crude and ungentlemanlike as to hint your wife's guest was unwelcome in your home. And if you were, you know I might well be unladylike enough to ignore the hint."

"It is not a laughing matter anymore, Pam."

She raised a hand as if to touch him, then let it drop. "Don't, my lord. I am frightened enough. Don't make me talk or think about this seriously tonight."

"If you are frightened, you must go, and at once. If you are afraid, you are vulnerable."

"Not for myself." Pamela flushed at the admission, more with irritation than with shame. If she had not been thick-headed with fatigue, she would have ended this conversation before she trapped herself. "Now, really," she added tartly, "in what way could I be involved or endangered? I am a stranger here."

"You pointed out yourself that you brought me the news of the pregnant maid. You are up to your neck in this. Curse me for a fool for letting Maud use you. It will be all over the village in the morning. This is the last straw. Pam, you must go."

Tired to death, knowing she was getting in deeper with every word, Pamela turned on St. Just, her eyes flashing and her firm jaw set. "You will have to drag me out of the house physically or lock the door in my face," she spat furiously. "I am not the type to run sly. There is something more at stake here than my absolute safety or yours. To sell love philters, to 'sing' good weather and good crops — I am perfectly willing to ignore such activity. I am willing to condone, even encourage, the herbalism. But the use of this power, if it is a power, against people must be stopped. St. Just, you cannot ask me to run away from a fight to oppose that, whatever the danger is."

"You are willing to ignore, to condone," St. Just murmured, his eyes lighting. "You are planning to stay with us, then, Pam?"

Cursing her unguarded tongue, Pamela shook her head. "Until this is over, no longer. It is useless to pretend that I have no feeling for you, St. Just. This makes my leaving Tremaire more imperative. I simply will not be involved in an illicit relationship with any man. Oh, it is not morality. I am not gothic, I am practical. Those things never work. The people end up hating each other. I could not bear to hate you, Vy. No," she added sharply, backing away, although he had not moved, "I will not talk to you any longer. I will not bid you a good night, either. It is too late for that."

CHAPTER 10

It seemed impossible to Pamela that anything more should happen. Her life had
always gone forward in a series of crescendos
and pianissimos, but previously she had
always had time to catch her breath between
periods of crisis. Even after her father's death
there had been several months of peace
before she realized the dreadful condition to
which she had been reduced.

Of course, she thought, as she struggled
upright in bed and tried to concentrate on
what Mrs. Helston was saying, her father's
death had been a numbing blow surmounting
a steadily rising anxiety about him. For a
moment the correlation of her fears for her
father and her fears for St. Just numbed her
faculties anew. Then she threw off the dream-
induced terrors and rubbed her eyes.

"Please wake up, Lady Pamela, please do.
Am I to tell his lordship?"

"I am awake now, Mrs. Helston. Tell Lord
St. Just what?"

"It was not my fault," the housekeeper said

defensively. Then her eyes slid away from Pamela's, and her voice grew sharper. "I daresay you will not believe me, but she was spirited away by witchcraft. Every door and window was locked and bolted last night — yes, and this morning too, because I went at once to check. And I had her sleeping in my own room. Yet this morning she was gone."

"Who?" Pamela asked, although she knew already.

Mrs. Helston's lips moved in reply, but at that moment there was a crash of thunder so loud and prolonged as to drown the words completely. Pamela did not repeat her question. She had asked it only to gain time to think, for her mind was full of the implications of the pregnant maid's disappearance. She did not believe the girl had been spirited away by witchcraft, in spite of Mrs. Helston's assertion. People always swore that a fly walking on the counterpane would wake them, when, in fact, a herd of horses trampling through the room would scarcely cause them to stir.

That all the doors and windows were firmly locked and bolted, she did believe. Therefore someone with access to the keys, an upper servant, was involved in the attempt to destroy St. Just. Or one of us, Pamela thought, and because she was clinging to words themselves, their clear logic being a bulwark against irrational fear, she added mentally: Well, it was not I. And it could not have been Hetty, because the dose of laudanum I saw her take with my own eyes would have subdued a horse. St. Just would not threaten himself; his distress over the pentacle could not have been feigned. And the servants were devoted to St. Just. That left . . . George.

"Lady Pamela, what am I to do?" Mrs. Helston was wringing her hands.

Pamela wrenched her mind from this freezing probability to the necessity for action. The longer they waited to set a search in motion, the less chance there would be of finding the maid. She was not due to deliver her child for a week or two more, but if she did, the two could be separated, and it was much easier to hide a baby than a woman. St. Just must be told at once. Even as Pamela made the decision, she recoiled from it. If he interfered in this, he would infuriate the coven even more. The wild notion of sacrificing the baby flashed through Pamela's mind, but she recoiled from that thought with even greater horror. Then she wondered if she could search for the maid herself. That idea too had to be dismissed. She did not know the people or the country.

"Very well," she said to the housekeeper. "I will attend to informing his lordship. You will not, of course, spread this story about the girl being taken by witchcraft," she added repressively. "I make no comment on the truth of it, but I am sure you would not wish to cast the lower servants into a panic. It will be safest to say that Lord St. Just removed her to a quiet place for her confinement, if a question is raised. If you can avoid mentioning her at all, I would do so."

"I will do my best, my lady," Mrs. Helston replied, but a shake of her head and her hopeless expression indicated how little belief she expected in the explanation Pamela proposed.

"Ring for Sarah, please, Mrs. Helston." Pamela's voice had been raised, for the thunder was growling and rolling almost constantly, but her last words seemed an unmannerly shout as a sudden, ominous silence fell. "I beg your pardon," she added in her normal voice, smiling. "I did not mean to shout at you." Pamela had been about to add a comment about the thunder, but the words never passed her lips. Mrs. Helston was staring toward the windows with abject terror on her face. Pamela's glance followed hers instantly, but there was nothing to see except the drawn curtain.

"No," the housekeeper breathed. "No, it is too soon."

"What is too soon? What is wrong?"

"The fleet is still out, and it is nigh on shore. The thunder cannot stop yet. The wind cannot come so soon. It is not a sea storm. It is not. The witches have sung this weather."

Pamela did not fully understand, but the housekeeper's fear communicated itself to her, and she found herself straining to hear the faint rumble that would presage another crash of thunder. Nothing. A silence as if the earth itself were holding its breath and listening. Pamela had just about recovered and was going to point out that there was no wind. Her intention was checked by the sight of Mrs. Helston, who stood before her with clasped hands, an image of entreaty. Tenseness returned, and with it, very faintly, came a whispering sigh, as if a great being had loosed his breath.

The housekeeper moaned and raised her hands to her ears to shut out the sound she knew was coming. Hypnotized by the waiting and listening, Pamela very nearly repeated the gesture. She shook herself free of the self-induced spell as the whisper changed to a moan. The sound was low and sustained, the groan of a giant unendurably hurt, in despair at the knowledge that worse was coming.

So strong was the impression, that Pamela rushed to draw her curtains. She almost expected to see the Cerne Abbas giant, club in hand, lying out upon the edge of the cliffs above the sea. There was nothing, of course, but the lowering gray sky, except that the water seemed to have drawn back farther than usual, exposing more of the sharp-fanged rock that made the Cornish coast so dangerous.

As she stared out, the moan rose in pitch to a wail and then to a shriek. Under the shriek of wind, which was blowing too steadily to rattle the windows, a low snarling arose, and suddenly the leaden sea leaped forward, smashing against the cliffs with a roar. The spume was flung so high that it formed a white curtain that temporarily hid the shoreline. Following the crash of the water came a prolonged boom. In the endless caves that honeycombed the cliffs, the air had been compressed and was voicing its protest. The shriek of wind cut off abruptly. Lungs emptied, the giant drew breath. The window frames creaked as the pressure of the wind relaxed, and the floor heaved under Pamela's feet as the water was flung outward by the imprisoned air. The very earth trembled in the violence.

"Good God," Pamela breathed, not without reverence, as the initial burst of violence settled into a more natural lashing of wind and wave and crashing of thunder.

The storm was a very bad one, but it was only that — a very bad storm, not a supernatural occurrence. The loud rattling of the windows drew Pamela to practical considerations. If the shutters were not closed at once, the windowpanes would shatter and the house would be flooded. The housekeeper was weeping and wringing her hands. Pamela subdued her irritation with an effort. She herself loved storms; they excited and thrilled her, but she knew that many people were terrified by thunder and lightning and roaring wind. It was necessary to soothe Mrs. Helston. To tell her sharply not to act like a child would merely shake her self-control further. Pamela moved toward the housekeeper and patted her shoulder consolingly.

"The noise is nothing but the sea and wind," she said softly. "You are quite safe in the house, you know. And the house is of stone, so that we are even safe from the lightning," she added. "Come, there will be less noise and less to upset you when we have the shutters closed. If the windows were to break, we would have a dreadful time cleaning up."

The woman lifted her face, exposing an

expression of agony and bitterness that shocked Pamela silent. "I have lived all my life in Cornwall. Do you think I fear a storm?" Mrs. Helston cried. "My son is with the fishing fleet. *You* are safe! You have no one out there to be drowned by the wind and torn to pieces by the rocks."

"Oh, I am sorry. I did not know. Sit down, Mrs. Helston, do. Surely, surely the men at sea heard the thunder before we in the house did. There must have been smaller rumblings, which we could not hear. They will have been warned. They know the coast. They will reef their sails. Surely they will be safe."

The housekeeper shook her head. The anger was gone from her face, and only the pain remained. "It is witch wind," she said dully. "All the sea storms are alike. First it is quiet, then the water grows restless but not angry. Then you see the lightning — far, far off to the west. Then the thunder softly, and that is the time to make for shore. There is time, for the thunder comes slowly, and it comes before the wind. This is witch weather — thunder and wind from the east, and without warning. Lady Pamela, why are the witches angry? Why did they steal a girl from this house?"

Pamela took the hand stretched out to her. "I do not know. I am sure no one in this house has deliberately offended them. Lord St. Just would not do that."

"Ah, well, it is not my place to question. We have always served St. Just, and we have been through hard times before. If my boy is spared, he will go no more to sea until whatever will happen has happened. I will see to the house now."

"Rest awhile," Pamela urged, for the woman's face was white. "You have had a dreadful shock. So violent a storm must soon be over, however. I will go down and speak to Hayle about closing the house."

"No, I had rather do it myself, my lady," Mrs. Helston said. "You are a stranger in a strange place, and you do not know our storms. This weather can rage for days. You mean kindly, though, and do not scoff — which is more than others do. It is better for me to work than to sit idle."

That was true, and Pamela made no further attempt to detain the housekeeper. She rang for Sarah herself, remembering that the onset of the storm had prevented Mrs. Helston from doing so. The maid was so long in coming that Pamela wondered if she were involved in singing the wind, in spite of denials. Sarah came at last, unhurried, and with the appearance of all her usual self-possession.

"You are up very early, Miss Pam," she remarked. "I thought you would sleep later, after the broken night you had."

The remark gave Pamela the opening she wanted, and she told Sarah about the abducted maid. "Maud would know where the witches would hide a person, would she not?" Pamela asked eagerly. It had occurred to her as soon as Sarah entered the room that if Maud could get the girl back or tell her where to look, St. Just need not be involved at all.

Sarah was behind her, lacing her stays, and Pamela could not see her face. Her voice was flat, without hint of surprise or even interest. "Perhaps, but I doubt she'd tell you such things. She'll be no help now, anyway. She's gone."

"Gone? Where? Why?" Pamela tried to turn and face Sarah, but the maid *tched* angrily.

"Stand still. How will I ever lace you if you jostle about? Maud's gone, because that business last night was a bad thing. While she was in here, the coven got out of hand. Ned Potten's wife sang that storm, with some young fools to help her, and many a good man will die if Maud cannot sing it quiet again."

The breakers were still crashing, the caves

booming, the wind howling, but Pamela had regained her balance. Spells could not affect the weather. Even if what Mrs. Helston said were true and this storm was not usual, there were freak storms all over England and the freaks had nothing to do with witchcraft. Her laces tied, Pamela turned and examined Sarah's face. It was useless, she perceived, to argue the point. Sarah believed that a witch had sung this weather and that a stronger singing would change it.

"Could you find out where they have taken her, then?" Pamela asked.

"I've always kept clear of the People, Miss Pam — as much as I could. I know their ways, though. I would not show you their places, even those few I know. It would not be safe."

"Sarah, a child's life is at stake."

"There won't be a child for some weeks yet. You stop fretting yourself."

"But every hour we delay in searching for the girl, they have an hour more to hide her."

Sarah frowned as one does at a fractious child. "Now, Miss Pam, she cannot be taken far away, and she must be fed and cared for. The longer she is hidden, the easier it will be to trace the trail that leads to her. It would be best if you would let this matter lie."

Again the suspicion that Sarah would rather sacrifice the child than fight the coven made Pamela stubborn. "I cannot," she said. "You know I cannot. Mrs. Helston has reported the maid's absence to me. If I cannot go and seek her myself, then I must tell St. Just. Do you want him interfering?"

The threat did not have the effect Pamela expected. She had been sure that Sarah would do anything to protect her nursling. To her surprise, the maid merely looked thoughtful and nodded her head.

"He must know, of course. If he does not hear it from you, someone else will tell him. Servants' hall is already connecting her with this storm."

"Oh, lord, I thought we had managed to keep it quiet."

Sarah looked pityingly at Pamela. "Potten never tried to hide the connection. Potten's wife is known. And then, the maid — a simple chambermaid — is removed to Mrs. Helston's own room. Not that it mattered. There's little enough not known in servants' hall."

The color rose in Pamela's face. So that was why she was always treated with such deference, was so easily accepted in a tight-knit, parochial household. There was no help for it, and no sense in trying to contradict the story.

Soon enough she would be gone, and the truth would be known.

In any case, what Sarah said was true. She could not have kept the tale of the maid's absence from St. Just. The noise of the storm had diminished a good deal, Pamela suddenly noticed with a sense of satisfaction. She had told Mrs. Helston that such violence could not long endure. Then, in spite of her worry over St. Just, she had to smile. The change would undoubtedly be put down to Maud's superior witchcraft instead of to natural causes. So much the better. Maud, no matter how unpleasant, was attached in some way to St. Just. If she was believed the stronger witch, the others would hesitate to attack someone under her protection.

The remainder of Pamela's clothes went on quickly, and she dismissed Sarah and hurried down to the breakfast room. Her expectation of finding St. Just there alone was not disappointed. He looked tired, as if he had not snatched even the few hours of sleep Pamela had. Outrage at the tale of the maid's abduction soon lent color to his cheeks and sparkle to his eyes, however.

"They dare come into my house! This is really beyond the line. I have always been rather favorable to the coven, but this is too much to be borne. I see that my father's too-gentle sufferance was a mistake. Power has gone to their heads, and they think to gallop curbless on their own path."

"St. Just, do not let your temper drive you into foolish actions. You will not begin a six-teenth-century witch hunt in this modern day. You will be a laughingstock."

"Last night you were the one who was anxious to fight these unpleasant practices. What makes you back down now?"

"I am not backing down," Pamela replied rather crossly, because the allegation was half-true. She was afraid for St. Just to tangle with the coven. "The maid must be found and her child saved, of course, but there is no need to persecute the witches as a whole."

"I have no intention of persecuting anyone," he replied coldly, and rose to his feet.

"Where are you going?"

"To change my clothes. Do you expect me to ride out in pantaloons and hessians in this weather?"

The sooner the task was undertaken, the sooner it would be done, but Sarah's hint that delay would not be detrimental had made Pamela hope that St. Just would not go out in the storm. It really seemed to be tempting fate. Her eyes went to the window, but the wind was no more than normal now, and the rain seemed very light.

"Where will you look?"

It was a foolish question, spoken to gain a few minutes, and it received the answer it deserved in an impatient shrug. He was gone. Pamela lingered at the breakfast table toying with the food and thinking of the day ahead of her. The servants would be in a state and would make the smallest accident into a crisis. Hetty would no doubt whine or wish to discuss endlessly the fright she had had. George would be his usual self, but Pamela could no longer take comfort in George's easy manners.

Pamela was frightened. Not of anything she could see or hear, not even of the witchcraft, which, in the light of day, had gone back into perspective. She was certain St. Just had done nothing to incense the coven; therefore, someone had convinced them to act against him. Only Hetty and George had any motive for doing that, and Hetty had neither contact nor influence with the witches. Fear makes some run and some hide; it lashed Pamela into a desire for action.

She returned quickly to her bedchamber and changed into her riding dress, then went again to the breakfast room and sat down to wait for George with what patience she could muster. If George was involved, he would want to know what St. Just intended to do. Pamela was even prepared to prod him into action. She was prepared to do anything, except sit still and wait.

CHAPTER 11

When George strolled into the breakfast parlor, Pamela's heart sank. She had not realized before how fond she had become of him. Now, looking at his face, where sleeplessness and strain marked his fair complexion and marred the cultivated vacuity of the expression — a combination that surely should have proved him guilty to her suspicious mind — she found she could not believe it of him.

"Up early, ain't you?" The voice was flat. George's attempt at his usual lightness was a failure.

"Oh, we have had another upset. I begin to think that Cornwall is as queer as you said it was."

George helped himself to sausages, fried fish, a slice of beef, and some frittered eggs. "Has queer effects on some people, too. Mistake to make people come to Cornwall. Some fall in love with it. Some . . . don't."

A clear warning that she did not belong here? Pamela lifted her head defiantly. "I have fallen in love with it. For all the queer happenings, I deeply regret that I will not be able to live here always."

"Don't know that you won't." George flicked a glance at her and dropped his eyes to his food again. "One way or another, you're the kind that does get her own way, Lady Pam." He began to consume his breakfast in a leisurely manner. "Never told me what happened that's made you think us queer," he said after a pause.

So he did wish to know. Pamela's heart was like a lump of lead in her breast, and its throbbing sent painful cramps up her throat. "One of the maids has been kidnapped. The girl was about to bear a love child, and Mrs. Helston was keeping a close watch on her."

How she got the last words out and what her voice sounded like, Pamela did not know. What little color the fatigue had left in George's face drained out of it, and his blank stare slid past Pamela's. Something had dawned behind those fishy eyes, but its passage was too swift for Pamela to identify the emotion.

"Seems rather like locking the door after the silver's been stolen to keep a watch on the girl now. Damage done. Pregnant already," George stated languidly.

Laughter rose to mingle with the tears in Pamela's throat, and for a moment she thought she would choke. It was horrible that George should continue to make disastrously funny statements of the obvious under the present circumstances. She could not command her voice to reply, and George sighed.

"Suppose Vyvyan's rushing about trying to retrieve the poor girl. So energetic. Don't it occur to you, m'dear, that the best reason for her to go was that she wanted to?"

"She may have gone willingly, but someone else had to suggest it to her." Numb with pain, Pamela no longer found difficulty in speaking. "She is simpleminded."

George scooped up the last of his frittered egg, but it seemed to Pamela that he was having difficulty swallowing it. "So's Vyvyan, so far as I can tell," George commented with disgust. "Why don't he leave things alone? Cursed restless nature he's got."

"He does not interfere for the sake of being a busybody," Pamela retorted heatedly. "Mrs. Helston is sure that the witches have taken the girl because they mean to make use of her love child on Midsummer Eve. Do you suggest he leave that matter alone?"

A convulsive movement spilled coffee from George's cup onto the spotless cloth. "Didn't know. Wish you hadn't told me." He met her eyes squarely, and he breathed sickly. "Oh, God!"

Anguish mingled oddly with relief. George was condemning himself with each utterance, but somehow it made a difference that, however evil his purposes, he was not depraved enough to sacrifice a helpless unborn child. Puzzlement added to the already chaotic mixture of emotions in Pamela, when George's expression changed suddenly to one of frowning disapproval.

"No, really," he said, "you cannot be planning to ride out in this weather."

"I cannot sit still in the face of this abomination," Pamela replied. "Besides, the storm is almost over. You can see that the wind has abated and the rain is almost gone. I daresay it will clear completely soon."

"No. No, it won't. Don't know Cornwall as I do. Only a lull. Be worse than ever in a little while. Good God, has that fool Vyvyan rode out?"

Pamela's breath checked, but it was useless to lie. George had only to go to the stables or ask the servants to find out. "He has indeed," she said as steadily as she could, "and since he knows the weather well, I presume he too expects it to clear."

An expression of revulsion, as at something indelicate, spread over George's features.

"No, he didn't," he contradicted flatly. "He won't care about getting wet, either. Ruin his clothes, mess his hair. No sense, that's what Vyvyan's got."

That George was truly disgusted at the notion of presenting a disheveled appearance, Pamela did not doubt. She saw, however, that George was laboring under some over strong emotion. His vague, staring eyes focused on her clearly then, and his jaw set in a remarkably firm and determined manner.

"You are not to ride out, Lady Pamela," he continued, the lack of his usual affectations of speech lending authority to his words. "Truly, it would be very dangerous for you to do so. For Vyvyan it is merely foolish. He knows the country and will know where and when to seek shelter. I assure you he will be quite safe, if he does not take cold from the wet. If you went out, however, it is ten to one you would be blown off a cliff or into a gully."

"But surely I should have time to find shelter too."

"You might, and you might not. Do you not remember how suddenly the storm broke? The process may repeat itself — several times, I should think, from the look of the sky — before it blows over."

"Very well," Pamela agreed reluctantly. "I shall not ride out now."

"Better go up to Hetty," George advised, his voice returning to normal. "Need you after what happened last night."

"I suppose I should."

Pamela rose, wondering if her docility was too great and would make George suspicious. She felt, however, that he was immersed in his own thoughts and would not concern himself much with the finer shades of behavior that might be uncharacteristic. It was probable also he would accept the fact that a woman would be obedient to a specific order, and also that she would not wish to be drenched in a downpour.

In fact, Pamela had no intention of riding out then, or of riding out at all, unless George did. If he were involved in the kidnapping of the maid, or if he intended harm to St. Just, he would have to go. She went upstairs, thanking God that the floors were uncarpeted. George could not doubt that she had followed his instructions that far. Making no effort to conceal her movements, she opened the door to Hetty's suite softly. As she expected, the countess's bedchamber was dark, her bed curtains still closed. A small sigh of relief passed Pamela's lips. She would have freed herself from Hetty somehow, but it was much better that her drugged sleep still held her. Still openly, Pamela returned to her own room and closed the door firmly but without a slam. Then she turned the handle with great care so that it would not click, and permitted the door to open a bare crack.

There was not long to wait this time. George's hessians could be heard clearly coming up, walking down the hall to his own bedchamber. Probably, if the door had been closed — the doors at Tremaire fitted well — and she had been seated beside the fire, she would not have heard him. Either he counted on that or on the fact that she would assume he wanted something from his room. After an interval of a few minutes, in which George had had a chance to begin changing his clothes, Pamela slipped down the stairs as silently as possible. She made her way to the billiards room, the windows of which commanded the paths to the stables from any part of the house. Here she waited, so eager for action she was able to forget that it was George she was spying upon and that the success of her venture would result — at the least — in a life of poverty and degradation for him.

A stab of regret made her hesitate when, clothed in rougher garments than she had ever seen, George strode toward the stables. The regrets could not hold her. Although St. Just might suspect George, he was too fond of him to take any action on a mere suspicion.

Pamela knew she could not leave Tremaire until the man who wanted St. Just's name, and perhaps St. Just's wife, could do no further harm.

Having permitted enough time for George's horse to be saddled, Pamela made her own way to the stable. A cautious survey showed George's handsome bay hack well along the path to the cliffs, and Pamela called to the grooms to saddle Blue Lady. Velvet was too skittish to be taken out when there was the possibility of thunder.

This concession to safety, however, was not enough to pacify the head groom, who argued against riding out at all and reproved her ladyship's foolhardiness for quite ten minutes. Pamela half-convinced him by saying, most untruthfully, that her errand was short, and insisting, somewhat more untruthfully, that it was necessary. A sharp order eliminated the remaining resistance. She was furious at the delay, but she could not blame the man, whose interest seemed almost paternal toward a lady who understood horses so well. The little time could not matter, Pamela told herself, as she rode off hastily in the direction George had taken. The country was so open on the sea side of the house that it would be virtually impossible to find concealment.

That would work both ways, she realized

suddenly, heartily annoyed with herself. If George could not hide from her, he would also see her. Her nicely thought-out plan was worthless; in fact, her common sense had been betrayed by her desperate need for action. Nonetheless, she rode on doggedly, still driven by that need and by the thought that seeing where George rode before he noticed her might give a hint of where the maid was hidden. Her presence would also serve as a safeguard for St. Just; once George saw her, he would probably turn back and find some innocent excuse for his excursion.

The trouble was, Pamela had to admit after keeping Blue Lady at a spanking pace for a time, that George *had* disappeared. Vision was somewhat obscured by the rain, which seemed a trifle heavier now, but it was clear that George was nowhere on the cliffs. Either he had changed his direction and gone inland — which meant that he expected or feared being followed — or he had gone down into the town. Pamela turned Blue Lady abruptly, thoroughly disgusted with herself. She was a fool not to have thought of the town directly. What better place to conceal a person than a well-populated area?

In her hurry and irritation, Pamela almost rode down a little knot of women apparently coming from the cliff edge. She reined Blue

Lady back on her haunches, and seeing that several of them were supporting and concealing someone in the center of the group, she dismounted hurriedly. With the reins looped over her arm, her eyes flashing dangerously, and her riding crop held threateningly, Pamela advanced. The women, she could see now, were all old, bedraggled by the rain, and appeared unutterably weary. Nonetheless, they closed grimly around the person they were shielding, and their eyes, glazed, red-rimmed, and rheumy though they were, glared defiantly. One lifted a hand.

"Let her be," an exhausted voice croaked.

"Maud!" Pamela exclaimed.

"What do you here?" the old woman grated irritably. "Get you home before you make more evil than the good you have done."

"I am looking for a maidservant who has been abducted from Tremaire. Have you seen her or heard of her?"

"Fool," Maud muttered under her breath. "Does no one outside the coven see with the eyes or hear with the ears God-given?" She swayed on her feet, her fat face gray and sagging. "Seek if you will," she said in a louder voice, "but after the storm. I have held it back these few hours so that the men could come safe to harbor, but others are singing it awake again. Death wind and death weather it was meant to be. If it fails of its purpose, I have won another point. If it succeeds, you will have given a great weapon of fear into the hands of your enemy. Go home."

As always in Maud's presence, Pamela's certainty about the basic impossibility of witchcraft faltered. She came closer to Maud, and the other women, as if they knew without words Maud's willingness, fell back. "St. Just is out, and George Tremaire also," she said in a low voice.

Maud's dull eyes stared, then dropped. "Do not trouble yourself for Master Vyvyan. He is only a man, but the right blood flows in his veins. George Tremaire" — she shrugged — "knows the country. He must chance what chances. But you are the one who touched the Saturn pentacle, and all know that. It was not meant for you, but such things are not certain in their workings, and if it takes you, you have given a strength where you meant to make a weakness. Go home. Quickly."

Pamela opened her mouth to protest, but Maud turned away.

"Then do as you will," the old woman spat over her shoulder. "And consider what you have done to Master Vyvyan as you die."

The women closed around Maud, and the group moved slowly forward. More shaken than she would admit, Pamela began to look for a rock or a stump from which she could mount. Behind her she heard a ragged sing-song muttering begin. There was no raised object immediately available, and Pamela began to plod over the soaked ground toward the cliffs, where she might hope to find a mounting block among the tumbled rocks. At first there was nothing useful, but in the distance, rough-shaped shadows could be seen through the now-driving rain. Pamela moved in that direction, noticing nervously that the sky was darkening very rapidly and the wind rising. Fear made her regret what breakfast she had eaten, and she stopped to draw deep, steadying breaths. As the rain-wet, sea-tanged air filled her lungs, she remembered George's remark that these storms customarily had periods of remission and renewed violence. If George knew it, the witches certainly must, and they would use the knowledge to enhance their appearance of power. Pamela began to hurry. Even if the part of the coven opposed to Maud could not sing a storm, they could certainly gain importance by claiming credit for its results.

Suddenly Pamela stopped dead. There was singing, or chanting, from behind those tumbled rocks. Her breath caught on a sob. She had been convinced of the hopelessness of her self-imposed task and of the wisdom of returning to Tremaire. If only the damned women had gone a hundred yards northward to sing their stupid spells, she would never have known about it. Now that she did know, she had to investigate, of course. Once again taking a sound grip on her riding crop, Pamela advanced cautiously to a straggling bush, to which she fastened Blue Lady. She had to make sure that these women did not have the abducted maid with them.

Pamela cast a backward glance at Blue Lady. She hoped she would not pull loose from the bush if startled by a peal of thunder, but it was better to take that chance than expect the witches would not hear the noise the horse would make. The animal seemed to be standing placidly, and Pamela did not plan to be gone more than a few minutes. She wished only to peep over the rocks and be sure of what the witches were doing. Stealthily now she ran to the protection of a large boulder and peered around it. She damned the rain, which was falling more and more heavily, because it prevented her from seeing the faces clearly. She was sure, however, that these women were younger than the group with Maud.

Slipping softly closer between the rocks, Pamela at last made out the faces of all but two. Of the two who squatted with their backs to her, the hair color of one was wrong, and the other, whose body she could see in half-profile, was not pregnant. The maid was not there. Pamela sighed softly with relief. To her chagrin she found that she had not wanted to find the maid. She would not have known what to do. She was afraid again.

More hurried and less cautious now, Pamela ran back toward her original shelter. She was aware that a few pebbles had rolled under her feet, but she hoped that the rising wind and the singing would cover the sound. And then, the voices stopped. For a moment Pamela hesitated, undecided as to whether to hide or make a dash for her horse. Neither alternative had much value. The witches could find her among the rocks in a few minutes, as soon as they saw Blue Lady. On the other hand, since she could not mount unassisted, the horse would be little protection.

The choice, she realized immediately, had never been hers. During her brief hesitation, a shower of rocks flew over her head to strike Blue Lady with a remarkable aim. Terrified by a shock she had never endured previously, the mare tore free of the bush and bolted.

"Stop that!" Pamela cried, pale with rage.

She leaped toward the horse, but Blue Lady was far beyond her reach, and she turned, riding crop raised threateningly, to face the half-circle of women who advanced toward her. There were eight of them, three on each side of a middle-aged harridan whom Pamela found even more repulsive than Maud. Her body was not so gross, but she was dirty and slatternly, and her expression could have curdled milk. Behind the evil-faced central figure was a younger woman, who seemed to be trying to stop the advance. Two more stones flew, striking the ground just at Pamela's feet with thuds sharp enough to warn of the force behind them. Instinctively Pamela stepped back. More stones. Pamela backed a few more steps.

She moved without thought, too outraged at the idea that these women would dare attack her to consider their purpose or evolve any plan of her own. Quite five minutes of stone throwing and backing passed before Pamela's surprise melted enough to permit reason to take the place of shock and rage. Since none of the rocks had hit her and she was closer than Blue Lady had been, it was plain that the women did not wish to hurt her.

"Stop that," Pamela repeated firmly. "If you continue to behave this way, I shall report you to the authorities. I understand that you wish me to go away, and I am willing to do so. I have no interest in your . . . your weather-making activities."

The youngest woman leaned forward and spoke urgently to the witch in the center of the group. Something about her was familiar to Pamela, but her streaming hair half-hid her face. The sense of recognition was wiped away almost immediately, because the next rock thrown hit Pamela's thigh painfully. She gasped and backed again, and another stone fell harmlessly at her feet. As long as she retreated, they would not hit her, yet they would not let her go away on her own. What did they want? To demonstrate their power? To make her run? Pamela knew she would have to do something to extricate herself from the situation, and, her mind busy with plans, she sidestepped to the right.

The move had not been deliberate; it was in response to something Pamela knew only subconsciously, but the reaction was immediate. Two rocks hit her right arm; another struck her right hip. Pamela cried out sharply, with pain and with sudden, terrifying knowledge. She realized why she had moved to the right. The roar of the surf, even louder in her ears, had told her she could back no farther. Behind her was a drop of a hundred feet or more. The witches intended to drive her over the cliff!

Not far away, St. Just reined his horse to an abrupt halt and lifted his head to listen. Was

218

that a cry? The sound was not repeated, and he looked out toward the sea, gauging accurately how long before the second wave of the storm broke. He wiped the wet from his face rather ineffectually and turned his head toward the clutter of rocks south of him. They should be there. He hesitated, wondering if he should take the time to make sure the witches were out on the cliff. If they were not, he might run into trouble. Then he nodded at the memory of the half-heard cry. They were there, all right.

Near him was an irregular break in the ground, centuries old, which contained a scrubby tree. There his horse would be both sheltered and moderately well hidden. He jumped off, tethered the horse, and moved forward a few feet more to where a rough crevice split the cliff until it appeared to end in a drop into the sea. St. Just leaped into it and started down along it, stepping carefully on rough patches of weed or bare mud. He was not overly concerned to be quiet. The rising wind would cover his footsteps if he did not send a rock crashing downward.

The path seemed to end abruptly, but about eighteen inches below, a ledge protruded from the cliff. St. Just stepped down, turned at right angles to the sea, and stepped down again. Two more similar moves took him to another path, this one completely hidden from above. The wind was stronger now, but no particular danger to him, since it pressed him inward, against the cliff to his left. The sudden lulls held more threat, the unexpected relaxation of pressure having the effect of sucking him outward. St. Just, however, was accustomed to the vagaries of wind along the Cornish coast and continued along the path with surefooted caution.

Quite suddenly a cave yawned. It was low, forcing the earl to stoop, but it continued a considerable way into the cliff. In some distant geological period, a whole stratum of rock had been washed away by the sea. Whether the sea had sunk since then or the cliffs been thrust upward was a problem that had puzzled St. Just as a boy. Now, however, he was concerned with human rather than geological vagaries. He paused, listening. Then he sighed with mild disappointment. The maid was not here. He had hoped she might be, because this was one of the more secret places of the witches, one he was not supposed to know. To be sure, St. Just made a thorough survey, although he did not go back far into the cave. The passages were endless, leading one into another. If one lost sight of the light at the cave mouth, one could wander in those passages until hunger and thirst brought the release of death.

The storm was now whipping itself into a new fury, and St. Just hurried toward the outer ledge. There he paused, wondering whether he should return and shelter in the cave or make a dash for the nearest cottage. It would be unpleasantly cold and damp in the cave, he decided. He turned half-right toward the path, tensed, and leaped suddenly sideways in the other direction.

A rock, flung from above, struck him a numbing blow on his left shoulder. With the agility of a trained athlete, St. Just flung himself backward; with the intensity of a hunted animal, he lay perfectly still. A moment later another stone, much smaller, struck the ledge several feet to the right.

Very slowly St. Just rose to a crouching position, facing the path. Above him on the cliff a man turned toward the crevice that led to the cave. He took two steps toward it, then looked over his shoulder. A gasp of fear was wrenched from him, then a low curse, and he set off running as fast as he could inland.

Meanwhile, St. Just had risen to his feet, his face puzzled rather than anxious or angry. He turned his head slowly from the position where he had originally stood to where he had been when the first rock hit him. Then he looked across to where the second rock had struck. Chagrin replaced puzzlement on his face, and he moved hurriedly up the path, jumping the steps. His head cleared the edge of the crevice in time for him to see a flicker of a dark coat as a man dodged behind an outcrop of rock. He opened his mouth to call, then shut it. A fat riding cob lumbered out on the other side of the rocks but was lost to view almost immediately. Simultaneously, St. Just was aware of women's voices raised in an altercation. He sprinted for his horse, leaped into the saddle, and spurred him rapidly in the direction the cob had taken.

After the single cry of pain and fear, Pamela became mute. Now that she knew what the witches intended, she could feel an impact more painful than the bruises the stones had left. The pressure of combined wills, driving her to her death, raised a panic that nearly achieved its purpose. Pamela whimpered softly, flooded with the desire to turn and leap onto the fanged rocks below rather than face the inexorable force driving her back step by step. That single, pitiful breath of sound saved her. Shame and fury that she, Pamela Hervey, a noblewoman in her own right, had been brought to whimper before a bunch of ragged, dirty peasant women, totally blocked her terror. She gasped for breath and ran forward toward the encircling women, her whip raised to strike. The rain-soaked, voluminous riding skirt tangled her legs, and with a cry of despair, Pamela fell forward into the arms of her enemies.

CHAPTER 12

Pamela felt her hat torn off, felt hands tangle in her hair, grasp at her clothes. But now, although there were eight against her, she was not nearly so frightened. Fury at the indignities visited upon her person at first wiped out every other emotion. Then, as a shriek of pain was drawn from one woman in response to a vicious kick that Pamela launched, she was stimulated to fight in earnest.

She rolled over, lashed out with both feet and whip so violently that the women were surprised into drawing back a trifle, and leaped to her feet. The quick success surprised her somewhat, but she realized that these witches were, first of all, unused to opposition, and second, afraid of personal combat. They would never have touched her had she not fallen right into the group. It was also clear now that they were not really united in the way the women with Maud had been. The youngest witch, whom Pamela recognized with sick shock now as Hetty's maid, in spite of her disheveled appearance, was crying, "No! No!" and trying to draw one after another away. On the faces of others there was fear and uncertainty.

Nonetheless, Pamela knew her danger had grown even more acute. Having attacked one of the gentry, who had powers beyond the ordinary folk, the witches had laid themselves open to reprisals. It would be more important than ever to silence her permanently. The vile-looking leader stooped for a stone. Pamela reacted instantly by charging with raised whip. Startled, the woman dropped the rock and backed away.

"Mrs. Potten," Pamela cried, "you will hang as your grandmother did if you harm me. You fools," she spat at the others, "will you let her make you guilty with her in a quarrel that is not yours?"

There was a momentary hesitation. The witches' faith in their leader had been even further shaken by her retreat from Pamela, but Potten's wife was no fool.

"You *are* fools." It was an oily whisper, but somehow it carried clearly over the wail of the wind. "We have gone too far to go back. Who's to know we hurt her? Stone her and drop her over. What the rocks do to her will hide our work. And for a stranger to fall from the cliffs in a Cornish storm will surprise no one. The pentacle delivered her into our hands. If we do not use that power, it will turn against us."

Every superstition and buried resentment the women had was touched. Pamela's cause was lost, and she knew it. Though some were sickened, fear and determination hardened in the faces around her. She glanced around, seeking a sign of weakness, but Hetty's maid was gone. Perhaps she had gone for help, but Pamela doubted it, and besides, help could not come in time. Several of the witches now stooped to find stones. Pamela ran at them, struck right and left with her riding crop. Those whimpered and retreated, but still a thrown rock hit her shoulder, drawing a gasp of pain from her. Pamela knew she could delay the inevitable but not escape it. Sooner or later a stone would hit her head and render her unconscious, or she would faint from pain and exhaustion.

The knowledge gave her no desire to yield, nor was she afraid any longer. The single emotion that she felt was regret that she could not take these tormenting fiends with her. Eyes burning, she rushed and struck, rushed and struck, using the full strength of her powerful body. One blow laid the witch Potten's cheek open; another left a moaning fury with a disabled arm. They were drawing farther away, out of range of her short leaps, and she could not really run because of her hampering garments. Again they were ranged in front of her and her back was to the cliffs. Pamela dared one swift glance behind to be sure that a step or two backward would not send her over the edge, realized how painfully little she had gained by her attack, and turned to face the final onslaught.

The witches were gone. Gone! For one horrible moment, fear of the supernatural, belief that the witches had really disappeared into thin air or had flown away, nearly sent Pamela plunging into disaster. Then a cool, detached voice tinged with distaste set the world spinning firmly on its axis again.

" 'Pon my word," George remarked, "you are as bad as Vyvyan. Thought you were a woman of taste. What are you doing here in this condition?"

"Did you see the witches?" Pamela gasped, her first necessity being to assure herself she had not made up the dreadful things that had happened.

"No," George replied, dismounting, "but that don't mean anything. Probably off in those rocks. Did they annoy you?" he asked calmly, leading his horse toward her.

"They tried to kill me."

"No? Really? Well, glad I came along. Told

you not to mess about outside. Must get you home now. Another big blow due soon."

At the same moment that George was helping Pamela onto his saddle, St. Just was reining his horse to a skittering halt on the road. Neither in the direction of the village nor that of Tremaire was anything visible. It was not surprising, because the rain was falling in sheets and the road was by no means straight. St. Just cursed furiously, but not for long. He turned his mount's head toward the village and spurred him forward again.

Beyond his remark that he had told her not to mess about outside, George said no word of blame or disbelief about Pamela's story. His only commentary was silent, in that he kept his eyes turned away from her as if there were something indecent about her. Of course, she was soaked through with rain, and filthy with mud, her hat gone, her hair streaming. That might pain George sufficiently to make him avert his eyes; guilt might also do so. He had told her not to go out, but he did know her fairly well and might guess she would not obey him. Had this whole scene been set up to frighten her? No, there was no purpose to that, but it might have been arranged to enrage her so that she would tell St. Just she had been attacked with intent to kill. His natural reaction would be to start a real witch hunt, thereby setting the local people against him as well as some of the witches. She could hold her tongue, but if George intended St. Just to know, he would tell the tale himself, and somehow, in his languid, half-amused fashion, he would make it seem worse than it was.

They arrived to find Tremaire in an uproar. Blue Lady had returned to the stable riderless, and frantic arrangements were being made to search for Pamela. The fact that the men were willing to do so touched her deeply. They knew the danger of the weather, and more, they were ready to ride out in spite of their superstition and fear of meeting the witches. Pamela was responding as well as she could to the anxious queries directed at her when she was interrupted by a small irritable whirlwind.

"Pam! What happened to you? Where have you been?" Hetty yelped.

"I was so foolish as to ignore George's advice that the storm would start up again. I went out to look for a maid who . . . who wandered away. Something frightened Blue Lady, and I took a tumble. Nothing serious, Hetty," Pamela answered hastily, not looking at George but hoping his expression would not give her the lie, and that he would not contradict her openly.

"Yes," he agreed smoothly. "And we are both soaked and mud all over. Women! Stand here and gab while we both take cold too."

"No, you must both go and change at once, of course. Run up, Pam, do. It would be dreadful if you fell ill. But I must say you would deserve it. Imagine, running about looking for a servant girl in this weather. I suppose that is where Vyvyan is too? And you, George! I should have thought you would have more sense."

"No such thing," George protested. "Do have more sense. Went to look for Lady Pam."

They were both trapped in their lies. Pamela could not refute George's remark.

"Then you are just as silly anyway," Hetty said with a sharp touch of spite. "Pam's the same kind as Vyvyan. Nothing ever happens to them."

Having had the last word, Hetty shooed them out with irritated cluckings. George held the door politely for Pamela, and allowed her to precede him up the stairs. Just before they separated, he smiled at her.

"Very clever, what you said. No need to alarm Hetty."

"That's all very well," Pamela snapped, "but I would like to know why you did go out, George."

The fair brows lifted slightly, changing George's usually amiable expression to one of icy hauteur. "I could ask the same question, but I think it well for you to attend to your affairs and leave mine to me."

"You lied to Hetty."

"So did you."

"My reason for doing so was obvious," Pamela said desperately, seeing her advantage evaporating. "St. Just might want to know *your* reason."

"I hope he will not, but if he does, he will have a right to ask," George replied nastily.

"Well, he will know nothing about it, if . . ." The expression on George's face now brought a tide of color up Pamela's throat, until her cheeks were flaming. Nonetheless, she continued as steadily as possible, ". . . if he does not ask me about my meeting with the witches. You did not see them, George. Perhaps I only imagined it."

The contempt and distaste faded from George's face, leaving his expression more than ordinarily blank. "Think you're a cursed fool," he remarked blandly, "but your business, not mine. Can't keep him from knowing you were out. Grooms will talk, you know. I won't tell him more than they will. Suit —"

The remainder of his sentence was drowned in a new crash of thunder. George shrugged and walked down the hall. Pamela was left biting her lips and wondering if she had fallen into another trap. George's ready agreement seemed too easy, but twist it as she would, she could find no purpose in it. She could not really concentrate on the problem, however, because of her anxiety over St. Just's safety. The storm had reached a second pitch of intensity very little less than its original outburst. The wind was screaming like an enraged giant, the hidden caves booming with the rush and recession of the water, the rain falling in sheets. Sarah, who came to undress Pamela and see that she took a hot bath, seemed uneasy.

"Will he be safe?" Pamela could not help asking, her eyes turning to the shuttered windows, which, even with that protection, rattled under the impact of the wind.

"I am sure he is sheltered, sure he is protected. I am sure."

Pamela choked back tears. Sarah's words sounded more like a prayer than a reassurance. "Maybe I should leave this house at once," she said. "I have done nothing but add to his troubles." She shivered uncontrollably, although the bath water was still hot.

Sarah held out a large towel as Pamela stepped from the tub, but she did not wrap her in it immediately. First she ran her eyes over that magnificent figure. "Too late," she said. "Master Vyvyan has seen what he wants, and he is not the type to give up or forget. If you went now, God knows what desperate things he would do to get you back. Master Vyvyan is not always so reasonable as he should be. There is passion in both lines of his blood. The late earl and my lady were neither of them mild."

"You must stop talking and thinking this way, Sarah," Pamela said quietly but with determination. "St. Just has a wife, and I do not take leavings from someone else's table. I have only stayed this long because I cannot bear to leave while St. Just is in danger."

Sarah's eyes flicked at Pamela, flashing that odd, bright green, then were discretely lowered. "Then stay until after Midsummer Eve," she said soothingly. "I never meant you to be Master Vyvyan's leman," she added with a grim smile. "That wouldn't suit him. Only that while you were here, he wouldn't act foolish."

The old-fashioned word "leman," more delicate than "mistress" because it had been so long out of fashion, amused Pamela. She wondered if the word was really current in Sarah's vocabulary or whether she had used it to spare what Sarah considered highborn sensitivity. In fact, she was so diverted by thinking of the difference between what the lower classes thought the nobility was like and what it really was, that it was some time before she began to wonder what Sarah meant. If she did not intend that Pamela should become St. Just's mistress, just what did she intend? Where did that leave Hetty?

A shudder of fear had actually shaken her before Pamela rejected the notion that physical harm was intended. The servants all believed that Hetty was in love with George. Sarah intended to spy on them until she had evidence for a divorce. Pamela smiled sadly to herself. It was safe to make no protest. Hetty might indeed be trapped by a clever servant, but not George. His name brought back her original source of disquiet. Should she break her word and tell St. Just of his behavior? The grooms would back her statement that he left the house before she did, but what did that mean? She had told him about the pregnant maid; he could say he had also gone to look for her.

A blast of wind, which shook the house, struck. One fear replaced another, and Pamela paced the floor restlessly. Would there be a St. Just to tell anything to? Pamela stuffed her fingers in her ears to deaden the sounds of the storm. The violence that ordinarily excited her so pleasurably now brought her only pictures of St. Just swept from his horse, battered on rocks, or unconscious and drowning in a flooding gully. She understood all too vividly how and why Mrs. Helston feared the storm.

"My lady."

Pamela jumped under the hand that shook her shoulder, pulled her hands free from her ears, opened her eyes, which had been screwed shut, and turned around. The sullen, dark face that she had last seen over the witch Potten's shoulder stared back at her.

"My lady," the young woman said calmly, "her ladyship would like you to attend upon her in her room."

"Attend upon her" was language one used to a servant. Hetty had never used those terms before, and Pamela suspected she had not used them this time either. She had probably said, "See if Pam can come to me now," but this girl wished to reduce Pamela to her own status. Pamela's brows went up, her eyes flashed their danger signal. Then she remembered that Mary had tried to save her when the witches attacked.

"You keep bad company, Mary," she said quietly. "Apparently you had sense enough to realize that what your companions were doing this morning was both wrong and dangerous to them. Since you took no part, I will smooth the matter over as best as I may, but I must tell your mistress to keep better track of you. Lady's maids cannot wander about whenever they like."

"I don't know what you mean, my lady. I have not been out of the house at any time today."

The sullen face was utterly blank. Had the girl shown surprise, been anxious or fluttered, Pamela would have wondered if she should have trusted her eyes under the circumstances. She could have believed that she had seen wrong or misinterpreted a family likeness. What she saw in the maid's face, however, was not innocence but a contemptuous security that was as good as a confession. Actually, Pamela had not intended to say anything to Hetty. She did not think Hetty would care that the maid was a witch — she certainly had not minded the information that her groom was related to the People. Furthermore, providing proof of her accusation would be difficult, because she did not wish to tell Hetty of the murderous attack upon her. There were, however, other tacks one could take. Pamela walked into Hetty's room fully determined to tell a lie in a good cause.

"Really, Pam," Hetty whined as she entered, "you know I do not like to remind you of your position here. I wish our relationship to be that of friends. But when I am completely neglected, when the meanest servant girl is set above me in importance, I feel I must say something."

"I did not mean to neglect you, Hetty," Pamela said, thoroughly mortified. She was not troubled by the reminder of her position but because Hetty usually was so careful not to hurt her feelings. She, on the other hand, had become so involved with St. Just and the life of Tremaire that she had begun to regard Hetty as a casual encumbrance to be sloughed off on George whenever possible instead of her main purpose for being there. Part of her reason for going out this morning had, in fact, been a desire to avoid Hetty's conversation.

"Well, I do not know what you did mean, then," Hetty snapped. "After the terrible fright I had last night, I wake up to find you gone. Don't tell me you rode out for exercise."

"No, of course not. I did tell you. A maid had been —"

"So I have heard, and from everyone in the house. For heaven's sake, Pam, what does it matter? What if a maid does run away? Perhaps she became homesick, or quarreled with another of the maids, or did not like her work."

"She is a foundling. This is the only home

she has ever had, and she had nowhere to run off to. There seems to be more in it than a simple running away."

"I have heard that too — all about it. Really, now, who can believe such nonsense? No one is going to kill a newborn baby at the dark of the moon and drain its blood or render its fat, or anything else. Not in this day and age. And even if they did" — Hetty's voice rose suddenly with hysterical overtones, and her face turned red and ugly as some excitement gripped her — "even if they did, what affair is it of yours? What difference does one feeble-minded, unfathered brat more or less make? There are too many of them in the world as it is."

"Hetty!"

"You are as crazy as Vyvyan! You are! He was always involving himself with the slaves — just as if they were people like us. I tell you, if they wish to chop up their own children, it is their affair, not ours."

When the initial shock of hearing Hetty profess such unchristian sentiments had passed, Pamela began to wonder how she had learned the fate planned for the maid's love child. As far as Pamela knew, only St. Just, Sarah, and herself had discussed it before she mentioned it to George this morning. Probably Hayle and Mrs. Helston guessed. The other servants were frightened, knew the maid was involved with the witches, but did not realize in what way she was involved, or their panic would have been greater. George had had no time to talk of this to Hetty. That left only Hetty's maid. That meant that Hetty probably already knew the maid was a witch and did not care.

"Whatever people's condition," Pamela said collectedly, controlling her revulsion at this new aspect of Hetty's character, "it is against the law to abduct maids and murder children, and I feel obliged to uphold the law. It is true, however, that you have been neglected, Hetty, and I am sorry. But how could I know your maid would be out this morning?"

The countess's eyes slid away from Pamela's suddenly; her color receded, then returned higher than ever as she looked into Pamela's face again, most innocently. "Mary? But Mary was *not* out this morning. She sat up with me most of the night and then slept on the sofa in my room. She was there when I woke."

"But I saw her with my own eyes. She was with Potten's wife, and they st . . ." Pamela clamped her teeth hard into her lips. Hetty was the last person to tell what had happened.

"They what?"

"Stole away when they saw me coming," Pamela completed.

"Then you could not have seen them clearly," Hetty insisted. "You must have been mistaken about Mary. I know you were, because she did want to go out this morning. That was why I was so cross with you for being away. Mary wanted to go to the witches' meeting and could not, because she would not leave me alone."

"What?"

Hetty's face had turned to stone. "You do not believe me, but my life is in danger. Mary says the coven has been asked to 'hex' me. I am not afraid of that, of course, but if they do, some peasant with a sick cow or ailing baby might . . . might try to please them by eliminating me."

Could the death that was planned be Hetty's? But St. Just had received the pentacle. And the maid *had* been with the witches that morning. Pamela's own eyes and Mary's manner confirmed it. Then Hetty was lying. Hetty? Lie for a maid? Because the maid and her companions had been instructed to kill the "other woman"? Hetty was no jealous wife, but she meant to remain the Countess of St. Just. Hetty could not! Would not! Pamela drew a deep breath as her reason conquered her fear and revulsion. Hetty was certainly innocent of any attack upon her; it was Mary who had tried to prevent the other witches from harming her.

"Whatever is wrong with you, Pam?" Hetty asked crossly. "You have turned quite green."

"I am sorry," Pamela breathed. If the witches were not supposed to attack her, Mary might have been present for the reason Hetty gave. Hetty would deny Mary's connection with the coven, however, for fear that it might be used as an excuse to dismiss her. Pamela knew she had to be alone to think. "I suppose I was shaken up by that fall more than I thought," she muttered.

"And I have been scolding you. I am sorry! But that was all that happened? You only took a fall? Nothing else?"

There was genuine anxiety in those questions. "Nothing else happened," Pamela agreed. She would have agreed to anything. To escape was all-important.

"Then go and lie down. You still look very queer." Hetty followed Pamela to the door. "I am sure when you think it over you will realize you could not have seen Mary," she pleaded.

CHAPTER 13

During the next lull in the storm, St. Just returned, soaked and exhausted. Nonetheless he took the time to walk from stall to stall in the stable, fingering the horses' manes. The condition of Blue Velvet and George's hack drew sharp questions; the answers brought even sharper instructions. Then his hand fell on the bailiff's cob.

"Who's been out on *him* in this weather?" St. Just snapped.

The grooms looked at one another.

"It's witch weather, my lord," the head groom mumbled at last. "No one of *your* household has been out."

"Oh?" St. Just drawled.

But the eyes turned to him showed too clearly the agony of conflict between fear and loyalty, and the earl asked no more questions. In fact, his rigid mouth relaxed a trifle, and a gleam, which might have been satisfaction, lit his eyes. He had not found the maid and now had little hope of finding her, but if his suspicions and the little bits and pieces he was adding together were correct, she would be safe enough for a while. Things might work out for the best, after all.

Filled with a mixture of fear for St. Just and suspicion of him, Pamela made one more effort to deal directly with the witches. She went to Maud's cottage the day after the storm to appeal for her help. The old woman, still gray-faced and exhausted, let her in and listened to her, but no expression stirred in her opaque eyes. "You do not understand these things. As for Master Vyvyan, tell him that nothing has changed. Let him mind his affairs and leave the coven to mind its own," was all the response that Pamela received.

In desperation, Pamela transmitted the message to St. Just. He did not fly into a rage, but raised his brows and smiled wryly. "That means that Maud has her finger in the pie," he said, "and she will have nothing to do with baby-killing, that's sure." Then he shrugged. "I wish I were equally sure that her power over the coven is as strong as she believes it is. Besides, if she thought she was helping . . ." He stopped abruptly. "Maud has different values than ordinary people. I think I had better continue searching and see if I can find that girl."

Fear immediately overcame suspicion.

Pamela urged St. Just most strongly not to ride alone. He laughed with genuine amusement.

"Good lord, do you want to turn the whole coven against me? I am allowed a little license because of my . . . er . . . connections. If I am circumspect, no one will trouble me, but if I brought another person into some of the places I plan to go, even Maud would have no mercy on me."

Pamela had not known it was possible to be so sick with worry over someone with whom any relationship was out of the question. One thought steadied her. When St. Just rode in one direction, she would ride in another. She did not know the "special" places of the witches, but it was certain that if she poked her nose into enough nooks and crannies she would strike some at random. Some of the animosity of the witches was already directed at her. By meddling, she could draw still more attention away from St. Just. It was something to cling to — until she tried to put it into effect. Then she found that St. Just had already taken precautions against another accident befalling her.

Had Pamela been less familiar with the devotion of Tremaire servants to their master, she might have done her pride some damage by wheedling, attempting to bribe them, or flying into a rage. She knew, however, that no protest of hers could move them once they had orders from St. Just. So she merely looked from one groom to the other, her brilliant eyes glowing brighter and brighter and her generous mouth thinned into a tight smile. When she left the stable, the head groom whistled softly between his teeth. "I wouldn't want to be in his lordship's shoes — not I," he murmured with a deep, heartfelt respect for something he knew he could not handle.

It was, in the end, a mere accident that St. Just came out of the confrontation with honors in spite of his careful planning. Although he was not accustomed to the rage of a woman who neither wept nor became hysterical, he was prepared. The brief exchanges of the past had demonstrated that Pamela had a temper. Admittedly, however, they had not exhibited her full capabilities. In a deceptively level voice, she described to him his own character and antecedents in terms that would not have flattered the illegitimate idiot son of a drab and a drunken lecher. Well-launched, she then spoke for ten minutes — without, so far as St. Just could tell, taking a breath — on the subject of his present behavior, intelligence, and intentions.

He had listened in wide-eyed, openmouthed admiration at first. Few men had such a command of vituperative language, let alone women, who, in this mealy-mouthed age, usually pretended total ignorance that a word worse than "bad" existed. Shortly, as Pamela branched out into even more personal criticism, his detached attitude became shaken. A sense of injury began to overtake him, because she was hitting sensitive, well-concealed feelings of inadequacy. St. Just's lips drew back in a snarl; his eyes narrowed; and just before he went overboard, he saw the briefest flash of satisfaction under the icy overlay of Pamela's expression. His sense of humor came to his rescue.

The snarl relaxed into a genuine smile of amusement. The devil! Naturally she had learned of the prohibition against riding in the morning. No doubt she had actually lost her temper then, but Pamela was not a brooder or a grudge carrier. She had had plenty of time to swallow her rage and think. This display was purposeful. St. Just wished he could let her win, but he could not afford to have her running about loose, perhaps fouling his plans.

"I love you, Pam," he said.

Like a striking snake, her hand flew out to lash his face.

"I love you," he repeated.

"Then show it by having some faith in my judgment."

"You have none, because you love me too."

To deny something that was now so obvious would merely make her ridiculous, Pamela knew, yet she was frightened by the calm conviction he held. "I shall go mad. St. Just, I shall die of frustration if I am chained here while you and . . . and George are free. You must allow me to do something to occupy my mind."

"There is Hetty," he said with an odd quirk to his lips. He would not say anything else, and upon the subject of Pamela's riding out, remained adamant.

To her astonishment, Pamela found herself thrust back in time to the period before Mrs. Helston had mentioned the pregnancy of the unfortunate maid. Once again she did menus and discussed minor household problems with the housekeeper. She talked of furniture, clothes, and ton parties with Hetty and George. St. Just rode out every day and returned, as he had in the past, abstracted and silent. The only thing that prevented Pamela from wondering whether she had had a brief spell of lunacy was the attitude of the servants. They were frightened, and much of Pamela's time was devoted to soothing them. Hetty, on the other hand, seemed to have thrown off her fears, but this helped not one whit. The peace had gone out of Tremaire, and Hetty's good humor only magnified the contrast. Below the smooth-functioning surface of the house, tension rose as if a slack cord was being slowly but inexorably tightened. Sometimes Pamela felt as if the cord was around her neck, and soon . . . soon it would choke off her breath.

The days crept by, some sunny, some gray. May melted into June. The new moon swelled to full and began to wane. Often Pamela stood at her window in the night and stared at it, sometimes wishing she could arrest its motion, sometimes wishing it would hurry, hurry, to its moment of extinction, so that they would know the best or the worst at once. Neither halting nor hurrying, the moon pursued her course, night by night growing thinner and more wan, until on the twenty-third of June only the most tenuous silver thread appeared among the scattered stars.

"Miss Pam."

Pamela spun away from the window and stared into the dark room with blind eyes. Sarah had entered so softly that she had not heard her. "What is it?"

"You must dress and come to Maud's cottage."

Surefooted and certain in the black room,

Sarah chose a dark dress and began to help Pamela clothe herself. She seemed to have no doubts of Pamela's compliance, for she offered neither explanation nor apology, and she had judged her mistress's character quite correctly. Whatever she was needed for, it would mean action of some type, and Pamela was trembling with the need to act.

"There is nothing to fear, Miss Pam," Sarah said softly. "I would not let harm come to you."

"I am not afraid," Pamela hissed. "Let us go."

Out of doors, the starshine was sufficient to see a little after the blackness of the house. It seemed to Pamela that a dark figure gestured at Sarah, and then moved away as they came out of the scullery door. Since Sarah nodded and said nothing, Pamela also held her tongue, following unfalteringly to Maud's cottage. She had little time to wonder what she would find, but what she saw was so ordinary that disappointment rose in her throat like the prelude to tears. Four old women sat cozily together before a glowing fire. A small kettle steamed on the hob. A large cat purred on the hearth rug. Maud's glance, opaque and inscrutable, turned to her.

"Did you ever touch the maid who was with child?"

It was a most peculiar question, but as usual when Maud questioned her, Pamela felt no desire to question in return. She considered, then said, "Yes, I believe I did, once. I took her hand."

One of the old crones grunted, "Better than nothing."

"You remember her face? How she looked?" Maud asked.

"Yes, of course," Pamela replied.

"Do you like animals?"

"Yes."

"Go away, Sarah," Maud said. "I will send for you when I want you." The maid hesitated uneasily, and Maud's lips parted in what she might have thought was a smile. "Your nursling's leman will come back safe . . . tonight. And that is as much as I can promise for any of us," the old woman muttered as the door closed behind Sarah. She levered herself up from her chair and brought a stool forward so that it faced the fire. Two of the witches sat quietly on one side; Maud's empty chair and the third witch were on the other. "Take the cat in your lap and look into the fire," Maud said to Pamela.

It was a very large cat, not black, but handsomely tiger-striped, and it purred loudly, kneading the hearth-rug now with long, efficient-looking claws. Pamela felt somewhat cautious about disturbing it. Cats did not like to be handled by strangers. She put out her hand to be sniffed, and the animal raised its handsome head and stared at her, its pupils slowly contracting to slits, leaving its eyes the same glowing green as St. Just's. The purring had stopped, but the cat obligingly arched its neck to touch Pamela's extended fingers with its nose. Then it rose to a sitting position, blinked sleepily, and yawned. Hoping the creature was as docile as it appeared, Pamela lifted it, sat down, and set it on her lap.

Under her fingers, the whipcord muscles tensed. She stroked the top of the head between the ears, ran her finger down along the jawline. The cat shifted slightly, then deliberately curled up, fitting its body to the curve of her thighs. It looked up again for a moment, then dropped its head. Ridiculously, Pamela thought that it was fortunate she was so large; the cat would never have fit in a smaller woman's lap.

"So," Maud said softly. "So. Now do you stroke him, steadily. A stroke and a breath, a stroke and a breath."

The smooth fur was silky and soothing. A minute passed in silence; another minute. The cat began to purr in a regular, unvarying cadence. Pamela had not been sleeping well, and the dancing flames hurt her tired eyes. She closed them, strangely quiescent, her world narrowing to the ruddy light beyond her lids, the purring of the cat, and the silky caress of the fur against her fingers. Her empty hand was lifted, and a goblet, faintly warm, was pressed into it. Pamela opened vague eyes.

"Drink," Maud purred, softer than the cat, her voice blending with that sound. "You are tired. You will be refreshed. Drink."

The contents of the goblet smelled very pleasant, a mixture of aromatic spices, and Pamela drank as she was bid. Her left hand never faltered in its regular stroke, and the cat purred, purred. Her eyes closed again. Then, soundless, insistent, a question came to her mind.

"Where?" Was she asking herself that? Was someone asking it of her? "Where?"

Annoyed, Pamela forced open her heavy lids. The room seemed to have become very dark, the flickering firelight drew her eyes. The flames danced, dark areas changing with bright, bright with dark, until two eyes looked out of the fire at her. They were blank, guileless eyes in a pretty, empty face — the pregnant maid. Where was she? The face melted, and Pamela saw a house with a peaked roof on a steep street. Oh, yes, she must be in the town. Pamela remembered she had decided that a long time ago. Then she wondered if the girl had had her child. Well, she must have, the slow thoughts came. Poor little thing, Pamela thought, stroking the cat, listening to the numbing purr, an idiot mother and a vicious father. Poor little life. What would become of it? The flames darkened and swirled. Eyes again looked out, dark and angry in a pale face marked with a single slash of red flame along one cheek.

"Oh!"

The soft cry, which came from her own throat, the instinctive recoil that rocked the stool backward, brought Pamela to reality with a snap. The cat leaped from her lap and stalked off into the shadows. Pamela shook her hand to free it of the loose fur that clung to her fingers. Four pairs of eyes, old and rheumy, but keen nonetheless, were fixed upon her.

"You have not rested quiet, lady," Maud said in her ordinary flat voice. "What did you dream?"

"I don't think I was asleep."

"No?"

"I did have some odd thoughts, but . . . Did you give me some potion?"

"There were herbs in the cup to make the inner eye see clearer than the outer one. What

253

did you see . . . with your eyes closed . . . lady?"

Pamela felt, not frightened, for it was plain that these women meant her no harm, but awed. Somehow, without making a sound, the witches had asked her a question. But had she found the answer to it?

"I will tell you what I saw," she said, "if you will tell me what it means."

There was a moment's silence. Although the witches' eyes never moved from her face, Pamela felt they had somehow consulted each other.

"If you wish to know, we will tell you," Maud replied.

"I saw the face of the maid who had been taken away. Then I saw a house on a steep street — a street in the town of St. Just, I am sure."

"That picture was clear?"

"Yes, very. If I saw that house again, I would know it."

Maud pursed her lips. "Go on. Until I hear the end, I cannot tell what the beginning means. You saw more?"

"Very little. I began to think of the child, and I felt sure it was born, but I did not see it. Then I wondered what would happen to the poor creature and . . . and I saw another face I knew."

"Whose?"

"I am not absolutely certain, but I think it was Potten's wife. I marked her with my riding crop last month for . . . for something." Maud glanced at Pamela quickly and almost smiled, but did not interrupt. "The mark was there," Pamela finished.

A sound of indrawn breath seemed to come simultaneously from the other three witches. "She is strong, Maud. She is very strong," one muttered.

"Strong enough to block the lady's seeing," Maud said calmly. "But the lady is not one of us and had no touch with what she sought." No one spoke, but Maud continued, as if answering an argument, "It is better this way. It is time for a reckoning and a cleansing."

"You said you would tell me what this meant," Pamela said firmly.

Maud shrugged. "I took the maid from your house for safekeeping. Sarah has the keys. And I kept her safe until the child was born. Late — it was born very late, as if something held it back until the time was ripe. That was not here. It does not matter where it was. The labor was long; the girl was weak; I was tired, and there was much to do. We had her safe, where none could come to her, but I was too sure — this once. Perhaps I am growing old at last. I forgot she had been called before, and she is the kind that answers a calling. She went. Of herself she went, taking the child with her."

"You had her, and you let St. Just search and search?"

"It did him no harm, and showed his enemies that *he* did not know where she was."

"Oh." Pamela had never thought of that aspect of the searching. In a way, it had been a device to increase St Just's safety. Pamela repressed a flicker of doubt that the earl had known all along that Maud had the maid and had only pretended to search.

"Now we know where she is," Maud continued, "but the clarity of the vision shows that it is of no importance. The babe is not with her, and it is the babe who will be used. When you sought the child, then you were blocked — by another face. So be it. The challenge has been made openly. The coven must hold by its old faith, or take a new one." Maud's dull eyes changed in the sudden way they could, glittering bright and hard.

"May I ask what the old faith is?" Pamela asked with grave respect.

"God is over all, but under Him there are Powers. They raise the corn from the earth, quicken the seed in a woman's womb, heal the sick. There are Powers that stir the winds in the heavens and the waters on the earth."

"And blight the corn, and loosen the

womb, and waste the life of man and maid," another old voice added.

"Ay," Maud continued, "there are bright Powers and dark Ones. And you must know them both to use either, but you must worship the Devil to use the dark Powers, because he alone can master them. I do not worship the Devil. More than that you need not know."

As if the words were a cue, the door opened, and Sarah stood waiting. Pamela rose. "Is there anything we can do to save the child?" she asked.

The old witch's eyes were again dull marbles fixed on nothing. "Do not meddle," she replied.

It was what Pamela wanted to hear. Although by the time she returned to the house her awe was lessened, because she realized that there were rational reasons outside of witchcraft for what she had "seen," she was content to leave the last-minute rescue of the love child in Maud's hands. One did not have to believe in Powers to know that Maud had a real power of her own. Without witchcraft, the strength of her personality was such that she could probably force the coven to obey her. St. Just, who was an outsider, could only raise animosity if he tried to interfere. Pamela could not admit she was more afraid of a deliberate involvement on his part, an involvement concerning Hetty, than she was of any personal danger to him. He had ridden the fields and hills for over a month, he had been abroad in the storm, and no attempt had been made to harm him. She could not acknowledge her doubts, but she could accept the impulse to tell him of her meeting with Maud and see his reaction.

Propriety warred briefly with impulse and lost. Pamela silently let herself in the door of St. Just's bedchamber, which was opposite her own door. Soft-footed, she groped toward the darker darkness of the bed curtains, stretched a hand to draw them aside.

"Vy," she gasped in a terrified whisper, "don't! It is I."

The dully glinting barrel of the dueling pistol dropped. "Pam! What is wrong? My God, I could have killed you."

Pamela drew a shaken breath, weak with a double relief and a renewed fear. A man did not sleep with a pistol under his hand unless he had something of which to be afraid. "I am glad you are so well prepared," she whispered. "Don't you sleep at all?"

"I sleep very lightly these days," St. Just replied briefly, and reached for the tinderbox beside the bed. When he had lighted the candles, he added, "Now, tell me what is wrong and hand me my dressing gown, love."

Was it better to protest what he had called her or to ignore it? With a sudden renewed sense of grief and loss, Pamela realized it did not matter. Tomorrow night was Midsummer Eve. Within the following week, she would be gone from Tremaire for good.

"There is no need to get up. I am not sure what I have to tell you means, but you don't have to do anything about it right now." She told him then what had happened in Maud's cottage, her confidence fading as she saw his lips tighten. When he gestured impatiently toward his dressing gown a second time, Pamela handed it to him. "Do you think Maud would lie?" she asked desperately at last.

St. Just had been pacing the floor. He stopped with his back to her at the question and squared his massive shoulders. Then he turned. "Lie? About the child? No. But not because she cares about the poor creature, nor about you, nor even about me. She cares for nothing besides the coven and her power over it. Do you not see that she used you? How could you go without telling me?"

"Because Sarah asked me to, and I trust Sarah."

He made an impatient, rejecting sound. "Sarah is completely under Maud's thumb.

How could you expose yourself in this way?"

"Expose myself to what?" Pamela asked calmly.

"Any one of those women could have 'looked' for the child as you looked, and far more successfully, because they know how. None of them would, because to meet their antagonist — Potten's wife — would permit her to 'see' them . . . see, in the sense of knowing and therefore gaining an advantage."

"St. Just," Pamela protested soothingly, "you must know I did not really see anything." She was not so sure, but he was too sure. "I cannot believe in those things. I have no doubt that Maud gave me some stimulating or dream-inducing potion. I was thinking about the maid and the child — after all, I have thought about little else for a month — so I saw them. I had already decided in my own mind, long ago, that she was hidden in the town. Everything I 'saw' was a natural result of my own anxieties, my own imagination, nothing more."

"And Potten's wife, with that mark on her face? Had you seen that?" He did not give Pamela a chance to confess what she had previously concealed, continuing passionately, "Damn them! Damn them all! I told Maud I did not want you mixed into this. I did not mind them using me as a point to squabble over, particularly when I realized that Maud would be able to put down the unhealthy influence Potten's wife has been exerting over the coven. God knows how she convinced the others, how she kept them to their purpose, once Maud arrived. I suppose it is because there have been clashes between the Tremaires and the coven in the past. They have long memories, the witches. It might seem good to a lot of them to be rid of a family who had hanged one of them. An object lesson for the future. Even, perhaps, preeminence of this coven over the others. That settles it."

"What will you do?"

St. Just laughed harshly, and his eyes slid away from Pamela's. "Exactly what they want — nothing. You are quite right about one thing. If anyone can save the child now, it is only Maud. But none of us are going to be here to act as focal points in a private war."

CHAPTER 14

Morning brought a total release of the tensions that had been tormenting the servants of Tremaire. Pamela saw it in the face of the chambermaid who brought her washing water, in the smile Hayle gave her as she passed him in the corridor. She heard it in the easy tone in which Mrs. Helston was giving instructions to a parlor maid in the drawing room, and in the light tripping of the maid's footsteps as she trotted away to carry out her orders.

The servants' personal relief was comprehensible. If disaster was to overtake the family, it was no longer likely to be in the form of a catastrophe that would sweep them all away. There would be no storm so violent as to uproot the house, no lightning bolt that would burn Tremaire, and them with it, to ashes. Even if sudden death was meant for the master alone, it would not strike in a place or in a way that might force them to interfere because of their loyalty and therefore involve them.

"I have been waiting for you," St. Just said as Pamela entered the breakfast parlor. "I wanted to tell you all at the same time that I have decided to take up Sir Harold's offer of combining forces at his house for Midsummer Eve in view of the massive restlessness of the covens. We will leave at two o'clock, which should bring us to the manor in good time for dinner. We shall stay a sennight."

"What the devil ails you, Vyvyan?" George burst out, startled out of his pose of indifference. "Mean you're going to leave Tremaire empty on Midsummer Eve?"

"The servants will be here, and Allenby's place is only ten miles away. He is a justice, too, you remember, and can furnish us with official sanction to react against any violence."

"No!" Hetty exclaimed. "No, I will not be dragged out like a sack of hay. You should have told me yesterday. I cannot prepare for a week's visit in a few minutes."

"You need prepare very little," St. Just replied indifferently. "This is scarcely a major social event."

"It may not be to you," Hetty spat, "but it is to me. I have not been out of this house for nearly three months. I will not have my first outing spoiled by your disgusting lack of consideration. I will go tomorrow, and gladly, but not all in a hurry."

"Hetty's right, Vyvyan," George said. His eyes dwelt upon his cousin with unusual fixity, as though he were searching for something. "Damned short notice. Could have told us yesterday."

"I did not wish to tell you yesterday," St. Just remarked caustically. "Nor do I intend to endure any argument on the subject. I do not often tell you to do something, George, but I am telling you now."

George's eyes narrowed, but whatever he had been about to reply remained unsaid. Hetty drew all attention by thrusting back her chair and rising to her feet. "I will not go! I will not!" she cried.

"Why?"

"Because you are doing this to make me ridiculous. The whole plan is designed to disgrace me. You know my clothes are not in order. You know that I cannot go from now until two o'clock without eating, and that taking so much as a nuncheon will make me sick if I travel ten miles in that horrible carriage. What will the Allenbys think of a person who causes such a disturbance? A person who cannot come to dinner the first evening of a visit and must be catered to and nursed?"

"Knowing Lady Allenby, I should say she

would be delighted," St. Just answered, but his voice was less hard. "I am sorry," he added. "I admit I did not think of that. Nonetheless, I cannot alter the arrangements. Lady Allenby will understand."

"You cannot make me go!" Hetty screamed.

St. Just rose to his feet. "You are mistaken," he said, his voice icy with threat. "I most certainly can."

"St. Just . . ." Pamela began uncertainly.

George stared fixedly at the coffee service without lifting his head.

The countess cowered back, away from her husband, and licked her lips. "Let me drive myself," she whimpered. "Let me start early and drive myself. The pony cart does not make me sick."

"I'll go with you, m'dear," George offered.

A sensation of unease, of incipient threat, stirred and coiled tight in Pamela's breast like a snake about to strike. Somehow the mixture of George and Hetty seemed dangerous.

St. Just shrugged. "It is a long way for you to drive, Hetty, but if you prefer it, I cannot see why you should not take your pony cart. Sarah and your maid can go in the carriage. If you get tired, George can drive. You can drive a mule, can you not? And if the weather changes, you can change places with your maid. I presume you will wish to ride, Pam?"

Pamela saw the earl's eyes flicker from George to Hetty, and her sense of unease grew. She knew that the combination of George and Hetty spelled danger but she was afraid to guess whether the threat was against them or against St. Just. She thought of offering to go in the cart instead of George, but knew that Hetty would reject such an idea indignantly, and in the end she agreed to St. Just's arrangements with a wordless nod. Her discomfort increased steadily because it seemed to her that St. Just was also unhappy about the arrangement although he said nothing. Finally Pamela ran him to earth in the garden and made her offer to take George's place.

"Hetty would not like it," he said with veiled eyes.

"But you do not like her driving there. Why did you permit it, then?"

"So that we can be together." He uttered a forced bark of laughter. "Could anything be more obvious?"

Only, what was obvious was that St. Just did not want to be with her. There was no teasing in his laughter, and no feeling behind his words. All through the ride to the Allenbys, it was as if he was not with her at all. Whatever was Vy, the true being, had gone, retreated into some inner fastness within the big body, to shut her out, reject her completely. The mind that directed the lips that spoke in answer to her questions was withdrawn. The green eyes, when she demanded they turn to her, were shuttered and soulless.

Whether or not the move to the Allenby manor would have the effect intended and foil the plots of the witches, certain side benefits were immediately apparent to Pamela. No one could be sunk in a morass of doubts and fears in Lady Allenby's presence. There was fussing and clucking to reply to civilly, cups of tea to be drunk, a house to see and comment upon. Most of these benefits accrued to Pamela alone, because the ride in the pony cart had been a mixed blessing. Hetty was not sick, it was true, but she was much exhausted. Soon after she arrived she had retired to her bedchamber to rest. Pamela had no sensation of guilt. Although pale with fatigue, it seemed that Hetty had enjoyed her ride. In spite of her weariness, she was much excited, and anticipation of coming pleasure looked out of her round blue eyes.

The excitement was even more noticeable when Pamela was summoned to give her opinion on Hetty's dinner toilette. The countess was still pale and very fluttered, but so pleasantly, that when Pamela directed the removal of most of the jewels Hetty was wearing in her hair and on her neck, arms, and gown, she did not protest. She giggled merrily and commented that it was proof she still could not do without her dear Pam. The remark brought a pang of regret to Pamela. Within the week Hetty would have to do without her. She hoped she would be able to find another adequate companion.

All through dinner Pamela tried desperately to prune Hetty's speech as she had pruned her ornaments. It was a losing battle. Every time Pamela covered one of Hetty's lapses, the countess said something even more shocking and improper. She did not seem able to understand that it was bad manners to denigrate Cornwall in comparison with her own lush West Indian estates; that she offended the Allenbys' morality by praising slavery; that she touched their pride when she said she could buy and sell them, if Vyvyan did not control her money; that she attacked their sense of decency when she hinted broadly how unsatisfactory the relationship between herself and St. Just was. Pamela writhed internally with shame. Had Hetty learned nothing from her? How many times she had told her to talk as little as possible until she knew her company!

Lady Allenby was a chatterer herself, and

neither she nor her husband would have blamed Hetty for the spate of words that poured from her, had the sentiments been more in accord with their principles and feelings. The look of recoil and pity in William Allenby's face as he realized the price St. Just had paid to retain his estate was all too clear. Even the older couple were unable to master their feelings completely. There was a faint expression of distaste around Sir Harold's eyes and around Lady Allenby's mouth as they listened to Hetty give tongue. Once Sir Harold's eyes moved to St. Just's stony countenance with sympathy; once Lady Allenby's eyes met Pamela's, and she looked away hastily, with the guilt that an impossible hope and preference brings.

Again and again Pamela tried to draw George into the conversation. In the past George had always seconded her efforts to school and protect Hetty, and his raised brow and languid voice had always curbed her best. Tonight George was just as usual except for one thing — he seemed totally deaf to the improprieties Hetty uttered.

The agonizing dinner at last came to an end. The ladies withdrew and left the gentlemen to their wine. Pamela braced herself to draw Hetty aside and tell her bluntly that she was making a fool of herself. The trouble was that Pamela feared that a direct warning, in the mood Hetty was in at present, might make her misbehave even worse out of spite. Before Pamela could find an excuse for a whispered word or two, however, she realized that a direct reprimand would not be necessary. Hetty had suffered another change of mood, and she fell silent as soon as they came into the drawing room. A civil question from her hostess brought several short, unexceptional sentences from her, pleasant but lacking in animation. The next question, however, received only a monosyllabic answer and a deep sigh.

"Is something wrong, Lady St. Just?" Lady Allenby asked.

"No, only . . ."

"What is it?"

"I am ashamed, but I am so very tired."

"Hetty is a very poor traveler," Pamela confirmed, not wishing Lady Allenby to think Hetty was insulting either the dinner she had eaten or the company she was in.

"I suppose I should not have allowed you to come down to dinner. It was thoughtless of me," Lady Allenby said. "You must go up to bed at once."

"I could not think of being so rude," Hetty protested faintly. "If I sit quietly, I am sure my strength will return."

"No, no, for then you will exert yourself to make conversation or play cards, and then you will be more exhausted than ever tomorrow. If you go to bed now, you will be fresh as a daisy in the morning."

Was there, Pamela thought caustically, a certain relief in Lady Allenby's manner? Pamela was ashamed of it, but she certainly felt relief herself. She hoped Hetty had not noticed, and watched her keenly for a sign of hurt. There was, she discovered, not hurt, but a sense of satisfaction under Hetty's feeble protest.

"Let me ring for your maid," Lady Allenby urged now.

"Oh, no, do not trouble, please. She is probably waiting in my room already. She is a most excellent creature, most considerate of me. Indeed, she said that I did not look myself and that she would be ready in my room if I wished to retire early."

Lady Allenby blinked a little at this panegyric, which was in direct contrast to Hetty's previously voiced complaints about Cornish servants, but good manners made comment impossible. Pamela covered the awkward pause and made any remark at all unnecessary by rising to help Hetty from her chair and saying smoothly, "I will go up with you."

"Oh, no, do not trouble, dear Pam. Really,

it is not necessary. It is silly to disturb yourself and leave Lady Allenby alone. I am not such a dolt that I cannot find my bedchamber."

"But I must." Pamela laughed. "You are so tired you cannot see straight, Hetty. We cannot have you tumbling down the stairs again, you know."

As she said it, a qualm of fear seized Pamela. She knew why Hetty was rejecting her attentions. Mary had gone to the Midsummer Eve gathering, and Hetty was covering for her. And still there was that double, tearing doubt. Was Mary's work to harm St. Just or to protect Hetty? Both St. Just and Hetty were behaving peculiarly.

"Let Lady Pamela go with you," Lady Allenby put in. "I can support my own company for half an hour. I am quite used to it, and indeed, you are paler than ever."

That was true, although it seemed to Pamela from the one glance Hetty gave her before she lowered her lids that she was more angry and frightened now than tired. However, it was clear that to object further to Pamela's company would raise questions in Lady Allenby's mind. Hetty went out docilely, leaning on Pamela's arm. Pamela considered telling her that she would hold her tongue about Mary's whereabouts, but she could not make such a promise. She would be unable to keep it if harm befell anyone at the gathering.

The maid was not in Hetty's room, just as Pamela expected, but the countess's night clothes were all laid out; the fire, which Hetty never did without, no matter how warm the night, was burning; and Hetty's drops were ready on the table. One thing alone was out of place. A purple velvet dress of marvelous, if vulgar, splendor was carefully laid out across a chair.

"You see, she has just stepped out for a moment," Hetty said sharply.

Pamela looked away from the dress with an effort. She had corrected Hetty so often today that she was sure a comment on it would precipitate a quarrel. Nonetheless, if Hetty planned to wear that dress tomorrow, it could not be permitted. She had made a bad enough impression without that! Pamela opened her mouth to speak, and shut it again. Let the problems of tomorrow be dealt with tomorrow.

"Mary has gone for water for my drops. What are you waiting for?" Hetty cried. "Mary knows I like my water cold and fresh from the pump. Go away. I wish to be alone. I can barely keep my eyes open."

"Shall I help you undress, then?"

"Why are you spying on me?" Hetty

screamed. "Why can you not leave me alone? You know what a dreadful strain this day has been to me. Go away!"

Pamela wanted to say that she was not spying, but the allegation had struck her dumb. It was not that she was insulted, only that she realized if Hetty accused her of spying it was because there was something to spy about. It was impossible to say another word to Hetty; to remain in her room would throw her into hysterics. If the maid was gone, there was no way now of finding out what Hetty was hiding. Besides, it might be something totally innocent. Pamela returned to Lady Allenby in the drawing room with an abstracted mind. Her training in social behavior, however, held good. She heard her voice replying to questions and making conversation that her mind did not seem to direct.

The sun had set while Pamela was taking Hetty upstairs, and now, with the last of the light fading, Lady Allenby rang for the candles to be lit, remarking on how long it took to grow dark in the summer. "It is lovely outside, but in the house it is most unsettling," she chattered gently. "I hate to draw the curtains and shut out the last of the twilight, but one cannot really see in it, although it is so pretty. Usually we go and sit outside for a while, but on Midsummer Eve Harold does not like to do that."

"Midsummer Eve is a high celebration among the witches."

"Yes, something connected with the old druidical beliefs. I do my best to know nothing about these things and to urge our people to place their faith in God instead of these dreadful pagan rites, but they will cling to it. Of course, the few who are willing to talk about it at all tell me that there is no denial of God in the spells they say for a good harvest. They are very insistent that no black witchcraft is involved."

This subject had Pamela's full attention. A gleam of hope came to her. "Do they think that black witchcraft would spoil the harvest spells, or anything like that?"

"Perhaps they do. I don't really know, Lady Pamela. Truly, I try not to think about it at all. The best one can do is concentrate on teaching the children to have the right faith, and keep hoping. Do you know whether Lady St. Just intends to enlarge the Sunday school in the village? It has gone downhill sadly since Vyvyan's mother died. She did not feel quite as I do, but she had great influence among the people and did much good."

Pamela was disappointed at not receiving more information about the Midsummer Eve rites, but anything concerning St. Just was of interest to her. Every bit of information would be something to think over and remember when she was gone.

"Lord St. Just's mother died very young, did she not?"

"Yes." Lady Allenby's face developed an expression of reserve. "It was a great pity. However, the foundations of her work are still there, I am sure," she said briskly, "and if the present Lady St. Just would only . . ."

The voice became an indistinguishable murmur in Pamela's ears. She had been warned quite definitely off the only two subjects that could interest her tonight. Or was it that Lady Allenby, desiring only too much to discuss these things, was too well-bred to do so with a stranger? Pamela made a suitable reply about Hetty's probable interest in the Sunday school and began to pray that the gentlemen would not take much longer over the wine. Lady Allenby was a very kind person, and at any other time Pamela would have been deeply absorbed in what her experience could teach of the Cornish people, but not tonight.

Fortunately, the men did join them before Pamela disgraced herself by wandering attention and lost Lady Allenby's obvious good opinion of her. Their presence did not do much to enliven the evening, however, since the gentlemen were not exactly gay themselves. They all looked unpleasantly grim and seemed to find difficulty in concentrating upon the game of whist they sat down to. In fact, they had hardly completed one rubber when Sir Harold twitched the curtains aside from the window, pulled them back sharply, and called for the tea tray.

"Now, my dear?" Lady Allenby asked in surprise. "But we have barely swallowed our dinner."

"Yes. Well, we must ride out, and I would like a cup of tea before we go."

"Ride out!" his wife exclaimed, glancing from her husband's face to her son's and back. "In the dark of the moon? Harold, really —"

"It is necessary, mother," William Allenby said firmly.

Meanwhile, Pamela's eyes had flown to St. Just's face and read the answer there. A ready fear, born of her love for him, leaped to life, but still she could have wept with relief. He was not going alone. That George should be of the party was unfortunate. He could, however, do nothing to harm St. Just if Sir Harold and William Allenby were present. Pamela longed to be able to go with them, but only because she hated the traditional woman's role of waiting and passivity. She knew Sir Harold and his son were a surer protection than she could be, and made no attempt to propose her accompanying them. Women did not do such things, and the men would consider her damnably in the way.

Lady Allenby, for all her chatter, was no fool. "Are you going to break up the gathering?" she asked in a rather thin voice.

Pamela could have kissed her. Once the topic was broached, it could not easily be put aside, and it was the greatest relief to be able to discuss it.

"I hope not, my dear," Sir Harold replied. "We are going to hold a watching brief. If no more than the usual harvest rites take place, we will not interfere. No harm in that. Makes the people happy."

Under cover of the protests Lady Allenby was voicing about attachment to a pagan faith and the immorality that the faith spawned, Pamela made her way to St. Just's side. "But there will be more than that," she said. "Do they know?"

"Yes, of course. There is no sense in alarming Lady Allenby. Sir Harold prefers that she know as little as possible about the witches. She is religious, and the whole idea offends her. Don't worry, Pam. We will not meddle if Maud can turn the trick herself.

That would be best, because it will discredit the evil practices far better than outside intervention. The matter has become more serious than that one child's life. If there is a power struggle in the coven between black and white witchcraft, and the black should win, there will be a reign of terror in the whole countryside. That sort of thing can spread from coven to coven, too. It cannot be permitted to start."

"I can see that."

"I am glad you are not going to fuss and try to come with us. I was afraid you were going to ask. That was why I did not tell you what I planned."

That was part of it, Pamela thought, but there was something else, some haunted trouble behind St. Just's eyes. "I thought you meant to go alone, and I was worried. Of course, I wish I could be with you. I hate being left behind to knit when all the excitement is going on elsewhere, but poor Sir Harold would be so shocked. I shall hold my tongue."

That won a smile from him. "I cannot imagine you knitting, Pam. If only I were sure Maud would be successful, I would like to take you." His eyes glittered briefly, but some pain or guilt dulled them again. "It is too dangerous. If she and her group are overpowered, we may have to round up the whole coven and prefer some charge against them."

"I hope it does not come to that."

"I also. It will make living in these parts very uncomfortable," St. Just responded dryly.

The tea tray having arrived, silence fell upon the party until the servants left the room. Lady Allenby was pouring, Lady Pamela handing cups, when the butler reappeared in the doorway. His expression was stiff with disapproval as he announced that Lady St. Just's groom wished to speak with the earl.

"Lady St. Just's *groom?*" Sir Harold asked disbelievingly.

St. Just's nostrils spread, his eyes took on a feverish light. "Excuse me, sir," he said more sharply than respectfully, "I think it is important that I see him. Have him up here, Johnson."

Every eye in the room turned to him, but St. Just seemed unaware of the attention. His eyes remained fixed on the door until the groom had appeared. The young man stood stolidly, his cap in his hands, his eyes on the floor.

"Well?" St. Just prompted.

"I thought you should know, my lord," he started, then flashed pale eyes at the ladies and gentlemen watching him, and fell silent.

"Know what?" the earl prompted again.

The pale eyes lifted, slid suggestively around the room, and fell again. "Maybe you would like to hear me in private, my lord."

"If you have something to say, say it," St. Just snapped. His voice was harsh, as if the words were being forced through a tight throat. "These people are my friends. I am sure I have nothing to hide from them."

Lady Allenby's mouth fell open. The whole scene was incredible — a groom in the drawing room, and Vyvyan Tremaire justifying his actions to a servant.

"As you like, my lord," the groom replied sullenly. "Her ladyship is off to the gathering."

"Impossible!" Lady Allenby cried. "Why, she went up to bed not an hour ago, so tired that she could barely keep her eyes open."

"I don't know about that," the groom said stolidly, "but I harnessed the mule to the pony cart for her, and she went off in it with Mary Potten, who's a witch like her mother, to show her the way."

"When?" Sir Harold bellowed.

"My wife's maid is Potten's daughter?" St. Just roared.

"How do you know they went to the gathering?" William Allenby cried.

The groom was frightened by the violent

reactions induced by his news. He cowered back toward the door. The only man who had not spoken was George. He had briefly covered his eyes with one hand when the groom made his announcement, but the hand dropped almost immediately, and he stepped forward.

"It's all right," he said in his soft voice. "Just tell us plainly. No harm will come to you. How do you know they went to the gathering?"

"Where else would they be going? Mary Potten's a witch, like her mother — like I just said. She has to go. Her ladyship isn't likely to be driving for pleasure or visiting at this time of day."

"Perhaps they have gone back to Tremaire," Lady Allenby faltered. "Perhaps I offended Lady St. Just. Indeed, I did not mean to do so, but it is possible."

"I am sure you did not," Pamela soothed, "but it is easy enough to determine. I will run up to Hetty's room. If she does not intend to return, she will have taken at least her toilet articles."

A single glance showed Pamela that all Hetty's linings were intact. Another, when she pulled back the bed curtains, almost convinced her that Hetty was in bed. Certainly there was a humped figure under the bedclothes. A gentle touch indicated an unnatural flaccidity in the figure, and Pamela drew back the blankets with an indrawn breath of fear. Her breath sighed out with relief. For a moment she had thought that Hetty was dead, but the limp figure under the bedclothes was composed of bolsters. For a second Pamela wondered whether she should remove the bolsters and remake the bed. It was unlikely that anyone else would enter the room, however, and a new idea made time precious. She dropped the bed curtains, hoping that if anyone did come in they would conceal Hetty's perfidy, and hurried to her own room to tear off her evening dress and throw on her riding clothes.

"She is gone," Pamela said when she returned to the drawing room, "but all her things are laid ready for the morning. She could not have gone back to Tremaire."

"And she has been gone nearly an hour, according to the groom," William Allenby said in an exasperated voice. "He could not decide at first, he says, whether it was right to tell tales about his mistress."

Pamela wet her lips. "I don't think there is anything to worry about," she said. "I believe Hetty was very curious about the doings of the witches. She must have convinced Mary to take her, and I am sure Mary would not have done so unless she was sure Hetty would be safe."

"Then why are you in riding clothes, my dear?" Sir Harold asked keenly.

"Because I am also sure that Hetty has overestimated her strength. With all the traveling she has done, and the excitement, I am certain she will be unable to support herself. She will need a woman with her."

There was a wordless protest from both William and Sir Harold, but Lady Allenby silenced them. "Indeed, Lady Pamela must go if she feels she is able. I would go myself, if I could, but I cannot ride."

The men glanced at each other, and at Pamela. Their knowledge that this would be more than an ordinary Midsummer Eve gathering was a two-edged sword. It made it more dangerous for Pamela to be there, but it also made it more likely that Hetty would need a woman's attentions. George broke the deadlock.

"Very sensible," he said. "Needn't worry about Lady Pam. Equal to any exertion. Very steady, high courage. She'll do. Hetty will need someone discreet. The maid can't drive the pony cart — even if she isn't too busy witching. Go down to the stable. See about getting the horses saddled."

When the men had changed their clothes

and the party was mounted, they rode back in the direction of Tremaire. Of necessity they moved slowly, for there was no moon, but after a time their eyes did become accustomed, and the faint starshine of a clear night permitted them to increase their pace. About two-thirds of the way back, St. Just went into the lead and moved off the road. Once again the horses were held to a cautious walk, for rabbit holes and low out-croppings of bare rock laid invisible traps for the unwary. Soon the increasing sound of the surf told Pamela that they were approaching the cliffs above the sea. In another ten minutes they were among a group of scattered boulders and bare teeth of rock vaguely similar to those near which Pamela had been trapped by the witches. The familiarity was discomforting. Pamela began to regret faintly the mixture of curiosity and desire to action that had induced her to force her company upon the men.

A darker shadow in the blackness, St. Just stopped and the others halted behind him. Wordlessly, he dismounted, wound his reins in some scraggy bushes that grew in the shelter of the rocks, and weighted them with a large stone as quietly as possible. One by one the other shadows who made up the group followed suit. St. Just came to lift Pamela from her mare and fasten her similarly. Close against him, Pamela parted her lips to ask a question, but she was quickly silenced by St. Just's hand upon her mouth. They walked now, still silent, and in irregular bursts of movement and stillness. It seemed a very long way to Pamela, who stumbled repeatedly and was steadied by St. Just's arm around her waist, but at last he stopped, staring forward and listening intently.

Slowly Pamela became aware of a murmur that rose above the sound of the surf, but yet seemed to come from the sea. Simultaneously she was aware of a strange glow, a barely shimmering veil of rosiness. The murmur rose and swelled, became distinguishably women's voices raised in a chant. The witches were singing strength into the crops, freedom from blight, the fulfillment of a bountiful harvest.

CHAPTER 15

It was obvious to all that this was not the first Midsummer Eve gathering St. Just had attended. Silent, unhesitating, he led them through the dark at those moments when the witches' voices were raised highest and would cover their footsteps. He found places of concealment on a narrow ledge that over-hung the path that led still farther down in a sharp curve forming a rough U. The other leg of the U was another ledge, much larger, and so deeply undercut into the cliffs as to form an enormous cave mouth.

On the lip of this mouth, a huge bonfire burned. It was that which had reflected out into the thin sea mist and had produced the rosy glow, Pamela told herself. She was clinging desperately to one single piece of normality in a scene in which everything else seemed abnormal. The fire itself was not nat-ural. The loudest sound that came from it was a continual hissing, as if the grandfather of all serpents lay coiled in its heart. Occasionally it spat like a malevolent, giant cat, and once it exploded so violently that the figures that danced around it scattered backward for shelter.

The very flames of that fire were not right. Sometimes they were yellow, with little tongues of orange and red, like a proper fire, but mostly they were contaminated with sickly streaks of blue and glaring flashes of green. After the explosion, a veritable river of queer, unfirelike sparks had shot to the summit of the flames and cascaded down again, lighting the faces of the witches and their male companions with a weird, multicolor glow.

The witches. Pamela fought to repress the feeling that discovery was imminent, that they were far too close. Actually, the distance between them and the fire was not great, but they were at least five feet above it, and separated by the interior of the U, which presented a drop into the sea below. For the witches to reach them, it would be necessary to travel around on the path and then climb to the overhanging ledge. On the other hand, her own party had only to scramble across a steep strip of barren ground to reach the path still higher up. They were safe, she knew, but to be so close as to be able to make out the expressions on the faces and hear individual voices of those partaking in the gathering made her nervous.

Yet the expressions themselves were not evil. They were rapt and exultant, marking a deep belief in a rite that would bring plenty to their fields and flocks. The older women, grouped around Maud's gross figure, swayed and chanted. The younger women and men danced around the fire, which was plainly smaller than it had been. There were no old men present. Occasionally a man or woman, more daring than the others, would leap directly through and across the flames, casting something into them. The hour was now approaching midnight, Pamela guessed. The fire sank steadily, and as it died, the dancers grew more frenzied, more and more of them leaping across, crying out either with pleasure in their success or pain from being singed. The chanting rose in volume, rose to a near shriek, and suddenly stopped.

In the startling silence, Maud stepped forward, holding before her an odd-shaped bundle of sticks or possibly a rag-wrapped club. Simultaneously, from the other side of the fire, the side closer to the cave's blackness, Potten's wife also advanced, holding a similar instrument. There was a rush of low sound. A mass whisper? A mass moan? And overriding it, a cackle of laughter that held no mirth. Had either woman faltered? Pamela could not tell.

Both were moving steadily, although very slowly now. On the sea side of the ledge, a strange form was being lifted into the light, a wheel, but knobbed and misshapen by things that were tied to it. Pamela stared in horror, but a glance at her companions showed that their attention was all on the witches. Whatever was tied to the wheel could not be important.

Both women had reached the fire, which was scarcely more than bright embers now. Both paused and stared at each other, and the cackle of laughter, which Pamela now saw came from Maud, broke the silence again. Both together, as if it had been planned and practiced, thrust their instruments into the embers. There was a roar and a flash as both burst into flame. Potten's wife held a red-and-orange inferno that belched a black pall of smoke, but through it — clear, brilliant, incredible — burned Maud's torch, a hissing, spitting, glittering *green*.

There was a gasp, an incredulous cry, from the watching people, and before anyone had recovered from the surprise, Maud walked calmly across the fire and thrust her green-flaming torch into the center of the wheel. There was a hiss, a flicker. Maud began to chant again in words totally unintelligible to Pamela and to gesture over the wheel with her free hand. Within seconds another cry arose, and other voices picked up the chant. Flame had run along the spokes of the wheel to the rim, and there . . . it burned green! Those who had held the wheel upright released it when the rim began to flare, and with an action too quick for Pamela to perceive clearly, Maud twisted it and set it rolling toward the cliff edge.

Pamela pressed both hands to her lips to repress the exclamation of wonder she could feel rising in her throat as the wheel, wrapped in glaring green flame, struck a stone, bounded upward, and arched out into the night. The entire gathering rushed toward the cliff edge to watch it fall into the sea, and then a cry of joy, almost a paean of exultation, rose. Caught on a rock, the wheel still burned. The green was gone now, and the warm yellow flames lit the swirling waters of the incoming tide.

"A bountiful harvest on land and from the sea is promised us. Let us be fruitful, earth and water, beast and man."

Possibly it was Maud who spoke, although the voice was full and rich, like that of a younger woman. She alone had not moved from the side of the dying fire, and now, as if in response to her voice, it flared up again. A slight restless movement from St. Just caught

Pamela's eye. He was peering intently, not at the people, but at the cliff itself, and Pamela heard rocks falling into the water below. "They shouldn't stand there so long," he muttered. "They'll have the whole cliff down."

By the time Pamela turned from him to look fearfully at the people on the ledge, they were gone. Indeed, most of the participants in the ceremony had disappeared. They had melted so suddenly into the shadows of the path that for an instant Pamela doubted her eyes, terrified that the cliff had collapsed and precipitated them into the sea. The fear was gone as soon as it came; such a catastrophe could not have taken place in silence. And in the next instant the sounds her ears had been recording brought meaning to her brain. She heard the people making their way upward on the path, and stiffened with a new apprehension. That too did not last long. There was nothing to fear, because those climbing the path were intent upon their own affairs. Giggles, slaps, smothered shrieks, and uninhibited comments indicated very clearly what those affairs were. Man was about to be fruitful and multiply in earnest. Pamela spared half a thought to hope that weddings would follow the matings, before her attention was drawn back to those who remained on the ledge below her.

This, she realized, was the hard core of the witches' coven. The others had not been adepts, but country folk joining in an age-old rite to ensure fertility. Sixteen women remained. Maud was probably the oldest of these, although half a dozen, at least, approached her age closely. The largest proportion were women in their late-middle years, a few were younger, but there were no girls present. Mary, whom Pamela could now see clearly near her mother, was the youngest among them. Then Potten's wife slipped away, back into the cave. Pamela turned her head toward St. Just, but his hand closed on her arm, and she remained still.

Something more serious than the joyous dancing and leaping of the Midsummer rite was now being readied. The witches were drawing in on the ring of embers. Nine of the oldest, Maud excepted, were holding vessels of some liquid, muttering softly to themselves as they searched the circumference of the fire and finally settled irregularly around it. Maud looked up, gathering the coven together with her eye.

"Ready?" she asked.

"One of us is lacking," Mary Potten replied sharply.

"There is no need for all of us to be here,"

one of the women holding a jar said, looking anxiously at the fire. "If we wait, we will be too late."

"Then —" Maud began.

"I am here!"

It was a sharp, vicious whisper that carried with startling clarity. Potten's wife now stood at the edge of the light given by the dying fire, holding a bundle in her arms. Apparently she had come out of some recess in the cavern. Behind her was another figure, too much in the shadow still to be distinguished.

"We have promised business to do," the witch Potten snarled. "What are we? Corn maidens? Old straw wives? We are women of power, and that power must be used to take final revenge on those who have offended the coven."

"I know of none — outside the coven — who have offended it," Maud said.

"You! You seek . . . Old, weak, and mewling that you are, bound by blood first instead of by the greater ties of power as you should be, you seek to save your daughter's nursling. The Tremaires are a family accursed! And a Tremaire still lives!"

Once again Pamela pressed her hands to her lips. Here, out in the open, was the threat against St. Just. But where was Hetty?

"The curse your grandmother, with just

294

cause, laid upon the Tremaires has been ful-filled," Maud replied calmly. She said no eldest son should inherit until the heir married a witch, and a child of that union bore the name."

"Lady St. Just was no witch! Not once did she sing with us or dance around our fire."

"She was witch blood. She had the eyes; she wore the colors; she had the power over life. Her voice could call the wild beasts from the woods, and her hands could heal. Who should know better than I what she was? She was sister's daughter to me."

"There you have it." Scorn dripped in the angry voice of the witch Potten. "Sister's daughter's son! And you are tied to him instead of to the good and the power of the coven."

"No." Maud was still calm, scornful on her part now too. "The Powers accepted me and cast you out. My torch burned with the true color. The wheel took life from me, and promised rich abundance. I walked through the fire without hurt. The Powers cannot be befooled. Would they choose me if my heart was turned from them? When you can do what I did, then you may challenge me."

The face of Potten's wife, which had been evil enough in ordinary daylight, now crumpled and distorted until it was no longer human. Pamela understood the tales of vampires and werewolves. She was repelled and frightened, but not of the supernatural. The woman was insane, and from that point of view, something to be feared. It was Maud, however, facing that raving thing with monumental calm, who induced awe.

"Charlatan!" the madwoman shrieked. "I know the way to real power, the path to a summoning that will bring her heart's desire to every woman here."

She moved forward while she spoke, and laid her bundle on the ground near the fire. Pamela gasped as she saw the bundle move feebly, and realized it was the baby. The small sound that had been wrung from her was swallowed in a rising murmur from the rest of the witches. They had drawn together, away from both Maud and Potten's wife. Pamela could feel St. Just tensing, and guessed from the sounds the other men were making that they were getting ready to leap to the path and intervene.

"That path leads to hell," Maud said clearly. "If we draw such power without need, and against the innocent, it will turn and rend us." Maud's hands seemed to twitch at her skirt, and she drew closer to the child and raised her arms so that one was directly above the little bundle and one stretched toward the dying fire.

"It will not be raised against the innocent. The power will be called in a just cause — yours and mine. Let the power be sent to me. Then it will rend me if it is ill-used."

The new voice, high and shrill with excitement, was terribly familiar to Pamela. She did not need to communicate her recognition, however, for there was a muffled murmur of distress from her companions as Hetty moved forward into the light. She was gowned in the purple velvet dress Pamela had seen on the chair in her room, and Pamela had to admit that Hetty's taste had been impeccable in this case. The dress was most suitable for the occasion. Maud dropped her arms and turned her head.

"What right have you at our meeting?"

Was there a note of satisfaction, of relief, in the old witch's voice? Certainly Pamela heard a long breath sigh out of St. Just.

"I am come to crave this summoning," Hetty replied boldly. "I am come to prove that it is right and just. Vyvyan Tremaire is evil. He murdered my brother. He has threatened to kill me. I bring witness. One of your own — Mary — heard him."

"I heard him," Mary said clearly from the other side of the fire, where she stood with her back to the sea.

"Nor was it an idle threat," Hetty continued. "He once pushed me down the stairs. I am a woman, and weak. I need your power to protect me. Also, I am your friend, and he is your enemy. He has spoken against the coven — said you were useless, powerless old women who could be driven away at his will. I believe in your power. I am ready to be your instrument, to save us all. Give me a weapon a woman can use, and summon your power to protect me against his tools in the household."

"You lie," Maud replied, quite unshaken. "If he spoke against the coven, the protection given him would have been broken. I saw the pentacle drawn against him change its color in the fire, black against white, to white against black. He is protected."

"Not against the Power I will summon," Potten's wife screamed. "Give it to this woman. She is not one of us, but she offers herself for our use. If his protection holds, the Power will turn against her, not against us. Let the Powers war and decide. I have the weapon here — a poison that lacks only a baby's blood to make it perfect."

Suddenly a long, gleaming knife seemed to leap from the witch's clothing into her hand, and she bent toward the baby. Maud's hands flew up, one of them striking Potten's wife in the face so hard that she was jerked upright. A witch on the other side of the fire shrieked, "No!" and all drew farther away from Potten's wife and closer to Maud.

"She has violated our covenant!" Maud cried. "She would act in a death matter without the approval of the coven. Cast her out! Deny her, ye Powers who give all life! Save the child! Drive her back!"

As the men with Pamela leaped to their feet, Maud opened her hands, which had been clenched, and shook them once, violently, over the fire. The flames roared into renewed life, leaping into the air. Pamela was also on her feet, screaming with horror, then stumbling along in the wake of the men. It had all happened too fast. The baby would be burned alive. Even as she thought it, Pamela saw that there was a dent in that roaring inferno, a dim recess in which the little bundle lay quiet and untouched.

"You!" Potten's wife snarled, raising the knife and turning toward Maud. But Maud's hand moved again as she stepped back swiftly, and a sheet of flame raged between her and her enemy. The demented woman whirled about. "I will redeem my rejection," she screamed at Hetty. "You brought me to this. You told me he was evil. You lied."

Hetty did not even see the danger so close to her. She was staring wide-eyed, openmouthed, at the four men running toward the fire. The knife came down, slashing across Hetty's white breast. She screamed with pain, became aware of the insane witch; she turned, stumbled, began to run.

To Pamela came a moment in time, immeasurably short, which seemed to stretch infinitely, so that every action stood out with minute clarity. Between one step and another, she was frozen, and engraved into that moment was a picture of St. Just's face holding the knowledge that all he need do to be free and rich was to remain silent instead of warning his wife of her danger.

"Stop!" he roared. "Hetty, stop! You are going over the cliff!"

At the same time, he grabbed for the witch, but she struck at him with the knife and tore loose. The flames had died as suddenly as they had risen; all were blinded. Dimly Pamela saw Hetty's face, a white blur, as she turned to look behind her, and trembled, paralyzed by the black depths she saw. The pale face was blotted out in the same instant by a shadow that leaped toward it. Sir Harold cried out; then there was an unbelievable, ululating double scream that ended sickeningly in dual thuds.

"My daughter! Die, Tremaire! Die!"

Pamela saw the mad witch dart forward

toward St. Just, who did not even turn his horror-filled eyes away from the cliff edge, saw the knife rise, saw George leap across the fire. St. Just staggered back, fell with George on top of him — George, shielding his cousin's body with his own. William Allenby, who had halted long enough to snatch up the child and thrust it into Maud's arms, and Sir Harold were now advancing on Potten's wife. She backed away from them, knife raised, darted to the left, toward the path. She was clear of the men and would have run free, but suddenly her way was blocked by the witches. Blank-faced, in a solid phalanx, shoulder-to-shoulder, they advanced toward her. Not one sound was uttered; not one hand was raised in threat. When they were between her and the Allenbys, they stopped. They stared, silent, demanding. With a single despairing cry, Potten's wife turned and leaped out into the night.

Helplessly, Pamela retched, but she found there was no time even to yield to the body's demands and be sick. George was struggling to hold St. Just, shouting, "No! No! Damn you, it's too late. You can't go over that cliff. You'll just be another body to fish out of the sea." And Pamela went to help him hold his cousin.

"Stop that!" Sir Harold ordered sharply.

"We need ropes and torches and boats, not another corpse."

After that, memory yielded nothing but vignettes: the witches calmly forming the irregular circle Potten's wife had interrupted, pouring the contents of their jars on selected places in the fire; Maud singing softly, circling the embers, pulling fagots from the quenched spots and wrapping them tenderly in her skirt. Pamela found herself with the child in her arms, rocking it, and listening to a heated argument between St. Just and George. St. Just wanted to go down on the ropes. George opposed him, saying he was too heavy and that the cut the witch had inflicted on his arm would hinder his agility. Who went down, Pamela never knew, nor could she remember feeling any apprehension on the subject. Whoever did found nothing. The tide was coming in, and the bodies could have been forced into any one of hundreds of crannies, caught under the rising waters. Certainly none of the three women was alive. Morning, when the fishermen could bring the boats around from the port of St. Just and there was light to see, would be soon enough to institute a more thorough search.

That was Sir Harold's reasoning. There was a heated argument about that, too, St. Just's voice rising in near-hysteria and Sir

302

Harold barking remonstrance and orders. Pamela rocked the child and wept, not with grief or horror — there was no grief nor horror left in her — only because she was so tired and she could not see how she could ride home carrying the baby. Then a witch came and tried to take the child, and although she wanted to be rid of it, Pamela clung to it fearfully until Maud made her understand that she would return it to its mother. And then she was weeping in George's arms, begging his pardon for what she had thought of him. Nothing, it seemed, could discompose George. He held her gently, patted her sympathetically, and uttered his light laugh.

"Nonsense, m'dear. Knew what you thought. Silly. Told you I was fond of Vyvyan. Understood, though. Was acting odd. Knew that. Knew what Hetty was about, you see. Trying to stop her without raising a dust. Besides, loving a man makes a woman silly. Nice that Vyvyan has a woman to love him again. Needs it. Take you back to Allenby Manor now."

"St. Just?" she asked anxiously.

"He's all right. Sir Harold will keep an eye on him. Won't leave here, though. Can't blame him."

And then Pamela was up on her horse, clinging to the saddle with the desperate instinct of habit. Somehow, next, there was Sarah, thrusting a warm cup into her hand, peeling off her clothing. And bed. And oblivion.

CHAPTER 16

"Get up now, love, do," Sarah said caressingly, and Pamela opened her eyes in surprise. She had not known the grim maid could use that tone. "There's a pretty," Sarah added, pushing a pillow behind Pamela to help support her, and placing a tray across her lap.

For a moment Pamela blinked at her, wondering, but content. She started to stretch her hand toward the tea, and her eyes widened. "St Just!" she exclaimed.

"Down below." Sarah gestured with her head, her expression changing.

"Hetty?" Pamela faltered.

"They found her — what was left of her. Drink your tea, Miss Pam."

"I must go down." Pamela made to thrust away the tray, but Sarah pressed her back and shook her head.

"Not now. Sir Harold is taking depositions. When they are finished, you can be ready. And pay no mind to what Master Vyvyan says. He's in a rare state."

"Is he taking her death hard?"

Sarah shrugged. "He blames himself — more, of course, because he is glad of it. That makes it worse but he was always the kind, from a child, who felt that his actions made the world turn. He cannot understand that some things are meant. I told you, that woman brought a death wish into the house. Death wishes are dangerous things."

Pamela lifted her cup, but found her hand was shaking and set it down again. "Does he blame me too?"

"For what? You only tried to help."

"Oh, I did help," Pamela said bitterly. "Once he was ready to send Hetty and me away to Plymouth, and I convinced him to let us stay."

Sarah laughed. "I did not give you credit for so much sense. Don't fret yourself. Master Vyvyan never blames those he loves — only himself. Whatever you said, it was his decision to make, and he made it."

"But she is dead!"

"Good riddance. You know, Miss Pam, I have no proof, but I think that wife of his arranged his father's and brothers' deaths."

"That's ridiculous," Pamela whispered. "Hetty was not even in the country. There was a storm."

"A storm, yes, but Master Arthur and

Master Charles had sailed through many a worse storm. I have no proof, and never you tell Master Vyvyan, or he'll go mad. I only know this. A special messenger brought a letter from that woman saying Master Vyvyan was dying of yellow fever. Why send a messenger? The letter would have come as fast or faster by the regular mail. And that messenger went on board the yacht with the Tremaires — to tell them more of Master Vyvyan's condition, he said. Only the dinghy that went with the yacht was never found, and we heard through the covens that a man in a dinghy came ashore at Sennen. Only we heard it weeks later, when it was too late to catch him. What's more, Master Vyvyan never had yellow fever, never at all."

"Oh, God," Pamela breathed sickly, and closed her eyes.

"Now, you forget it," Sarah advised. "I told you because I didn't want you to get any ideas about giving Master Vyvyan up. She got what she was owed."

"And the Pottens?"

"Good riddance to them too. The daughter wasn't so bad, but she was bound to try to avenge her mother. Maud wouldn't have hurt her, but she was just as glad when she went."

"Maud! Why, Maud is your mother," Pamela exclaimed, matters that had been

307

submerged by Hetty's death coming to mind. "And St. Just's . . . St. Just's great-aunt. Heavens! Why are you a servant in Tremaire, Sarah? That is a disgrace."

"I am not exactly a servant, Miss Pam, but I have no right to be more. Madam — Master Vyvyan's mother, I mean — was not ashamed of us, and always wanted us near. She was a proper gentlewoman. Don't think the late earl married beneath him, because he didn't."

"But how could that be?" Pamela asked, distracted in spite of herself.

"It was all Grandam — my grandmother. She was a gentlewoman, but wild — wild as bedamned. She had the blood in her, though where she got it . . . well, her mother wasn't all she should be either, perhaps. Anyhow, we only know about Grandam. She took a lover. That wasn't so strange for those days."

"Nor for these, either."

Sarah glanced at her and half-smiled, but then she shook her head. "Oh, that wasn't good enough for Grandam. She didn't have a nice, proper lover. She took up with a horse coper, a gypsy witch's son."

Pamela's lips pursed in a soundless, appreciative whistle.

"My mother, Maud, was born of that union. It was kept quiet, of course, and later Grandam married, all right and proper. Lady

St. Just's mother was a child of that marriage, and Lady St. Just was a true gentlewoman, nor mark or stain on her. She was no witch, either, only a large-hearted woman who would not turn her common relations away."

In spite of the weight of tragedy hanging over her, Pamela burst out laughing. "Oh, Sarah, are you trying to prove to me that St. Just is respectable? Dear Sarah, I don't care if his mother was ten times a witch. I wouldn't care if he took to capering around Midsummer Eve fires himself." The laughter left her. "I would be a witch myself, if that was what he wanted. I am afraid that he won't want me. There are so many ugly memories I would bring back to him."

"He wants you. Master Vyvyan never changes. I haven't spoken to him, but I know from that woman's groom what happened. If Master Vyvyan acts odd for a while, just you be patient."

Pamela was comforted then, but somewhat later, when she went down to join the others, she began to fear that patience would not be enough. St. Just's eyes were blank and cold as glass when he looked at her, and it was George and Sir Harold who set a chair and led her to it. Lady Allenby fussed about her too, showing her concern for the experience to which Pamela had been exposed.

"It was a terrible thing, my dear," she murmured, "terrible. And terrible that you were there."

"Perhaps I deserved it," Pamela replied with stiff lips. She was shocked by the totality of St. Just's rejection.

"No, no, my dear. How can you say such a thing? How could you be at fault?"

"I . . ." Pamela found she could not say what she had intended, that she had known of Hetty's connections with the witches. "I should have gone to see how she was earlier. Perhaps I could have stopped her. I should have gone . . ." A flash from St. Just's eyes froze further words on her lips, and drove what little color she had from her cheeks.

"Don't you go vaporish on us, Pam, it don't suit you," George remarked with lifted brows.

Sir Harold frowned at him repressively. "Indeed, you must not blame yourself. You could not have stopped her. We know that Lady St. Just went to the gathering of her own accord and that she left this house only a few minutes after you parted from her in her room. Her death could not have been prevented by anyone. It was purely an accident."

"An accident?"

Sir Harold hesitated, and it became significant to Pamela that he had not called it an unfortunate accident and that in all Lady

310

Allenby's cluckings not a word of regret for Hetty had passed her lips.

"I saw the whole thing very clearly," Sir Harold continued. "When Vyvyan called out, Lady St. Just stopped and looked behind her. It was apparent that she was frightened at being so near the cliff edge, too frightened to move. Then that young wi . . . woman, her maid, seized her wrist. Obviously she intended to pull her away from the edge, but the cliff crumbled under the maid's feet. It must have been weakened when that crowd stood on it watching the burning wheel."

Pamela had a brief, vivid memory of the sound of falling rock.

"It is most fortunate it did not collapse then," Sir Harold went on. "That would have been a mass catastrophe. When the maid felt the ground going, she clutched Lady St. Just even tighter, as one does when one fears to fall. Instead of pulling Vyvyan's wife to safety, they both went over. If there can be blame attached to anyone in an unforeseeable accident, I suppose it is really mine. I should have gone to Lady St. Just's assistance myself."

"No!"

"How could you?"

"Not at all."

"Nonsense."

"Blame silly thing to think of."

Everyone spoke at once, and Sir Harold glanced coolly around at their faces. "It will not disturb my sleep at night," he remarked dryly. "I acted with consideration for what I decided would be best. I thought if I rushed at Lady St. Just, she would be further startled. It seemed wiser to leave it to her maid, whom she trusted. No one could guess the cliff would give way at that particular spot."

"And Potten's wife was demented, of course," William Allenby added with a cynical grimace. "Clearly she committed suicide while of unsound mind."

His father turned on him sharply. "I am a Justice of the Peace, William. If you saw one gesture or heard one word of threat against that woman, change your deposition and I will call up the whole coven and charge them."

"They willed it," William said stubbornly. "I saw Lady St. Just fall, and it was as you said. The maid was trying to help her, and then pulled her over when she fell herself. But the other woman was murdered."

"Old bean," George remarked lightly, "I thought Miss Austell was a Cornish girl. Planning to emigrate? She wouldn't be happy, you know."

William bit his lip. "I do not intend to emigrate, but neither do I think it right for those women to take the law into their own hands."

"Nor do I. Had they done something I could charge them with, I would charge them," Sir Harold repeated. "Do you deny that Potten's wife was of unsound mind?"

"No, she was mad — at least temporarily."

"And so you would have to testify. A fine laughingstock I would be at the assizes if I told the judge that a group of witches willed a madwoman to jump off a cliff."

"And she deserved what she got, William, you must admit that. There are not often deaths within the coven. The witches have other methods of discipline."

It was a relief to hear St. Just's voice. Pamela turned toward him at once, to be met with another icy glare.

Sir Harold harumphed, came toward Pamela. "My report will close the case. You see, there is no need to blame yourself. You won't think any more about it, will you?"

Pamela smiled wanly. "I cannot promise that, Sir Harold, but I certainly feel somewhat better."

"Well, I wish you would pull yourself together completely, Pam," George said fretfully. "There are a million things to be done, and thus far they have all fallen upon me. Vyvyan's no use."

Lady Allenby cast him a monitory glance.

"What will you do now, my dear?" she asked Pamela gently.

"I don't know. I suppose I will go back to London and find another position."

"Not until you have recovered from this shock," Lady Allenby protested.

"And not before you take care of the funeral arrangements and death notices and notes of condolence!" George yelped in a horrified voice.

"I think, if you can bear to exert yourself, Lord St. Just *will* need help," Lady Allenby urged. "I would offer myself, but I am so hurried with the preparations for William's betrothal that it is impossible."

There was a short silence while Pamela waited for St. Just to indicate whether he approved of these plans. Not a sound came from him, and Pamela was afraid to look at him again.

"I would be very willing to do anything I could to help," she said tentatively, still hoping for a hint of the tack she should take from St. Just. "Indeed, I think it is better to exert oneself in such a situation, but —"

"Good," George interrupted with satisfaction. "Get to work right off. Get a list from Vyvyan of the people in the islands who have to be notified, that is, if you can get him to open his mouth. No help at all in a crisis.

314

Crawls into a hole inside himself." There was petulance in George's voice, and under that, a warning. "Going to the stables to tell them to saddle my horse. Promised to ride into town. See about transportation, coffin, notify the vicar — that sort of thing." Pamela's fins pawed, and George nodded at her. "Be back for a final word," he added. "Weather getting warm, you know. Sooner underground the better."

"George!" Lady Allenby cried, revolted.

George's fishlike eyes moved around the company. "Sorry to offend, of course, but I ain't sorry about Hetty. Don't need to pretend among ourselves. Liked Hetty when she came, sort of. Sorry for her. Learned different. No need to give details, but she was a bad woman. Better this way all around. What happened . . . just as well that it did."

He left the room, leaving the air a good deal clearer. Lady Allenby looked at St. Just, and he lifted his head and shrugged his shoulders. Sir Harold walked over and patted his back.

"Heard some things about her ourselves, from our own coven, my boy. We didn't like to believe it, or interfere, but perhaps George is right. Put it behind you."

"Yes, it is true. We were worried sick about you, Vyvyan," Lady Allenby said. St. Just smiled at her, and she hurried to him and

315

embraced him, whispering something in his ear, at which he shook his head. Then she straightened up and looked at Pamela. "You have been under too great a strain to take a position soon," she said positively. "You had better stay here with us for several months. You can help me with William's betrothal parties, if you must have some employment. That will be cheerful for you, and it will be very nice for me to have a young woman in the house. I always regretted not having a daughter. Perhaps now —"

"My love," Sir Harold said hastily, having caught the gleam in his wife's eye, and afraid that her matchmaking fervor and her liking for Pamela would take her too far too soon, "your housekeeper has been waiting this half-hour past to know how many we will sit to dinner. And you and I had better see to the horses, William. I think the chestnut hack you used last night is throwing out a splint."

"Nonsense!" William said good-humoredly, but getting to his feet. "You always see faults in that horse because you were not by when I purchased him."

The Allenbys went out together, and Pamela was alone with St. Just. She sat with her eyes on her fingertips, waiting for him to speak, but still he said nothing. Grief swelled her throat, and she swallowed desperately.

"I did not know whether to accept Lady Allenby's invitation or not. Am I to go or stay, Vy?" She used the name he had asked her to call him deliberately, hoping to wake some emotion in him.

"Idiot," he responded.

Rage replaced Pamela's grief. Her head went up; her eyes blazed. "What right . . ." she began, and saw that he was smiling at her with besotted fondness.

"Why should I say anything, when everyone else was urging just what I desired? Besides, it is well and good for Sir Harold and his lady, who probably know a great deal more about you than you realize, to decide you would make a proper mistress for Tremaire and that we should make a match of it. They are obviously offering, in a tactful way, to forward our relationship. I imagine George has been doing some heavy groundwork on that score. It would be another thing entirely for them to think there had been an affair begun before Hetty's death." He said that lightly, but then a shadow crossed his face.

"Don't, Vy."

"No, it is purposeless. I did not plan it, Pam, although I knew more about it than you thought. I do not think — I hope — I did not even wish it. Not her death. Only to shame her enough to let me go."

"I am as much at fault as you. You were going to send us away, and I urged you to let us stay. But I never dreamed . . ."

"No, I am sure you did not. Only I profit from her death. That is dreadful, and I do not know what to do about it. Hetty would hate me to have her money scot-free."

"It is not scot-free. You will have scars to remind you all your life. I profit too, Vy. And she would hate me to have you. That will not make me give you up."

He laughed wryly. "We are in this neck-deep together. I will ease my conscience by giving a decent independence to George. Hetty would like that. She did plan to marry him, you know. He told me last night. In some ways George is so sophisticated that he is innocent. He could not understand Hetty's utter directness about something she wanted. He is so skilled in polite flirtation and dalliance that he could not believe Hetty was in earnest. She told him right out what she intended, and he thought she was joking . . . for a while."

"What did she intend, Vy?"

"To poison me, although I don't believe she would have trusted to Potten's wife's concoction. She had a few West Indian tricks up her sleeve, I think. She had heard about my mother, you see."

"Your mother was poisoned?" Pamela's eyes went wide. "Did no one in the Tremaire family die a natural death?"

"Not really, but Hetty must have heard the story from the witch, and she must have said so."

"How *did* your mother die? I want to know."

"Why?"

"George was talking about her, praising her, and when I asked what she died of, he was embarrassed and said to ask you. Other people too seem disinclined to mention her death."

"Oh, I see. My mother took her own life, Pam. She had an excruciatingly painful and incurable disease. She asked Maud for . . . for something. She fell asleep, very peacefully, and never woke. That was why Maud went away. She did not wish to be reminded, or to remind us. Perhaps my mother was a witch. She always said her life was her own, to do with as she pleased, provided she hurt no one else. It was only when she saw that her physical agony hurt my father and me more than her presence could help us that she decided it was time to die. Does it matter?"

"That she was a witch? Not in the least. Sarah was busy explaining about your family and proving you lily white and unspotted by sorcery this morning. I told her I didn't care if you took to capering around fires yourself, so long as you let me caper with you."

He smiled faintly. "No, I meant about her being a suicide. It was hushed up, of course. There was no difficulty about that, because she was so ill. George would prefer not to say anything. He doesn't like to lie, but George is the soul of propriety, and suicide" — St. Just's lips twisted — "is very bad ton."

"The things George worries about!" Pamela exclaimed. Then, seriously, "No, of course I don't care about her suicide, although I'm sorry for its cause. How could I evince indignation when my father blew out his brains for a far more shameful reason?"

"I'm sorry, Pam. I didn't mean to remind you of that. And I have done George an injustice, too. I'm sure that is why he would not tell you. It was consideration, not propriety."

Pamela frowned. "George's propriety takes odd forms. Why did he continue thick as thieves with Hetty, once he knew?"

"I don't think he knew she planned to poison me. He thought she was going to try to get the witches to 'sing' my death. George continued to cosset Hetty so that she would confide in him. As long as she did not threaten me with physical harm, he felt there was no need to inform on her. He just assumed you would become my mistress — if he ever believed that you weren't already. That wouldn't offend George's sense of propriety. To have a mistress is perfectly good ton. He hoped that if I was content in that way we could patch up the marriage on the surface. George is, as I said, scandal-shy."

"Anything George is, is all right with me," Pamela asserted in answer to the faintly apologetic note in St. Just's voice. "I saw him save your life twice. I'm just dreadfully ashamed of suspecting him, and I keep trying to find excuses for doing so. I couldn't forget that accident in the gully, and you seemed to have thought it was deliberate yourself."

"Only while my brains were rattled loose, and perhaps for a few days after that too. I was finally convinced he was innocent that night before the storm. Do you remember how distressed he was when he knew I had called Maud back? Until then he had not believed that Hetty could get the witches to act against me. He knew nothing about the power struggle or what Potten's wife planned, because he deplores witchcraft and avoids them like the plague. I should have known better than to suspect him anyway. I have known George for nearly thirty years."

"He must have been furious with me."

"Not at all. He never blamed you for thinking he was trying to grab the succession. Thought you were funny and rather touching, in fact. Hen with one chick, he called you, and said it was time for you to have children."

"It is most forgiving of him, especially since I never voiced my suspicions of Hetty, and I did have some. I knew her maid was a witch. Oh, Vy, that was how the pentacle got into your room. Mary must have put it there."

St. Just nodded. "I knew Hetty must have had something to do with it after that screaming act and the face-at-the-window bit. She could not have seen anyone. You thought I was frightened by the pentacle. I wasn't, although I was startled by it and rather disgusted. You see, I was so sure Maud would head the trouble off before it went that far. I still think she could have. She and Sarah hated Hetty with a violence I cannot understand. I think now she wanted" — he paused and swallowed — "she wanted Hetty to die. That was why she let Potten's wife sing the pentacle and deliver it. If I had only known then."

That was a painful and useless line of thought, and if Maud's and Sarah's reason for hating Hetty was true, she had received only her just deserts. "What was the pentacle made of?" Pamela asked quickly, to divert Vy. "It felt like skin, and smelled like it too, when it burned."

"It probably was — no, don't shudder, love — just lamb or chicken or kid. You know, Pam, Hetty was the oddest mixture, stupid and shrewd at the same time. She never could understand loyalty, and thought that if she gave the estate people presents, they would abandon me and look to her. Of course, they told me at once she was in contact with the witches. Incidentally, that groom was spying on Hetty, not on me. His mother was one of Maud's cohorts. That was why he took so long to tell us Hetty was gone. Maud wanted to be sure we would not interfere with her getting to the gathering. Poor Hetty, she could never have accomplished anything."

"The stupidest thing of all," Pamela said hastily, "was to think you were the type the witches could frighten to death."

"You know, Hetty never thought that. The only reason she dragged the witches in was to frighten people like Sarah and Hayle and Mrs. Helston, the people who might give evidence that we were not a loving couple, or that I was not the type to take my own life — in other words, people who could mess up her cover story. How she thought she would fool Sir Harold, who is the local justice, I cannot even guess."

"And what about George and me?"

"George was going to marry her and get all that money. He would never tell and spoil his chances. You were going to be sent back to London, either just before my untimely demise or before the investigation started. Perhaps she would have tried to accuse you of it — scorned love. To her mind, you were nothing but a hired girl."

"I suppose she threw herself down the stairs to gain sympathy. She almost convinced me that you had tried to kill her. How could you be so inconsiderate as to wear boots instead of slippers as an invalid should?" Pamela laughed, then sobered at once. "Was she mad, Vy?"

He looked haunted. "In a way. It all started with my stupidity, of course. I hated being sold like a parcel of land, and I showed it by acting superior. That bruised Hetty's pride; she had plenty of that. At first she reacted sensibly enough. She loathed me, and showed it — which was what I wanted, I suppose. But her brother . . . Oh, God, he took me at my own evaluation and worshiped me. Perhaps it went to my head. I was the youngest of three brothers, and no one showed me much adulation. I never meant to harm him, Pam, but when he died, it *was* my fault. Hetty loved him. She really believed I murdered him by intention. I did murder him. I killed them both — both!" He covered his face with his hands.

"Nonsense!" Pamela said sharply. "You sound like a bad play. Stop dramatizing yourself. I heard you call out to Hetty to stop. You could have let her go over that cliff. And even if you did handle the brother unwisely, people do not usually die of a fall from a horse. The animal did not savage him, did it?"

"No. He broke his neck."

"Well, so might I have, twenty times over, when hunting. Still, my father, who taught me to hunt, would not have said he murdered me, no matter how badly he felt about it. How many times have you been tossed from a horse? Would you have said George murdered you if you died in that gully?"

"No."

"Then give me no more imitations of Garrick acting a Shakespearean tragedy."

St. Just laughed, seized her, and kissed her soundly. "How am I going to wait a year to marry you, Pam? Must we wait?"

"I think we must."

"I will not have you slaving as a drudge in someone's household."

"No, I shouldn't care for that myself," Pamela remarked with a smile. "Perhaps it need not be so long. The Allenbys can be our guide, and George, of course. He will tell us what is quite proper."

"Can you never be serious?"

"But I am. I shall stay here, and there will be frequent occasions for our meeting. It will not be thought odd if you seek to fill your time with company. After a time I can confess my love to Lady Allenby, and you can do the same, or use George as your messenger. From what I have seen today, no impediment will be placed in our path."

"Certainly not. Lady Allenby seems ready to drag you to Tremaire by force if you should prove unwilling. Pam, I think you should go to my sister in October or November and stay in London. I will come too, of course." His arms tightened around her. "Alice always loathed Hetty. She will be delighted to forward our purpose. Perhaps we could marry by the new year."

Pamela would have agreed, but her lips were covered and St. Just's embrace was too stringent to permit even a nod.

"Vyvyan! Pamela! 'Pon my word, right in the middle of the drawing room! And before lunch, too! You will undo all my careful spadework, my delicate hints of a growing affection rigorously suppressed." George's face bore a perfect rendition of a painful and shocked surprise, while his eyes twinkled merrily, "Bad ton, very bad," he intoned.